DESCENT: LEGENDS *of the* DARK

Terrinoth: an ancient realm of forgotten greatness and faded legacies, of magic and monsters, heroes, and tyrants. Its cities were ruined and their secrets lost as terrifying dragons, undead armies, and demon-possessed hordes ravaged the land. Over centuries, the realm slipped into gloom…

Now, the world is reawakening – the Baronies of Daqan rebuild their domains, wizards master lapsed arts, and champions test their mettle. Banding together to explore the dangerous caves, ancient ruins, dark dungeons, and cursed forests of Terrinoth, they unearth priceless treasures and terrible foes.

Yet time is running out, for in the shadows a malevolent force has grown, preparing to spread evil across the world. Now, when the land needs them most, is the moment for its heroes to rise.

ALSO AVAILABLE

DESCENT: LEGENDS OF THE DARK

The Doom of Fallowhearth by Robbie MacNiven
The Shield of Daqan by David Guymer
The Gates of Thelgrim by Robbie MacNiven
Zachareth by Robbie MacNiven

The RAIDERS *of* BLOODWOOD

DAVIDE MANA

First published by Aconyte Books in 2022

ISBN 978 1 83908 155 2

Ebook ISBN 978 1 83908 156 9

Cover art by Asur Misoa.

Map by Francesca Baerald.

Distributed in North America by Simon & Schuster Inc, New York, USA

Printed in the United States of America

9 8 7 6 5 4 3 2 1

ACONYTE BOOKS

An imprint of Asmodee Entertainment Ltd

Mercury House, Shipstones Business Centre

North Gate, Nottingham NG7 7FN, UK

aconytebooks.com // twitter.com/aconytebooks

For RV and the Sevagram Boys

Mounts of Morshan
Sudanya
Applewood Forest
Aerendor Keep
The Bloodwood
Vynelvale
Sundergard
Methras
Morshan River
The Greywood

PROLOGUE

The city no longer had a name.

The city was burning.

Flames rippled through the fields outside the walls, the wind spreading the fires and burning the crops. Flames ate at the buildings, engulfing the thatched roofs, consuming the beams, thick oily billows of black smoke choking the air. The low, continuous drone of the fires drowned the screams and the wails of the men and women lost in the inferno.

On the top of the hill, they watched. They had been gathered there, one hundred strong and more, seven scores of warriors, away from the fight and the plundering. And there were others, hungry, in the trees, calling. But they did not care about what was in the thickets. They were looking at the flames eating the city that was no longer a city, but just a trap of fire and fear for their enemies.

"We should be there," one of them growled.

He was the largest of the warband, tall and broad-muscled, his thick skin scarred, the rocky bone spurs on his arms and shoulders sharpened by battle.

"Why are we denied the slaughter?" he said.

Some of his companions grunted in agreement. From where they stood, they could barely smell the flames and the carnage.

Beneath them, without any apparent sound, a tall tower leaned to the side, broke, floundered, surrounded by a rising cloud of burning debris. For a moment the tower seemed to be frozen in time, and then it crashed into a nearby dome. A cloud of dust mixed with the smoke, churned by the wind, speckled with bright ember sparks.

The Cathedral was a pile of smoldering ruins.

The city was no more.

It was glorious, and it looked so far away.

"What are we doing here, hiding like curs?" the tall warrior asked. "What of the battle we crave? What of the deaths and loot that were promised us?"

Most heard the crack of the bone whip before they saw it. It cut through the air and wrapped itself around the neck of the one that had spoken. He gasped, and his scarred hands closed on the bone coils, the spines piercing his skin. He was yanked back, stumbled, and fell.

The warband stepped back as one, suddenly silent. Beastmaster Th'Uk Tar stood over the kneeling warrior.

"Deaths?" he said. "Battle?"

He twisted his wrist, his hand holding the end of his whip, that he called the Tyrant Lash, and the bone coils tightened around the neck of the warrior. "Loot?"

The beastmaster was not as massive and powerful as the warrior kneeling in front of him. He was taller, but his frame was limber and wiry, possessed of a rabid energy that seemed to burn from the inside. He was not like the others, his legs shaped differently, his hands larger, his features sharper. Spines grew out of his skull, pushing the pierced skin aside. His features were sharp, and merciless.

He Who Comes Back Stronger, that was the meaning of his name.

And he *was* stronger. That made him the leader. And more: his strength, yes, but also his sharp mind, his ruthlessness, the unquenchable hatred burning in his chest. Those that were around him, he had tested and marked them as his, one by one. Each carried his sign on their chest, etched in pain. He was the beastmaster, and these were his pack.

He would deal ruthlessly with their indiscipline.

The kneeling warrior tried to speak. Black blood dripped from where the whip cut through his skin, and from the corner of his mouth, staining his fangs. Now there was only abject terror in his eyes, his voice reduced to a whimper, his arrogance dead in his chest. Th'Uk Tar twisted the whip some more, and the warrior let out a gurgling sound, like a man drowning.

Behind the beastmaster, the huge, armored shape of a caecilian cast its shadow over the scene. It hissed, opening its strange jaws wide, and its long tongue lashed out, in imitation of its master's whip. Gorgemaw, Th'Uk Tar's personal war beast and companion, never far away when the beastmaster was about.

Breath caught in the throat of the kneeling warrior. He gurgled again, weakly. He lifted a hand, imploring for mercy. His companions waited for what was to come.

"I will fulfill the promise," the beastmaster said. He stared into the waning eyes of the warrior. "I will give you death."

He felt a pang of regret. It would have been good to explain his plans to the troops. Reassure them, fire them up. There would be deaths, and loot, and creatures to join his menagerie.

And fire and destruction for the hated Latari. All promises would be fulfilled, as his army marched east and south towards the woodlands where the elves hid in fear. Towards the Fountain of Purity, and the Well of Tears. But he owed no explanations to his underlings. Their natural bloodlust would be enough motivation.

Th'Uk Tar looked into the distance. Along the roads, far away and hazy, he could see the antlike shapes of the people running from their burning anthill. Scared and helpless. Doomed. Other warbands would take care of them, one by one. He had no time for that.

A knife-sharp grin split his craggy features, a glint in his flint-like eyes. But first, he needed to reinforce discipline. Strike one down to keep a thousand in line. He tightened his grip, and snapped the bone whip with a flick of his wrists.

The warrior's head rolled on the blood-stained grass. Gorgemaw greeted the sight with a purring sound, and set down to consume the body.

The warriors of the warband cowered under Th'Uk Tar's scowl, but he barely noticed them. The hunger and the fury of his beasts resonated at the back of his mind, as he watched the city that was no longer a city, but a blackened husk consumed by flames.

Soon, he thought, he would bathe in the Well of Tears, and make true its name. Soon he would crush the Latari, squash them, and twist the survivors into his tools. Soon, the beastmaster would be the master of Bloodwood.

His laugh echoed as the city burned.

Part One

RUNNING FROM THE FLAMES

CHAPTER ONE

People on the run. Alone, or in small groups, whole families or whole neighborhoods. As Terrinoth seemed to be going up in flames, they had taken to the road, heading west, hoping for respite and safety, and dreading the menace of the Uthuk Y'llan. They carried their meager possessions in baskets and bundles. Some had loaded a donkey, or piled the contents of their houses on carts. Many ran with what they were wearing and little else, too scared and desperate to hold on to their belongings.

Survival came first, and survival meant going west, and north.

There had been rumors, of course, but then again, there had always been rumors, ever since the First Darkness. Fearmongering was a healthy business for mystics and rabble-rousers and a florid trade flourished in the shadow of the barons' castles. Some said the Uthuk Y'llan had once again risen from the sands of their land and spilled into Terrinoth like the plague from which they had taken their name. It was like the First Darkness all over again, they said.

These stories had been dismissed as old wives' tales.

Terrinoth was at peace. Good citizens had kept working the fields and drinking in taverns, laughing at the stories.

And then the Uthuk Y'llan were there. The savages had broken into the land, clashing against the forces of the Barony of Kell, washing over villages and towns like a bloodthirsty tide, spreading like wildfire, hot on the heels of the rumors no one had believed. By the time news came of the defeat of Baron Fredrick, the Uthuk Y'llan were no longer a rumor, or a spook to put children to bed.

The barons and their soldiers had been caught off guard. There had been battles, and skirmishes, and the fate of the land was now hanging in the balance. Nobody knew what would come next, but they all feared it would be bad. What of the dwarves of Dunwarr, some asked? What of the Latari? There were no answers. There was only the horror, the people hunted and killed, the cities sacked and razed. The fires, the death and destruction. What else was there to do, but gather one's things and flee?

Grimald of Guyot stopped for a moment and stretched his back, his bones snapping like twigs. His big belly rumbled, reminding him of missed meals and happier days. He had lost the notion of time, and no longer remembered how long he had been on the road.

Three days? Four.

He rubbed his unshaven chin. Four days pushing the cart with his wares, eating poorly and sleeping rough under the cart itself, by the side of the road. He looked at his hands and rubbed them together. He had loaded on a pushcart the finer items in his shop; bottles of alchemical ingredients, bundles of virgin parchment and fine inks, and, under a cloth, a bunch of crude spellbooks, if that was what they really were, quite dubious in provenance but sure to fetch a nice price from the right people. Food too, but that was gone already. He rolled his head, working out the kinks in his neck.

He carried no weapon but the knife in his right boot. He was no fighter, and carrying a weapon you can't use, he had learned, was the best way to get in trouble with those that could. Maybe someone that wanted to steal your useless weapon. The world in which Grimald lived was rife with dangers, and the coming of the Uthuk had not discouraged brigands and highwaymen.

Grimald took a good look around. As far as the eye could see, the countryside was quiet. The fields were unattended, yellow, dusty and wild. Twenty yards away, a lone scarecrow looked at the traffic on the Old Road. It was leaning to one side. A raven perched on its shoulder, underscoring its uselessness. The sky was clear, with a hint of clouds to the west, and the tang of smoke in the air was gone. Autumn was pushing in. The nights were getting misty, and the cold crept in as the sun downed.

People walked by, barely looking at him, with pale faces and haunted eyes. Grimald took off his wide-brimmed hat and fanned himself. He should have listened to his old man, he thought. Nothing wrong in being an innkeeper. Or he should have stayed in school. Not that he had had much say on that front. He wondered briefly if his family's inn was still there, or if the Uthuk had already razed it. He wondered what had become of his father, of his sister. He sighed, and squashed the hat back on his black hair.

As for Greyhaven, he was sure the old pile of rock was still there. Even if the return of the Uthuk was the First Darkness come again, the universities would survive. He chuckled to himself. That had been the whole problem, right?

Horses neighed behind him, rumbling wheels approaching.

His hands already on the handles of the pushcart, Grimald turned and watched as a luxury coach thundered on the cobbled paving of the Old Road, pulled by four white horses with braided manes, and a swarthy man sitting in the driver's box, cracking a whip.

A minor noble or a major merchant, Grimald thought, fleeing like everybody else, but in style. And fast. Good for them.

A few men and women jumped into the bushes to avoid being run over. Showing unsuspected agility, Grimald pulled aside as the coach passed, careful not to upturn his barrow. He got a flashing impression of an auburn-headed woman with cat ears sitting inside, on red-upholstered cushions, and a younger woman in a white bonnet, holding on for dear life among the luggage piled on top of the coach.

Then the carriage passed him by, the tarp covering the boxes in the bag flapping like a loose sail. It left behind only the moaned curses of the walkers, getting back to their feet, and a cloud of yellow dust. Grimald coughed, and squinted at the coach. He shook his head, set down his cart again, and retrieved a water-skin hanging from one of the handles. Only half full. He took a mouthful of water, and spat it in the bushes. Then he drank. He would need to find a creek or a stream to replenish it. He could go for a while without food, but not without water. His belly rumbled again, and he patted it, running his short fingers over his waist. He patted his threadbare doublet, raising more dust.

No horses for him, he thought. He replaced the water-skin, picked up his pushcart again, and moved on, trying to remain in sight of the other people on the road but without getting too close. He pulled the brim of his hat down, hiding his face. Wherever they went, they were all going the same way. He just did not feel like listening to their whining, not here and now. Sundergard lay ahead, with its promise of safety. A promise that seemed to draw farther away the closer they came. Life was grim enough as it was.

He chuckled. Grim was what they had called him, back in the day. The wheels of his cart creaking, he marched on, steadily, under the unblinking stare of the scarecrow. The raven had flown away. Smart birds, ravens.

The next sound Grimald of Guyot heard was the coming of a number of people, on foot, wearing armor. He cursed under his breath.

Brix was knitting when the axle broke and her life changed forever once again.

She was counting the stitches, striving to ignore the bumps in the road and the incessant chatter of the children. Lysette, by her side, was busy playing Cat's Cradle with her brother, who sat in front of her, squeezed between his mother and father. The kids were laughing and kicking each other, oblivious to the gloom that pressed down on the adults.

On the other side of Lysette, Arnost Emery, the children's teacher, smelling of dust and book rot, had buried his bearded face in a small volume. Some chronology, or hagiography or history. Boring.

The blonde girl passed the knotted string to her brother, and in doing so pushed her elbow in Brix's side. Brix hissed, her ears flattening instinctively.

"Sorry, Mistress Brixida," Lysette said, in a tone of voice that made it perfectly clear she was not sorry at all. She was seven, and already showed more than a hint of the supreme indifference towards other people that her mother had often displayed as she prowled the corridors of the great house in Vynelvale.

Brix looked up from her work, worried her masters had caught her irritated reaction. A governess was supposed to be always calm and detached, an immovable bastion of security in the wilderness of the youngster's lives. Hissing murder at the little monsters was in her catfolk nature, but still not professional at all. The "quiet, dignified job" that her mother had dreamed for her had always proved demanding, and now it was turning into a challenge. For two days they had been traveling north along the Old Road, two long days during which the air had grown stale and the tempers frayed.

Enthroned on her velvet seat, dame Eulalie Petremol was lost in her dark reveries, a small kerchief in her gloved hand. She sometimes brought it to her eye, as if to dry a lonely tear, her haughtiness replaced by a mournful countenance. Her husband, master Galter Petremol the Second, head of the Petremol family and one of the richest men in the Free Cities (or so he claimed), was looking out of the coach window, a deep frown etched on his square face. Outside, the open fields of the Great Plains were being replaced by hills, and the vineyards were fading into thickets of wild trees. There was a faint smell of smoke on the wind, a sooty ghost lingering in the air, but Brix knew she was the only one keen enough to perceive it.

"Are we there yet?" asked young master Remin, his fingers entangled in the string. He was moodier than his sister, and despite being younger he had already developed the same authoritarian streak as his father. He would inherit the family business, and the lands and the houses. He would be a master of men, and he knew it. Like his sister he was dressed in blue and white, in clothes that were a miniature copy of the adults'. And that was how children were perceived in the Petremol household, as miniature adults, and raised accordingly.

When nobody answered his question, the boy kicked Arnost Emery in a shin. "Are we there yet?" he repeated.

The old man winced, and left his book to turn his sad brown eyes on the boy sitting in front of him. "I believe it is self-evident," he said, "that we are not yet, as it were, 'there'– wherever that may happen to be. Your question is not only badly formed and far too vague, but it is also exquisitely superfluous." He made a long pause, and then, "Young sir," he added.

Remin kicked him again. "And when will we be?"

"Maybe you should ask your father," Brix said. She traded a look with Emery, who gave her a brief nod. She had always considered it her duty to save the children from their teacher's dry notions and formal pomposity, and she had often been at odds with Emery back in the house; but now things had changed, and they recognized in each other the only ally they could count on in these strange new times.

"What?" Galter said, turning from the window and looking at them, like he was surprised at finding other people traveling with him. His graying hair framed a face pinched with worry.

"When will we get there?" Remin asked. His sister tried to take the string back from him, but he let it drop in his lap, uninterested.

Galter grumbled, and shook his head. "We should be in Sundergard by sundown," he said. The coach hit a bump, and the horses neighed. Estvan, the master's man, cracked his whip, as if that would be enough to keep the coach on the road. They were now on a badly maintained tract of the Old Road, and the going was uneven. People saluted their passing with a chorus of curses and coughs, and rude gestures, counting themselves lucky they had not been run over by the carriage. Not many refugees could afford a four-horse coach to escape the Blight.

"Sundergard is a dump," Remin said, stressing the last word. He had heard his father describe the town like that in the past, and now beamed proudly as he underscored the notion. "A proper dump."

Master Galter's frown deepened. The Petremol family maintained a house and an office close by the fortress of Sundergard, that with its troops and riders of the militia would grant protection to them. Or so Brixida hoped, as they all did.

Eulalie suddenly let out a long wail, and pressed her kerchief to her eyes. Her children looked at her with open curiosity. Lysette's eyes widened, and Remin chuckled.

Brix thought it was up to her to say something. She looked down on her knitting, her pattern forgotten.

A loud crack brought her back to reality. The horses neighed, the people outside screamed, the people inside screamed, and the world was suddenly turned upside down. Brix's claws dug deep into the side of the coach as it tottered and rolled on the side, in a chaos of tumbling luggage, scattered clothes and snapping branches.

The children were the first to run out of the coach, screeching and laughing, followed by Brix and then, limping, by Doctor Emery.

"Children, stay close!" Brix commanded. Duty and habit overcame her bewilderment and pushed back the ache in her bones due to the sudden tumble. She quickly took stock of the situation.

The children were running around, collecting bits and pieces that the accident had scattered. The coach was leaning against a tree, two wheels in the gutter by the road, one quite obviously broken. The four horses were snorting and shaking their heads, the harness pulling at them. The luggage that had been on the carriage top had been projected all around as the coach had lost its balance. The trunks and boxes had opened, spreading their contents about. Clothes and underwear, a scattering of silverware, mismatched shoes. A large mirror in a gilded frame had landed in a bush. A crack crossed its width, doubling the reflection. It was supposed to bring ill luck. As if they already didn't have plenty, Brix thought.

The door banged open once again. Master Galter helped his wife climb out of the wrecked coach, and then looked around. Estvan was crawling out of the underbrush, a large gash on his forehead, the whip still in his hand.

"What does this mean, you ruffian?" Galter exclaimed, and slapped his own hip with a hand. He adjusted his coat, and then cast a glance down the road.

The servant cleaned his face on his sleeve. "The front axle, master," he said. A large bruise was spreading over his face. "It broke."

"This is unacceptable!"

"Léa?" Eulalie called. "Where are you, you silly girl?"

Léa, the mistress' maid, had been riding on the top of the coach, among the trunks and baggage. Now stuck in the branches of the tree against which the coach was leaning, she squealed and waved her arms. In doing so, she lost her perch and tumbled down with a scream.

"Stupid girl!" Eulalie snapped.

Emery dove into the bushes, leaning on his walking stick,

and helped the maid to her feet. Léa was holding her right arm and crying. Brix righted a trunk, and patted it, signaling for the girl to sit down. Léa nodded a thank you.

"The children!" Eulalie called. "Brixida, please, don't mind the stupid girl. Look after the children."

Brix gave Emery a look, then nodded. Léa whined, and Brix patted her hand. Then she straightened up and scanned the stretch of road from which they had come. She squinted at the dark clouds on the horizon, knowing those were not thunderclouds, but the smoke rising from the burning shell of Vynelvale. She shuddered, feeling the fine hair down her spine raise against her camisole. Then she focused on the two brats, who were playing tug of war with one of their mother's frocks.

Brix clapped her hands. "Lysette. Remin. Order!"

She put as much authority as she could into her voice while still keeping her tone under control. The situation was complicated enough without her scaring the children further.

Remin looked at her, and let go of the silk sleeve he had been holding. His sister stumbled back and sat down heavily in the middle of the road.

"Get away from the road," Brix commanded. The children had learned to pay attention to the tone of her voice. Under her stern stare, they marched back to the coach, where Brix had them sitting on a box, in the shadow of the wreck. "You need to stay close," she told them, in a level voice.

"Why?" asked Remin, staring at her.

"Because–"

Léa screamed, and Doctor Emery took a step back, raising his hands to placate her.

"What now?" Eulalie asked peevishly.

"I am afraid the young woman's humerus is fractured," the old man said, to no one in particular.

"Well, set it," Eulalie snapped. "Aren't you a doctor?"

Emery glanced sideways at Brix. She felt a surge of sympathy for the old man. "I am sorry to inform you, my lady," he said, piqued, "that I am a doctor in letters and history. Setting bones is not one of my competences."

"I am surprised we pay you at all," Eulalie said. She turned to her husband. "Why is this man traveling with us when he isn't even a doctor?"

"Please, Lally," her husband said. "The man's been working for us for thirty-five years."

Eulalie shrugged and snorted.

"I can take a look at her arm," Brix said. Dislocated shoulders and sprained wrists had been a common occurrence in her father's school. And then to the children, "You wait here."

"I want to watch," Remin said.

"Yes, me too!" shouted his sister.

"You look after the girl, mistress Brixida," Emery said. "I will endeavor to keep the young master and his sister entertained in the meantime."

The horses neighed and kicked, as Estvan detached their harness from the coach, and then proceeded to remove the straps and belts, releasing them.

Brix tried to focus on Léa's arm. "Does it hurt?"

The girl nodded, tears streaking down her cheeks. She had lost her coif in the fall, and her pale hair was coming undone. Brix took a deep breath. The characters in the novels she usually read were always setting broken limbs and sewing or burning wounds closed. But this was not a novel, and her heart fluttered in anticipation, and fear.

The arm was swelling, a large bruise spreading, but the skin was unbroken. Brix tried to remember what her father used to do in similar cases. "Can you move it?"

Léa tried to lift her arm, and cried out in pain.

Brix took her hand. "Can you feel my fingers?"

Léa nodded.

Brix turned to where the children were being bored to distraction by Doctor Emery's droning voice. "Children!" she called. They looked up, and Emery turned to her. "I need your help."

Both jumped up, and walked to her, Emery two steps behind them.

"Is she bleeding?" Remin asked, with a bright smile.

"No, she is not," Brix said. "I need two long straight sticks." She placed her hands in front of her, about two feet apart. She looked sternly at Remin. "This long, and as straight as possible. Will you find them for me?"

The boy nodded. "Sure."

Brix looked up, and Emery nodded and moved to follow the child as he ran to the trees.

"I want to go too!" Lysette said.

"No, I have another mission for you, just as important, and fit for a young lady. Find me a strong silk shirt, one of your mother's. Can you do that?"

"What do you want a shirt for?"

Brix grinned. "I want to rip it to shreds."

Lysette's eyes sparkled. "I'll find it!"

The half-cat turned to Léa and smiled. Then she placed a hand on the girl's forehead, to check her temperature. Léa sniffed, tears running down her cheeks.

By the coach, master Galter was deep in discussion with

Estvan. His wife stood by his side, sobbing into her kerchief.

Brix looked at the sky and wondered how far behind them were those they had not dared mention. She pushed the Uthuk Y'llan to the back of her mind.

The children returned, Emery behind them, short of breath. Brix found two straight sticks in the bunch that Remin had collected, and then used her talons to rip the periwinkle shirt Lysette had fetched into a number of even strips. The girl gasped and looked at her brother, but the boy was watching Brix's desecration of their mother's garment, fascinated.

Brix looked Léa in the eye. "This will hurt a little," she lied.

She grabbed her elbow, pushed with the other hand on the shoulder, and as the girl screamed, she nodded and Emery was there, holding up the sticks and helping block the broken arm. Léa's gasps subsided as Brix tied the straps of silk around her arm. "This will have to do, for the moment," she said. "There will be a doctor in Sundergard, I am sure."

"And not a doctor in history and letters," Emery said, with a smile.

Galter called for his children, and they ran to him. Estvan had readied the horses, and Eulalie was pulling at the folds of her skirt, shaking her head.

"We ride to Sundergard," Galter said. He turned to his servants, who had come closer. "You will have to continue on foot."

Léa whimpered, and Brix stifled a hiss, training once again overcoming instinct. Outrage was like acid in her mouth. And yet, a voice whispered in her mind, why should she be surprised? She turned to see her own surprised fear in the face of Doctor Emery.

"See that you carry all the luggage you can," added Eulalie.

Estvan was helping Lysette sit on the back of one of the big white horses. She found her balance, and Estvan picked up Remin and sat him behind her. "You make sure your sister doesn't fall," he said. "Hold on tight."

"How am I supposed to get on a horse," Eulalie said, in her customary peevish tone, "when we don't even have stirrups?"

Estvan ran to her and offered her a leg up.

"We will send a ride back to you," Galter said. "As soon as we are in Sundergard. By tomorrow evening we will all be together again, and will laugh at this whole adventure."

Again Brix looked at the doctor, finding herself at a loss for words. Her head was reeling.

"By your leave, sir," Arnost Emery said, "but were young master Remin to ride with you, and his sister with her mother, then Mistress Brixida and Léa could share the fourth horse. In this way you would only leave one behind, and that one is admittedly old and not fit for such equestrian pursuits."

"Or Doctor Emery could ride behind Estvan," Brix said, taking a step forward. She was honestly surprised by the old man's selfless proposal. "He is light as a child himself." She turned. "With all due respect, doctor."

Galter cleared his voice. His wife was already on her horse, her skirts bunched up and her pale calves showing, and his servant was holding the reins of the two remaining animals. "I am afraid that we cannot load too much on these poor beasts," he said. "But rest assured, this is all for the best. You follow us at your leisure, and we'll send a ride for you–"

"Master–" Estvan said, looking south with a frown.

With a snort and a wave of his hands, Galter Petremol pulled himself on the back of the horse, and his servant handed him the reins.

"Everything will be fine," the merchant said, trying to bring the animal under control. "You just follow us–"

"And you will send a ride for us when you reach Sundergard," Brix said, her voice flat.

"Exactly. Everything will be for the best."

Estvan vaulted onto the last horse and kicked his heels. The others followed at a light canter.

By the broken carriage, the teacher, the governess and the maid watched the four horses and their five riders as they departed. In a few moments, they were vague dots in the distance.

CHAPTER TWO

Shuffling feet, voices talking, the cry of children and the creaking of cartwheels combined in a sound like the breaking of waves on a lake shore, and the call of wild ducks.

But the river was behind her, and there were no lakes between her and the Bloodwood.

Only a thin strip of the Plains, and a road.

Laurel did not like roads, as she did not like the artifacts of the men and their allies.

To her eyes, the landscape had always been crossed by simple paths that followed the crests of the hills and the course of the creeks, stretching from a standing stone to an old tree, past a notch in a cliff. It was along such a pathway that she had traveled in the past six days, looking out for signs of her enemies. She had left the mountains behind, and the green darkness of the Aymhelin. She had hiked through the woodland, early autumn tinging the treetops of brown and copper and gold. Red too, reminding her of home. And home she was going, in the hopes of finding news of her cousin, Redstar.

But now the wilderness had retreated, giving room to fields, orchards and vineyards, the land transformed by the work of the humans.

It was stewardship of sorts, Laurel knew, and she respected it. It was these people's way, and her mind was curious. What need was there for cobblestones and signposts, milestones and bridges? Why did they cut the landscape they were so lovingly grooming?

Laurel stopped by a tall oak tree. Below her, on the gentle slope of the hillside, was row upon row of rust-colored grapevines. The ground was clean of grass and wet with the previous night's rain.

Laurel sighed, and took a moment to center herself. Weariness and fear for Redstar's fate were at the surface of her mind. Things were as they were, and it was a warrior's mind that accepted such truths as they may come, wasting no time to color them with what-might-have-beens. The humans and their allies had settled these lands. They were looking after them in their own fashion. They had built cities and villages, and laid out roads to connect them.

This was neither right nor wrong. It simply was.

And now their fields were abandoned, their orchards grew unattended, and their cities and villages burned.

Laurel had witnessed the horror of the Locust Swarms. She had killed the Uthuk Y'llan in the light of a burning cabin, too late to save whoever had lived there. A new darkness was sweeping over the land, and now the people of the cities and the villages were fleeing along their ancient road, slowly moving west and north.

Or not so slowly. Four white horses galloped along the gray ribbon of the road, carrying their riders towards an imagined safety. People on foot hastened to get out of the way.

Laurel waited in the shadow of the oak, and watched the river of people pass by. Clouds were gathering. It would be raining again soon.

The dust of the horses had not yet faded in the distance, and Brixida was already rummaging in one of the trunks that had tumbled from the back of the coach. She pulled out clothes and scattered them in a multi-colored fan around her.

"May I inquire about what you are doing, Mistress Brixida?"

She turned and looked at Emery over her shoulder. "If we are to take to the road, I'll need practical clothes." She nodded towards Léa, sitting on her trunk. "The girl, too. It's not like we can walk any distance in these skirts and these shoes." She tucked a bundle of clothes under her arm and walked to the coach.

"You should do the same, doctor. Look for useful stuff we might need. Cloaks, hats." She eyed the sky. "We can't carry much, but the night is going to be cold. Food too, if they left something behind for us, which I seriously doubt. We must make haste, and travel light."

The old teacher mumbled. She ignored him.

She stopped, one foot on the step of the wrecked carriage, and turned to look at her companions. Stranded like the survivors of a shipwreck, she thought, and she shuddered at the idea this adventure would be real, and deadly. The adventures she had always read about, and dreamt of, had been a lot more fun. More people walked by. Arnost Emery shouted at a man who picked up an abandoned leather bag and ran. He shook his fist, and cut through the air with his walking stick, but the thief was running on. Someone somewhere laughed. The slow flow of refugees continued. Nobody stopped to help.

Inside the carriage, Brix found a way to keep her balance

on the tilted floor. She pushed her knitting bag aside with her foot, and quickly got out of her dress and underskirts. She kicked the shoes off and flexed her claws, scratching the carpet.

She put on a pair of master Galter's blue corduroy pantaloons, using her retractable claw to cut the seam in the back, for her tail. Next, a black loose shirt. She tied the laces on her chest and rolled up the sleeves at the wrists. Unfurling a golden sash, she rapidly wound it around her waist, like she imagined a pirate would. She weighed the red riding coat, with the silver finish and the large pockets. Those would come in handy. It would reach down to her legs, and might hinder her movements, but she liked the color. She'd be able to wrap it around her as a blanket for the night. Of one thing she was certain: she would not sit down and cry her eyes out, waiting for the Uthuk Y'llan to come and get her.

She paused for three heartbeats.

Having acknowledged the danger looming, she discovered a new determination building inside of her. She was not lost, she was not afraid. She would need a weapon, she told herself.

Arnost Emery used the end of his walking staff to push around the discarded clothes and snorted. Useful, the silly cat-woman had said. Thirty-seven years he had been a teacher for the Petremol family, trying to infuse some sense in the thick skulls of three generations of the family younglings. Thirty-seven years, not thirty-five like his master had said, he had spent suspended in that strange twilight world that was neither upstairs nor downstairs.

More than a servant, but so much less than a member of the family.

Young Brixida Lovell had said that. She had been hired to

look after the children, shortly after master Remin was born. A temperamental young woman, and a half-catfolk at that. Very unusual. Emery sniffed and cast a glance at the wrecked coach, into which Mistress Brixida was retreating.

Emery had not approved, but of course he had not been consulted on this issue, as on any other. Brixida had been too young, he believed, and came from an unconventional family. And yet that single phrase, spoken out of line one late evening, in the house library, had struck him. He had been looking for the third volume of Gilvert's *Concise Annals of Central Terrinoth*, and Brixida had been curled up in a couch, reading one of her old romances. Her passion for stories of swashbucklers betrayed her young age.

Out of common courtesy, Emery had asked her how she was finding being part of such an exalted household. Being part of the family, he had said, those had been his exact words. Family. And she had corrected him, the cheeky feline: "More than a servant," she had said, "but so much less than a member of the family." He had to concede that, for all of her dubious taste in literature and her eccentric manners, Mistress Brixida had shown, in that circumstance, a sharp mind and a much welcome penchant for concision.

He sighed.

Three generations of Petremols he had tutored, and each had been more spoiled, capricious and disrespectful, with eyes only for wealth and thoughts only for profit. He had spent his life in their service, and they had treated him like a cart horse. And now, after thirty-seven years, here was Doctor Arnost Emery, philosopher and erudite, rummaging in the laundry to look for a warm cloak. They had left him behind, discarded like the rags he was exploring.

He spotted one of his master's hooded cloaks, rich purple velvet, lined with black fur. He bent, his back creaking, to pick it up.

Léa squealed, and Emery straightened in time to see a young ruffian pick one of the master's leather bags and start running.

"Thief!" he shouted. "Stop him!"

The man laughed and kept running.

There were other people walking by, peasants and town-dwellers by their looks. A man leading a mule laughed. The mule pulled a cart. On the cart sat a woman and two children. The woman laughed too. The children looked at the old man shaking his fist, their eyes big and haunted.

The coach hatch slammed open and out stepped Brixida, wearing britches and one of the master's rust-red coats. She was tying her hair with a strap of leather, pulling it up in a thick ponytail, leaving her pointed ears exposed. "Come," she said to Léa, "we'll find something for you too."

Léa whimpered. The cat-woman looked at Emery. "Have you found something suitable? We must get moving."

"They will steal everything we leave behind!" he said, indignant.

"They can have it," Brixida replied. "Some things you can't take with you. Isn't that what they say?"

Léa made a gesture against ill luck because that was what was said of dead people. Then she spotted Emery looking at her, and blushed.

CHAPTER THREE

By dawn the following day, as the refugees slowed from exhaustion, a column of sorts had formed. Families fleeing from the burning cities, people leaving behind the small villages and settlements that dotted the countryside. Some traveled with their goats, and Brixida saw a man carrying a pig on his shoulders, inside a wicker basket. His children walked at his side, trying to keep up with his strides, but he was carrying his pig. There was a group of monks, clustered around their overloaded mule, carrying on with the rest of the refugees, the rising sun at their back. The monks sometimes tarried to help the elderly or the infirm and share the provisions they carried.

The men and women from the territorial militia walked along with the refugees, grim faced with weapons at the ready, and their officers ran up and down the road on their weary horses, checking for stragglers.

"This is not good," Brixida said.

Doctor Emery glanced at her. He leaned casually on his black wood walking staff, and was carrying a large leather bag slung over a shoulder. Brixida was surprised at the energy the old man was showing. They had stopped briefly for the night, before being rounded up by the soldiers and joining the column. They had no food but a bag of hard candies that Brix had brought along to bribe the children into some kind of disciplined behavior. They had sucked on the sweets, wrapped up in their cloaks, in a light drizzle that had started as the sun was setting.

"We are slow," she explained. Her mouth was dry, and her words came out clipped and severe. "And we are easy to spot, a multitude here in the open. We make a lot of noise. We might as well light a beacon to call the Blight upon us."

By her side, Léa stumbled, her foot caught in the hem of her long skirt. She had refused to wear more practical clothing, outraged at the idea. Brix had thought it useless to waste time arguing, but now the girl's choice was slowing them down.

Emery cleared his throat and worked his jaw. "The general wisdom maintains there is safety in numbers, and we have the militia with us now to protect us."

"What, twenty bumpkins playing soldier?" Brixida snapped. Children and old men pretending to be soldiers, the militia had not impressed her for martial deportment or warlike attitude.

Then she spotted a tall orc looking at her, hurt passing over his features like a brief shadow. He wore a mismatched breastplate and gauntlets over plain leather clothes, and carried a brutish ax over his shoulder, the handle blackened by use and the wide blade dented. The red scarf of the militia was tied to his arm. She looked away, and adjusted the satchel she carried. She was sorry he had heard her, but there was little she could do now. The orc gave her one more brief look, lengthened his stride, and moved on.

"And what would you propose, then?" Emery asked.

Brix eyed the muscular back of the orc. "We should scatter, and lay low."

The old teacher shook his head. "And be hunted like wild animals by the Uthuk, singled out and dispatched?"

Léa whimpered.

"The lady is right, you know."

A man was walking along with them, pushing a wheelbarrow loaded with boxes and parcels. He was short and heavy-set, with black hair under a slouch hat. His clothes were good but well worn, a leather sleeveless vest over a shirt that had once been white, and baggy trousers. A grin split his unshaven chin, and he nodded at Brixida. Brix started in surprise. She had been so caught up in the conversation, she had not seen him as he approached. "We make for easy prey here," he said, "bundled all together like this."

Emery looked at him and arched his bushy eyebrows. "I seriously doubt facing the Blight alone would make for a better choice, Master…?"

The short man nodded, and doffed his hat, one hand still holding the barrow. "Grimald of Guyot, at your service. And you are not wrong, because the Uthuk would surely kill us all, and relish the opportunity, because that is their nature. But what I am saying is, we should leave the road, and find a nice, secluded spot in the hills and go to ground. Weather the storm because we cannot stop it."

"Are you a master of the military arts, Master Grimald? Or maybe a natural philosopher, a student of the vagaries of the weather that you use so aptly as a metaphor of our current affairs?" Doubt and sarcasm tinted the old teacher's voice. Brix felt a surge of sympathy for the one standing on the receiving end of Emery's sarcasm. She had been there in the past, and it was not a pleasant position.

But the short man chuckled. "Not by a fair length, sir. I am in the trades."

"Indeed."

They advanced for a while in silence, the creaking of Grimald's cartwheels the only sound.

Once again, the commander of the militia ran the length of the column, barking orders to his soldiers. The shuffling of feet and the fragments of conversation, the coughs and the sighs, and the crying babies merged in a sound like a distant sea roaring against rock cliffs.

"What sort of trade?" Brixida asked suddenly. The short man intrigued her more than she would admit. There was a hint of craftiness underneath his geniality that made her wary but stoked her curiosity.

The short man looked at her. "I'm a vendor of mystical supplies. Alchemical components, laboratory equipment. Parchments and books, too. The occasional minor runestone. Honest Grimald, they call me, because I drive a fair bargain. I used to have a shop three streets down from the library–"

"What sort of books?" Emery asked, suddenly interested.

"Compendiums of formulas and recipes, mostly." Grimald shrugged. "A little natural philosophy. Sometimes a... spellbook. Tomes of an antiquarian interest, too, occasionally," his voice took a conspiratorial tone, "for a select clientele."

Emery opened his mouth to speak, but Brixida cut him short. "Is that a sample of your wares you are carrying, Master Grimald?"

Grimald nodded, and the wheels of his cart creaked. "But a fraction of what I had in my shop. I had to make a hard selection, and fast. A lot I had to leave behind, let the Uthuk burn it."

The orc with the axe was back.

"We are taking a rest," he said, passing by.

"Why?" Brixida asked.

The orc looked at her, his stare hard. "Fatigue kills just like the Locust Swarm, my lady. Ten minutes, no more, to catch our breath. Rest your legs and drink some water."

Then he moved on.

"He's not wrong, you know," Grimald said. He pushed his cart to one side, out of the way, and arched his back, groaning. "I wonder if we'll have time for a bite. I forget the last time I ate."

He looked at Léa, and winked.

No good deed goes unpunished.

Life had taught that to Grimald, and the importance of minding his own business. Fastest and farther the lone traveler goes, as the saying went. And yet, much as he felt fine when he was on his own, he also felt the need for company, and conversation, sometimes. He had spent long days pushing his cart and barely speaking to a soul. Now he had company, and the world looked brighter.

"Hop on the cart," his mouth said before his brain could stop it.

They were on the march again, and the flax-haired girl with an arm in a sling had been so miserable, dragging her feet in the dust of the road, he could not refrain from offering her a ride.

She looked at him like he was an apparition.

He shrugged and turned to the girl's two companions, a tall half cat woman in a red coat, and an old man in a purple cloak who was looking at Grim like he was some sort of cut-purse or smuggler. He wondered what was going on with these people.

They had sat in silence in the ditch until the militia had called again for them to move. They had shared a small water-skin, and talked among themselves in soft tones. There was an air of quality about them, and Honest Grim had a good eye for quality, yet he had still to figure them out.

"We are going the same way," he said with a grin, "and this young lady won't be a burden."

The old owl arched an eyebrow, and walked closer to the cart. He was leaning on a walking staff, dragging his feet, but to Grim's well-trained eye it was obvious it was not as much as a physical problem as the old habit of someone that had spent a lot of his time with slippered feet over thick carpets. "And you can take turns," he was hasty to add. "To bring relief to your legs."

The old man stopped, and pursed his lips. "There will be no need for any of that, Master Grimald, thank you. My legs are perfectly fine."

Meanwhile, the blonde had hopped on the cart, pushing a box of bottled mineral extracts to the side. Grim wished she'd be careful. That stuff cost good money. She arranged herself, pulling her legs up and smoothing her skirt. She leaned on a stack of books, favoring her injured arm.

"You are very kind," the cat-woman said. She looked like the brains of the outfit. "Léa, say thank you to the gentleman."

The blonde mumbled a thank you, glancing at him sideways. She blushed.

"My friends call me Grim. They think it funny."

"And are we friends?" the cat-woman asked, in an ironic voice.

Just like he had imagined, she was a smart one, and Grim liked that. He shrugged. "Companions on the road, if you will.

There are times when a man needs all the friends he can find. And a woman, too."

"I am Brixida Lovell," the cat-woman said, her eyes gleaming. She pushed her shoulders back. "My friends call me Brix. And these are Léa, and Doctor Arnost Emery."

"And my friends," the old owl sniffed, "call me exactly that. Or just plain doctor, for brevity's sake."

"And we are grateful for your kindness," Brixida added, giving a hard stare at the old man and shaking her head.

"You from one of the Houses?" Grim asked.

"We have the privilege of being in the employ of Master Galter Petremol," the doctor said.

"The merchant." Grim nodded. He had heard about the man, and hoped his distaste did not seep through his voice.

"Wherever he may be at the moment," Brix added, her tone tart. It was the doctor's turn to stare at her. On the cart, Léa had fallen asleep, her chin on her chest, her breathing regular.

"Did he leave you behind?" Grim asked. He was surprised at his own surprise. Of course the master had left behind his staff. It was a commonplace fact in this world that you could not trust management, or look at them for loyalty, or mercy.

"He had more important things–" the doctor began, but he did not sound much convinced.

"Like saving his own skin," the cat-woman said.

"And his family." Doctor Emery was indignant.

"He did leave you behind." Grim nodded. "The coin of the rich and all that, uh?"

The doctor opened his mouth, then closed it. "Are you quoting to me the poems of Guy deMere, young man?"

"Some things the coin of the rich cannot buy," Grim said. "But that won't stop them try."

And it was all right to let them try, he said to himself. Some of his best sales had come from letting rich patrons believe they could buy the impossible.

"Of course you realize the skald of Mere was referring to happiness, and not–"

"Loyalty. Or a family. Or plain common decency. Yes, I know."

Grim saw that Brixida was looking at him sideways, and wiggled his eyebrows. The doctor coughed. "Exactly."

Grim shrugged. "Yet I still think Guy spent a few nights on an empty stomach, and made poetry out of it. That's a poet's life, isn't it?"

"I thought you said you were a tradesman, not a man of literary pursuits, Master Grimald."

"It's Grim, doctor. Honest Grim, if you will. And no sane man is but one thing and that alone during his lifetime."

He bent down to push on his cart. The wheels squealed, but the girl kept sleeping, cradling her broken arm.

Later, the militia called for another stop, and they settled down for another night on the roadside, trying to sleep in the ditch. The militia commander, an old man with a sour frown and a spade-shaped gray beard, wanted to move as soon as the sunrise came. His soldiers moved up and down the makeshift camp, making sure nobody lit any fire, and noise was kept to a minimum. Sentries were stationed along the road, and up the brief slope of the closest hill. A light rain had turned into a proper shower by the time the sun was down, and Grim retreated underneath his pushcart, allowing some room for the two women and the old man. The forced intimacy was not conducive to conversation, and they sat on the ground, wrapped in their cloaks.

"Why can't we light a fire?" Léa asked.

"We don't want the Uthuk to know our position," Brix replied.

The blonde girl gasped. "Are they so close?"

"Maybe," Brix said.

Grim shrugged. "Better a cold night on the ground than knowing for certain."

He shared with them the last of his rock-hard bread, and a skin of wine he had saved for difficult times. The cat-woman had some hard sweets. They huddled together, rain falling in thick sheets all around them, and waited for the dawn.

When the dawn came, so did the Blight.

Like all elven hunters, Laurel carried a bullroarer in a pouch in her belt, and now, as she pulled it out, she wondered whether anyone of those on the road would understand. Keeping her eyes on the gray-skinned Uthuk Y'llan cresting the hill, she unfurled the string and twisted it.

Below, the men and women on the road, freshly awakened after another wet night, would not see the Locusts until they were upon them. It would be a bloodbath.

She could not allow it.

Like a child who steps on an anthill watches with horror and fascination as the ground raises in a crawling carpet of enraged insects, Laurel had watched with a growing sense of horror the Uthuk warbands move through the grass and the vineyards. Mostly skirmishers, clad in crimson rags and carrying mismatched weapons, and a few blood witches scattered in their number, already humming their chants, summoning powers to drive the warriors into a frenzy.

Laurel took a long breath. As she started to twirl the singing wood, second thoughts came to her, bone-dry and useless, like ghosts haunting an ancient battleground. Her mind grumbled with self-preservation and hunger. As soon as the singing wood started its call, the Locusts would spot her and come to take her life. She wondered if it was worth risking her own survival to warn the strangers on the road of a danger they were too silly to see coming. Were they not the same that were welcomed to the Bloodwood with arrows and pit-traps?

But she knew it was worth it. Lives were lives, and past squabbles were meaningless in the face of the Uthuk Y'llan.

The instrument started humming as it picked up speed. It buzzed, like a large bumblebee, like a whole cloud of raging bumblebees, but as she forced it to spin faster, the sound turned into a deep roar, like a bullhorn or an enraged deer buck venting his challenge.

It echoed in the trees and down the slope, carrying far and wide.

The people on the road heard it. The warriors escorting them heard it.

The Uthuk Y'llan heard it.

Somebody understood. A bugle sounded down below, and the scream of a hundred bloodthirsty Locusts responded.

Laurel let go of the singing wood, and pulled back her bowstring.

One of the blood witches that had driven forth the warriors caught her arrow in her neck. The one by her side turned, screaming a warning, and another arrow caught her in her open mouth, silencing her forever.

CHAPTER FOUR

"Is this some kind of bird?" Brix asked. She looked around, trying to spot the source of the sound. She squinted in the early morning light, and yawned.

"Sounds more like a deer looking for company," Grim chuckled, and winked.

Doctor Emery scoffed. "I am afraid this is the wrong season for romantically inclined ungulates."

The sound increased in volume, rising and falling like the heartbeat of a man running. And running a man came, the big orc they had seen the previous day. After him, the captain of the militia thundered by, waving his hand and shouting. A trumpet sounded. The soldiers looked around like they were lost in a mist.

Grim and Brix traded a look, recognizing each other's fear. Not a deer.

"Brace for attack!" somebody shouted.

Something bounced on the road by their side, and rolled with a wet crunchy sound. Grim squinted in the mist and made out contorted features, a severed neck. Then the roar exploded like a thunderclap and the Uthuk came at them, running down the side of the hill, screaming for blood. For five precious heartbeats Grim was paralyzed, unable to avert his gaze. The warriors sank in the mud, and the lines of grapevines slowed them down.

Coming back to himself, Grim pulled Léa off the cart and rolled on the ground with her as a large, scarlet beast leaped over the luggage and landed on the cobblestones, its talons clicking. Eyes glinted, a low purring escaped its throat and its maw opened to reveal row upon row of sharp yellow teeth. Léa screamed. Grim hugged her and tried to close his eyes, but she would not stop staring and screaming. He watched as the creature prepared to spring, and then two, three arrows slammed in its back. It turned its head and sprinted in the direction of its attacker.

"Get up!" Brix hissed, grabbing Grim by the arm and helping him up.

A mountain of gray flesh rose in front of them, roaring. They caught an impression of mud-caked skin and crimson rags, of wild bloodshot eyes. Doctor Emery lifted his staff to defend himself, intercepting the descending arc of a stone axe. The black polished wood shattered and the old man staggered, stumbled, and fell on his back.

Shaking with horrid mirth, the Uthuk took a step forward, raising his axe again. A horse thundered by and a sword bit into his neck. Black blood pouring down his chest, their attacker turned on the new assailant. The horse reared, and the stone weapon missed its side and slammed in the rider's leg. Again, the sword descended in a silver arc and got stuck in the Uthuk's shoulder. Eyes wild with terror, the horse sprang on. The Uthuk turned to where Emery was still holding his broken staff. He lifted it as the wounded warrior stumbled and fell on him, crushing the old man with his dead weight.

Too many things were going on around him. Blood roaring in his ears, Grim looked for a way out. He saw Brix run to the shrubbery on the other side of the road. A soldier stood in front of her, screaming, and was suddenly silent. They both fell, and when she rolled back to her feet, she grabbed the hilt of the man's short sword. She stood, the blade in her hand. A massive, squat raider confronted her, a savage grin splitting his misshapen head. She lifted the blade in front of her, and he pushed it aside with the bone claws he had tied to his wrists. He made to grab her, and an arrow struck him in the hollow between the neck and the shoulder. He made a surprised gurgle, and Brix pushed her blade under the bone plates of his chest, pressing with both hands. His blood sprayed out. He looked at her with eyes that were not human, and then fell back, tearing away the sword from her.

The whole scene had taken no more than two breaths. Grim tried to pull Léa away, but she was frozen in panic. Grim could no longer see the old man. Fear gripped his gut, and he pulled the blonde girl along by sheer force of desperation. They needed to run, now.

The Uthuk kept coming, a screaming, bloodthirsty horde of demons and beasts, gray and red and relentless. Some dragged along broken poles and lumps of dirt as they trampled down the hill through the abandoned vineyard. One pulled a post from the ground and hurled it like a spear. It clattered unheeded on the road flagstones. There was no method or strategy to their attack, only a boiling bloodlust that pushed them forward. Their shouts and screams drowned the sounds of the scattering refugees.

A shadow fell over Grim, and he turned, again pulling at Léa, but it was just the orc from the militia. He stood with his legs apart, and swung his woodsman's axe, pushing back against the advancing creatures.

"Run to the bridge!" he shouted.

What bridge? Grim wondered. It did not matter. He would follow the flow. The militia was forming a flimsy line against the Uthuk. Archers shot blindly into the incoming mass, and spearmen waited, their weapons braced, fear and shock on their faces.

"Come!" he said to Léa, and pulled her violently. She finally took one step, then another. They moved in the same direction as everyone else.

A running man crashed blindly into them. Léa stumbled and fell. Grim caught a flash of a blue scarf, a pale face. Then he was gone.

Everything was going too fast. Grim helped the girl up again, and in doing so looked back, trying to get his bearings. A tall, broad-shouldered Uthuk slammed down towards the orc with a huge rock hammer, loaded with all the momentum of his downhill run. The soldier parried with his axe.

His heart thumping in his ears, Grim watched in fascination as the giant swung again at the orc, and again the orc parried. Despite his bulk, he looked like a child in front of the Uthuk. Again they engaged their weapons, and this time the orc staggered, and went down on one knee under the force of the impact. The gray monster threw back his head, his laugh suddenly turning into an angry growl as a length of black wood pierced his thigh. A bedraggled Doctor Emery, his clothes torn and smeared in black blood, retreated under the stare of the monster which, with a rumble in his chest, pulled the makeshift spear from his leg and tossed it away.

The orc's axe caught him under the ribs, and the Uthuk screamed in rage. Léa whimpered.

Another of the demons landed on the top of Grim's cart, crushing the boxes, breaking the bottles and scattering the books about. Grim stopped in his tracks, and Léa bumped into him. All this running, and they were still here.

He cursed, and his voice caught a witch's attention. She turned to them and let out a screech. She wielded a long gnarly staff from which feathers and bones hung, and started reciting a long string of twisted, angular words. Her face was crossed by an ugly scar that exposed the bone underneath, and her teeth. A wind from nowhere rose around her, shaking her red sash and her ragged skirts, and Grim took a step back as pale ghostly shapes started milling around her. The ghosts' cry rose in intensity, claws and teeth started taking shape. The blood witch's single eye burned like an ember.

Fleetingly, Grim remembered the old stories that had circulated in the academy's dorms, about mages and sorcerers being gifted and cursed with a glimpse of their own death. This was what it must feel like. This creature was Death, and she was here for him.

The monster pointed her staff, her eyes still on him and the girl. A sob escaped Léa's lips as the haggard shapes of the spirits wailed and turned their ghost-light eyes on them.

Grimald of Guyot decided right there and then he would not die afraid. There was no barrier between thought and action. What is a cartload of wares compared to two lives? Grim let go of Léa's wrist and pulled an alchemist's firestarter from his belt.

"Just a glass straw filled with white phosphorus," his shopkeeper's voice recited in his mind the usual selling routine. He had sold loads of them to pipe smokers. The glass was slippery in his cold sweaty hand. He snapped the fire-making charm and with a sigh tossed it on top of his wares.

"Kellos have you," he mumbled as the flames caught the books and the parchments, spreading to the chemicals in the bottles. For a moment that felt like forever, nothing happened. Grim whispered an oath. Then, with a loud bang, a column of blue-green fire engulfed the blood witch, rising in the morning mist. The creature's screams were loud and brief, and its train of hungry spirits dissipated with bark-like lamentations.

Grim lifted an arm to protect his face and turned around, looking for Léa. She was gone.

As the column of green fire rose in the sky and spread in a great cloud, raining black ashes over the road, Brix spotted Léa moving like a sleepwalker amongst the chaos. Moving swiftly, the cat-woman ran to the maid, just as one of the Uthuk beasts caught their scent and approached them with the slow deliberation of the predator.

"Mistress Brixida..." the girl breathed, her eyes wide and tears streaking down her face.

The beast was upon them. Brix pulled Léa to the side of the road and shielded her, facing the monster. The thing was powerfully muscled, a crest of spine running down its back, a segmented tail flailing. Its crimson head was a nightmare of sharp teeth. Under the black glare of the creature, all of Brixida's carefully cultivated civility evaporated, her father's teachings vanished, and all that was left was the animal instincts of her ancestors. She hissed like a scared creature of the wild, ears flattened against her skull. Her vision tunneled. Her claws extended from the tips of her fingers, and for the briefest of moments, the monster hesitated, confronted with an adversary it had never faced before. Her blade lost somewhere in the chaos, Brix cut through the air with her claws, trying to scare it away.

The beast sniffed at her blood-smeared hands. Growling in curiosity, it moved carefully closer. It dug at the ground with a clawed paw, its tail snapping like a whip.

An arrow shot through its neck, and as it turned a second arrow caught it in the eye. It made a surprised twittering sound, like a bird, and then it crashed to the ground. Brix stopped, confused for a moment. Through the running crowd, she saw an elven woman, her head a mane of brown locks, red marks on her face. She was wearing a coat of some dull brown material, and a rust-colored cloak wrapped around her arm.

Brix remembered her father wrapping his cloak that way, for parrying during a street brawl.

The elf pulled a long dagger from her scabbard and tossed it at Brix, who caught it in midair, surprised at the selfless gesture. The elf gave Brix a brief nod, and pulled another arrow from her quiver.

A horse thundered by, the man in the saddle cutting left and right with a big battle axe. "To the bridge!" he shouted.

Brix did not know where the bridge was, but she started running in the direction everybody else was, the elven blade in one hand, and Léa's wrist tight in the other.

Laurel was impressed by the desperate courage of the cat-woman. To face a blood beast from the swarm with her bare hands was the sort of folly that songs were composed about. Rarely would the brave that inspired them live to listen to them, but that was the way of the world.

As the monster lay dead in the road, she and the woman looked into each other's eyes, and Laurel felt a spark of something. She was not familiar with the ways of the cat-folk, but in this woman a spirit burned that Laurel felt akin to. They were sisters in battle.

She pulled her dagger from her belt, and tossed it at her. The woman caught it easily. What else can you gift a warrior, in the thick of the battle, but a chance to fight for their life?

Her arrow sought another target, just as the horse galloped by, blocking her line of sight. She moved back, seeking higher ground.

She saw an old man, leaning on the shoulder of the man that had summoned the green fire. Behind them, a giant wielding an axe screamed his defiance to the Uthuk Y'llan. He was bloodied and fearless. Again, Laurel admired his bravery, but the Locust Swarm did not need an invitation to come for their lives. A reed-thin Uthuk warrior dug at the orc, sharpened animal antlers strapped to his wrists. The orc swung his axe, and felled his adversary like a dead tree, the blade biting into his hip and drawing blood. As he disengaged his weapon from the thrashing berserker, another came at him from the side, with a cruelly curved blade in his hand. The old man hit him with a chunk of black wood, and as the Uthuk turned to slap away that disturbance, Laurel shot him through the neck. She was rooted in this moment, and all she could do was help as much as she could.

A screaming woman slammed into her and pushed her back into the ditch. Laurel managed to keep her balance. A bone scythe, no more than an animal jaw tied to a tree branch, crashed onto the screaming woman's head, and a gray-skinned warrior pushed her aside, her face running red with blood. He stood over Laurel. Her hand went instinctively to her belt, in search of a dagger that was not there.

A sharp-toothed grin split the Uthuk's face as he raised his weapon. Then the monster screamed as someone stuck one of Laurel's own arrows in its side from behind. The short man in a black hat. The one that had made a fire. It was so sudden and unexpected, even Laurel's focused mind missed a beat.

The gray-skinned warrior turned and slapped the short firemaker out of the way. Laurel used her bow like a club, hitting the warrior in the back of his knees. He staggered, screamed, unable to cope with too many adversaries, and a swing from the orc's axe ended the fight.

And then they were gone.

The stillness was so sudden Brix felt the ground drop from underneath her, like she was falling from a cliff. Her mind reeled, her heart pounding in her chest.

Gone.

She turned around, catching Léa's pale features, the twisting smoke rising from the remains of a burning cart, the bodies scattered over the cobblestones. The smell of blood was suddenly thick and revolting in her nostrils. She dropped on her knees, retching. The elven dagger was still in her hand, the blade slick with the Uthuk's black blood. She had no memory of using it, no recollection of the creature she had stabbed. Her wrist ached.

Voices were calling, people crying. Bits and pieces were scattered everywhere, resembling the passing of a storm. Bags and baskets of food, ripped cloaks and broken bodies. Dead people. Militia, civilians, and the gray hulking shapes of the Uthuk. Brix shuddered violently and closed her eyes. She heard the voice of her father, coming from a long distance, and remembered.

"Close the distance, duck under their guard, stab."

She had stabbed a leering Uthuk under the armpit, as he lunged to grab her. She retched again, but she had nothing to throw up but her fear and the acid juices of her empty stomach.

Flashes of the elven huntress shot through her mind. The elf had not been scared. She had been strong, resolute, elegant. And she had helped her. Brix kept down on all fours, taking long slow breaths, and looked at the chaos surrounding her, trying to spot their companions, trying to quieten the thoughts screaming in her head.

The orc soldier had been wounded, a long gash along his arm and a cut just below the bottom of his dented breastplate. Knees cracking, Doctor Emery knelt by his side. "Are you all right, young man?"

The orc groaned.

Looking up, Emery saw an elven woman in a russet cloak. She carried a long bow over her shoulder, and was pulling arrows from the carcass of a downed beast. Her own arrows. Her face was painted with a star shape of sorts on her forehead. She had clear eyes, hard as steel.

"Can you help, please?" he called. She stared at him, frowning, as if surprised he would talk to her. "This young man seems to be in much pain from his wounds."

"Not much," the orc said, with a lopsided grin.

The elf woman's lips twisted. She looked around.

"Please," Emery repeated. Then he turned, "What's your name, boy?"

The orc gave him a weak smile. "Tanner, sir."

The elf shook the arrow in her hand to clean it from the gore, and came closer. Without a word, she slipped the arrow into her quiver, and then ran her fingers along the exposed cuts. She had a serious face, Emery saw.

"Keep moving!" came a voice, and the sound of hooves. A bugle bleated in the distance.

The captain of the militia towered over them. "Can that man move? Tanner, right? Look alive."

Emery glanced at the elf. She was crushing some dried herbs into the cut. The orc grimaced and groaned.

"I'll be right up, sir."

The elf looked at him but did not speak.

"We need to move," the captain repeated. "The bridge over the Morshan river is two miles away. Beyond the bridge we will be safe."

Arnost Emery looked around. "We have yet to pass the crossroads to Mayvale," he said, sniffing. "Which means by my reckoning we are at least four miles from the bridge, as the crow flies. An interesting expression, if you think about it, as the crow flies–"

The captain coughed and spat. "That's more reason to hasten. Get him up and going. Beyond the bridge we will be safe."

He kicked his horse and moved on, repeating his call to get moving.

"I seriously doubt crossing the bridge will do us any good," Grim said, coming closer. Emery nodded in agreement. There were burn marks on the shopkeeper's leather vest, and black smears on his face. He gave a long look at the elf, who had finished dressing the wounds of the orc, and was now standing. "You're quite handy with that bow."

She looked puzzled. "It's my bow."

"Damn straight," Grim said. He clapped his hands. "Help us get this big guy on his feet, will you? His captain wants him up and going."

She hesitated for the briefest moment, and then helped pull the orc up. Grim gave her a sign of thanks. Emery recovered the orc's axe and handed it to him. The big warrior thanked her too, and made to grab her hand. She pulled back, and he blushed.

"You're Latari, aren't you?" Grim said. The woman looked at him, a puzzled frown creasing her forehead. He waved a hand over his face. "The warpaint. You're what? Bloodwood?"

She straightened her back and nodded.

"I'm Grim," he said. "And this is Doctor Emery. Thank you for your help."

"First Lance Tharadax Tanner," the orc said.

The elf woman frowned, staring at Emery. "A doctor?"

"Not that kind of doctor, I am afraid," Emery said. "I studied words, not bodies. Your help was quite timely, mistress."

"I am no mistress," she said. "I'm just Laurel."

"Thank you for your help, Mistress– ehm, Laurel," Emery said.

With a last wave of his hand, Tanner walked carefully over to his fellow soldiers. Laurel watched him go. "I shall leave now," she said. "You should follow your captain. Or don't. It's your call."

Emery frowned. "What do you mean?"

"The road is not safe," she said. She nodded at the surrounding hills. "This side of the river, or the other. It's a box, it traps you."

"Just as I was saying–" Emery agreed.

"Damn straight," Grim stage-whispered.

The elf turned to go. "Be safe."

"Wait." Brix walked up to them, dirty and disheveled, with Léa still in tow. She gave a brief nod at Emery, and an even briefer look at Grim.

"This is yours," she said. Her hands were stained black. She held the dagger by the blade, and offered it to the elf hilt first. Elven handicraft, Emery noticed, utilitarian yet elegant.

Laurel looked down at the blade and then up at the cat-woman. "Keep it," she said. "You will need it."

Reforming the column and getting it to move was taking forever. Captain Ventner kept riding up and down the bloodied stretch of road, his voice raw from the orders he was shouting. Rage burned in his gut and helped him ignore the pain in his right leg, where a glancing blow from an Uthuk hammer had caught him. He would not complain about the pain. They had lost seventeen civilians and ten of his soldiers, and he was too smart a man not to realize they were alive because the Uthuk had passed them by. The bulk of the horde had washed over them like a wave over a rock, and continued in its advance. They were alive because they were too dismal a prey.

"Captain, if I can have a moment of your time, please..."

He reined his horse to a stop and looked down at the small band of civilians standing by the remains of a burned pushcart. He smelled a mix of smoke and chemicals. An old man in a purple cloak took a step forward. The man that had been helping Tharadax Tanner, he remembered.

"This young woman," the old man said, "might have some important information you need to hear."

The young woman was an elf, an unruly mane of brown hair and her face painted red with star patterns. Ventner wondered if it was blood, and whose blood it was. Not an Uthuk, for sure. She carried a longbow and stared belligerently at him. He had met her kind before.

"We do not have time–"

The old man cleared his voice, like he was going to give a talk to a classroom. "With all due respect, sir, I believe you should pay heed to one that has a better grasp of the lay of the land than ..." he hesitated, "than we have."

Behind the old man and the elf, a rotund man with black hair and a cat-folk woman in a man's clothes stood motionless, waiting. A young woman with an arm in a sling sat by the side of the road, rocking gently.

"What then?" Ventner looked up and down the road. His soldiers were spread out along the column, pushing the refugees to move. He had no time to waste.

"The Locust Swarm moved north and west," the elf said. She had a dark contralto voice, not what he expected from her lithe frame. "If you go to the river, you will meet them again."

"They will not pass the river. The banks are steep in this point, the water wide. And the bridge is defended."

Her voice was deadpan. "The men at the bridge are dead. There is only death for you at the bridge."

"Dead?" Ventner frowned, a chill settling in. "You saw it? Speak!"

She shrugged. "Some things you don't need to see. The ones that attacked you have gone forth to the bridge. They are following the road just as you do, and it points like an arrow to the bridge. The mud of the fields will not hinder them there. They will kill your soldiers."

Ventner tasted copper on his tongue. "You can't be sure. The bridge is a bottleneck. They will have to come at us in a column ..."

"Are you willing to run this risk, sir?" the old man asked.

"They are not soldiers," the elf woman said. "They do not march in column. They are the Blight."

"We should take to the fields and seek cover," the cat-woman said.

"I have my orders," Ventner replied, and hated himself for it. Orders were the last refuge of the incompetent. He gave a hard stare at the elven woman, and then turned to the old man. "What do you propose, then?"

It was the elf that replied. "Yonder lays a village–"

"Mayvale," the old man said. "Three days along a fair road, with a clear view of any incoming dangers."

"The Blight have been there already," the elf said. "They will not come back. Not for a while. You could rest there. Plan a defense. Then decide."

Ventner looked in the direction the elf had pointed, where the fields faded into a light woodland, and the hills rose in gentle waves. But that was uncharted territory, and he still did not trust the elven woman. The bridge would be guarded, and safe.

"I have my orders," he replied. "We go to the bridge, and then continue on to Sundergard, and from there to Riverwatch."

CHAPTER FIVE

"We are coming with you."

Laurel looked at Brix. "You don't go where I am going,"

The old man cleared his voice, but once again it was the woman that spoke. "You are going off this road, and away from the plains. We believe we'll be safe in the woods. Safer."

"I am going to the Bloodwood," Laurel said. "To my people. You are not welcome there."

And yet, she thought, they were not coming to burn and cut down trees and plow the land. They were not settlers, bounders to be pushed away, but refugees. Allies, maybe.

Brix nodded. "Taking our chances in the Bloodwood sounds like a better plan than the one our captain's so set on."

Laurel looked into her amber-colored eyes, reading what was burning there. "Spite is not a good master."

The woman turned to look at the old man, and he nodded. "We do not mean to spite the captain, Mistress– ehm, Laurel," he said. "That's not our purpose or counsel. We should move away from the Uthuk, not follow them. And as you said, the road is like a snare, and we are the rabbit. We want to get out of it before it is too late." He spread his arms. "For some of our companions it was already."

Laurel took a deep breath, and tried to weigh her own choices. Was she hastening to the Bloodwood to join her people in the battle to come, or was she just worried for Redstar?

She knew there was no honor in leaving these people behind, just as she knew the old ways had been broken, and it was not for her to decide who would be welcome in the Bloodwood, and who wouldn't.

"You will slow me down," Laurel said. "I will not wait."

"We won't," the cat-woman said. "And should we become a burden, you are free to leave us behind."

"Even if we'd rather you don't," the man in a hat said, and winked.

Curiosity whispered in Laurel's ear. Who were these people? What moved them? Where did they fit in the flow of nature? And truly, wasn't knowledge a worthy pursuit for a warrior?

Curiosity was what had brought her from the Bloodwood in the first place. It was curiosity that gave her the final nudge. She pointed at the top of the hill.

"When the sun touches the crest, I'll be gone."

The cat-woman nodded. "We'll be ready."

First Lance Tharadax Tanner could read the miles they had traveled in the lines on Captain Ventner's face, and the battle fatigue in his slumping shoulders and his limp. The old man turned to him and frowned. He patted the side of his horse, which answered the gesture with a snort.

"What now?" Ventner asked.

Tanner shifted his weight from one foot to the other, feeling like a schoolboy caught playing truant. His side throbbed where the Uthuk blade had caught him. The officer's frown deepened. "Speak up, man, or get moving."

"Those three," Tanner said. "And the elf woman." He pointed at the cat-woman and the old scholar as they conversed with the short man in a black hat. The old man was handling a short lance, looking at it like it was a venomous serpent. The copper-headed elf was standing by, perfectly still, waiting.

Ventner grimaced. "What about them?"

"Are we really leaving them behind?"

They were taking to the fields, following the elf. Ventner sighed. "It's their funeral." Then he gave Tanner a stern look. Tanner was a full head taller than the captain, but he felt like the blue eyes of the old soldier were causing him to shrink. "What's on your chest? Speak up."

"I think we should not…"

The young orc stopped.

"Should not what?" Ventner said, giving voice to Tharadax's own uncertainty. "They made a choice. Are we to tie them up and drag them along? Will you carry them on your shoulders?"

"No, sir." Tharadax scoffed. "But–"

Ventner snorted. "But what? They made their decision. And who knows, maybe they have a point."

"If you believe they have a point–"

"I believe they'll be dead by tomorrow evening. And if the Uthuk do not get them, the Latari will greet them with arrows, like they always do. And to be completely honest, one way or the other, their going means one less problem for us."

Tharadax felt like he had been slapped in the face. "And you are letting them go anyway?"

Ventner shrugged. "We have a duty here. Our duty is to protect the people."

"And aren't they people? Sir?"

"They are troublemakers, and you are slowing us down with this useless debate."

"We are supposed to protect all of these people, sir." It was strange, having to explain what was plain to see for him. He cleared his throat. "All of them. If we leave some behind, if we knowingly leave them to die… How can we say we are doing our duty, sir?"

Ventner looked up at the sky, and the lines on his face distended. For a moment he looked younger. "Our duty," he said. Then he looked at Tharadax, straight into his eyes. "This is not a night out in the fields, hunting for poachers, boy. This is a blight like in the old stories, this is the First Darkness all over again. A proper war. And in war one needs to take decisions, and make choices. Look for the greater good, no matter what. And that is the reason why there are officers. To take responsibility, and carry the weight of those choices. The weight of the dead, and the lost." He nodded at the four heading into the field. "They made their choice, they will carry the weight."

"But–"

Ventner shook his head. "A conscience is a luxury in war."

"We could leave behind someone to escort them," Tharadax said.

"We have lost enough men on this road. You want me to sacrifice, what, three fighters, for two schoolteachers, a shopkeeper and an elf? You want me to pick them, and order them to lay their life on the line in the Bloodwood?"

The orc straightened his back, raising himself to his full height. He managed to keep a straight face despite the pain in his side. "No, sir. Just one. I will escort the refugees to Mayvale."

"What do you believe you will find there, but burned houses?"

A good question, and one Tharadax had asked himself. Now he gave Ventner the only answer he had been able to find. "I don't know. But we'll go on to the Bloodwood. I will see them there safely."

Ventner grimaced at the name, but looked closely at the warrior standing in front of him. "You are crazy, boy. You think the Latari will welcome you? After centuries of hostility?"

Tharadax ignored his question. There had been talk, of course, among the soldiers, about Ventner's distrust for the elves. A good man, but he had spent too many years on the border of the Latari lands. But this was no longer a time for such prejudices. "We cannot leave people behind like this. If we do, we are no better than the Uthuk."

Ventner looked at Emery leaning on a lance, Brixida with her borrowed dagger, and short-legged Grim, turning his hat in his hands as he talked. He looked at Laurel, standing like a statue, holding her longbow, her face a blurred oval with red marks.

"They have the elf to protect them," he said. "She's good with her arrows, and knows the lay of the land. Maybe she'll talk her people out of slitting their throats."

Tharadax just straightened his back, and waited.

"This is foolish," the captain said.

"I swore an oath, sir."

"You swore to follow orders. You did not swear to die."

Tharadax smiled. "In fact I did, sir. We all did."

The old soldier looked up at the sky again, like he hoped to find an answer in the slate-colored clouds. Then he turned. "Quartermaster!"

The quartermaster hobbled by. Like the captain he was a veteran, and as a young man had served in one of the Baron's armies, three decades before. "We are ready to move, sir."

"Put it in your book," Ventner said. "First Lance Tharadax Tanner is hereby assigned a reconnaissance mission to the east and the south, to spot Uthuk activities in the direction of the elven enclaves. He will report back in due time, in Sundergard or in Riverwatch. He is leaving the column now. He is to receive rations for five days. His pay will be docked until he rejoins the force."

The quartermaster gave a long stare at the captain, and then eyed the orc. Then he pulled the book hanging from his belt, wet the tip of the writing stick, and scrawled some lines on a page. He had only three fingers on his right hand.

"Noted, sir," the man finally said.

"Fine. Prepare to move."

They watched the quartermaster go back to the column.

"Thank you, sir," Tharadax breathed, the full import of his decision only now starting to dawn on him.

Ventner shrugged. "Wait." He unhooked his great battle axe from the saddle.

"Here," he said, handing it to Tharadax. "This has served me well. And it's better than that lumberjack iron you carry."

Tharadax weighed the axe, surprised at how well balanced it was, how light it felt despite its bulk. The blade twinkled grimly, and the grip was well-worn leather.

"Thank you, sir," he said again.

"Be careful out there, boy."

For the third time, Léa shook her head. "I am sorry, Mistress Brixida. I can't."

She was sitting on the ground, with the former governess crouched in front of her, lithe on her long feet. Now she snorted. "Of course you can," Brixida said, in the same tone she had often used with the children. Léa wondered passingly where they were right now. In their father's home, in Sundergard, behind tall defensive walls, with strong, armed soldiers guarding them. Soft beds and warm food. She shuddered, and pulled her arms around her.

"The master said we should join him," she said. "In the house in Sundergard."

The cat-woman's ears flattened. "The master left us behind." There was a cold, cutting edge to her voice. "We have to fend for ourselves now."

Léa shivered. "The soldiers will protect us."

Brixida cast a quick glance at one of the militia as she walked by. A tired woman, her spear on her shoulder, the dented helmet hanging from her belt. There was a dirty bandage around her forehead. "Will they?" Brixida asked.

Léa looked at the governess for a long moment. She had changed. She was wearing the master's clothes, and had done her hair in a tail, like a street urchin. There was a long knife tucked in her sash, and she had laid a sheathed sword on the ground by her side. Léa did not recognize the weapon, but she recognized what Brixida was doing. She was acting like a swashbuckler from one of those stories she was so fond of reading. "Reading books instead of living her life," Cook had always said. A foolish little girl with dreams above her station.

But this was not a story, Léa knew. This was a cold road in the middle of nowhere, and there were monsters in the hills. A sword found somewhere would not help them.

"I am not an adventurer," she said. How could Brixida not see? "And neither are you. We are servants. We are not good at making decisions. We wait for instructions from our betters, and act accordingly. And we don't go adventuring."

"We are what we make of ourselves," Brixida replied.

Léa turned and gave a long look at Grim, where he was rummaging in the remains of his burned cart. The man had a knavish charm, she admitted to herself, for all that he was on the short side. And he was a man of means. A shopkeeper. But he, too, was taking the road to the woods, following the elf and Brixida's dreams of adventures.

"You dream above your station," she said, and only when she saw Brixida's stricken features did she realize she had spoken out loud. She felt her cheeks burn, and hated herself for that. And yet, they all said that, in the servants' quarters, that the cat-woman believed herself better than she was. She pretended she was a lady. Nothing good would ever come out of it, Cook had always said.

"You can't just up and go adventuring," Léa said, spite creeping into her voice. "This is not one of your silly romances, where serving girls become princesses, and marry a pirate."

"I don't want to marry a pirate!" Brix replied. Then she hissed. "This is silly."

Léa scoffed.

"We are not safe on this road," Brixida said, again in her scolding tone. "You heard what Doctor Emery said ..."

Léa cast a glance at the old man, leaning on a lance. "As if he knows," she mumbled, and shrugged.

Brixida's eyes widened in outrage and surprise, but Léa did not care anymore. She was not the one being unreasonable. "He's just a musty old man who's spent all his life reading musty old books."

"And he is right," Brixida said, anger seeping into her voice. "We have better chances in the woods. And with an elven hunter with us, we'll be able to ask for the Latari's assistance."

With some effort, Léa stood, and dusted the bottom of her skirt.

"Do as you please, mistress," she said. "I will not go running in the fields like some woodland sprite, chasing somebody else's dreams to go and live with the fae."

Grim came closer. "Our guide's going," he said. He had gathered what remained of his things in a satchel, and carried a rolled blanket. He was rubbing his fingers, blackened with ash. "We should move, too. She doesn't look like the sort that waits for others."

Brixida collected her sword and stood. "Léa will not come with us," she said, dryly.

Grim looked at her, and took his hat off. Like a beggar, Léa thought.

"Why?" he asked, in a soft voice.

"I think it's foolish," Léa said. She tossed her head, like she had seen Mistress Eulalie do a thousand times. "The militia is here to protect us. Sundergard is a fortress. Once we are there, we will be safe. We shall just follow their orders, and everything will be fine."

Grim worked his jaw, like he was trying to say something. Then he pushed his slouch hat on his head. "Take care of yourself, girl."

She watched him walk away, and Brixida too.

This was not a romance, she repeated to herself.

Brix gave a long hard stare at the orc soldier as he came for them, wading through the tall grass like he was crossing a river. He was carrying a big battle axe, and the red scarf of the militia was tied to a strap of his backpack. He had dropped his dented breastplate, and was wearing a leather armor instead. It did not fit him, and as he came closer she could hear it creak when he moved.

"We are not coming back with you," she said. Then she turned to her two companions. Both Emery and Grim nodded, neither with much enthusiasm. Laurel was already a hundred paces on, and did not seem to have any interest in them.

"You will slow me down," she had said. Brix was now set on proving her wrong. She had no time for the orc.

"I know you are not coming with me," he said. "In fact, I am coming with you."

He gave them a bright smile, his tusks white against his dark lips.

Brix scoffed. "What for?"

He ran his left hand over his head. His black hair was braided and dirty. "I thought you might need some help. So, I decided to come along."

Brix hissed. "Well, what if we do not need any help?"

He gave her a look. "With all due respect, my lady," the orc said, pointing at the sword on her hip, "it takes more than a sharp blade to survive in the wild. You people don't look like the sort that will be much good at foraging, if you excuse me saying so, and you're not used to sleeping rough."

"While I guess you are, right?"

He gave her a lopsided grin. "I might have done a bit of poaching in my day."

"Will that help us sleep more comfortably?" she asked.

The orc opened his mouth, his eyes wide. "Uh, I mean–"

Grim took a step forward and placed a hand on Brix's shoulder. "Mistress, have you looked at this guy?" he stage-whispered. "The man has more muscles on his bones than the three of us together, and he looks like he can work that cutting implement he's carrying. And at least we can talk to him and hope for a reply, which is more than the elf is going to give us. Of course we need his help."

Brix shrugged Grim's hand off and eyed the orc. The short man had a point, she admitted to herself. They would need all the help they could get. "Do you have a name?"

"Most people do," he replied with another of his lopsided grins. "Mine's Tharadax Tanner."

He offered her his hand, but then thought better of it and pulled it back. He rubbed it on the front of his cuirass, as if to clean it. He stood there like a big schoolboy. He shifted his weight from one foot to the other. A six-foot tall schoolboy with tusks, she conceded, but a schoolboy nonetheless. She tried to keep a straight face.

"Tanner sounds like a stone-dweller's name," Grim said. "Were you a poacher or a rat-catcher? Nothing wrong in neither, mind you."

Tanner's eyes widened and his cheeks burned. He babbled something, and Brix was no longer able to hold back her laughter. "I'm Brix," she said, putting her hand forward. "These are Doctor Emery and Grim."

"We've met," Tanner replied, and nodded at them.

"Do they call you Thar?" the shopkeeper asked.

"Tanner, actually."

"Tanner it is, then. Welcome to our little venture." They shook hands. "As you may have guessed, Mistress Brixida is the brains of our company, the one that keeps us in line," Grim said, grinning. "And Doctor Arnost Emery is a much-needed beacon of wisdom in these here wild parts."

"And Grim's a jester, despite his name," Brix said. But the shopkeeper's words had stirred something warm in her chest, just like Tanner's naive attitude. She turned, and was surprised to see that Laurel had stopped, and was looking at them from a distance, waiting in the tall grass.

"And as for Laurel," she said, and then shrugged, "she's an elf, I guess."

A bugle sounded on the road behind them, and slowly the column of refugees shuffled on. Brix tried to spot Léa, but the young girl was lost in the crowd. She pulled her coat closed, trying to suppress a shiver. The sense of betrayal and the worry for the girl were pulling her in opposite directions. She watched as the column moved slowly. The captain of the militia lagged behind, reining his horse in, and lifted a hand. Tanner waved back. Then the captain rode on, shouting orders.

"They think we are the strange ones," Emery whispered, standing by her side. He had tried to talk a few others into joining them, but they had just looked at him like he had lost his mind. They were like sleepwalkers, desperation smothering their minds.

Brix sighed, and started again. "We are not."

"It will rain by dusk," Laurel said as they approached.

"Tanner is coming with us," Brix said.

The elf looked at the orc for the space of a long breath. Her eyes lingered for a moment on his axe. "Good," she said. Then she turned and started again towards the distant line of the woods.

"Not much of a conversationalist," Grim said.

"Let's move," Brix replied.

CHAPTER SIX

They crossed the field and headed for the woods, the dirt road to Mayvale to their left as they marched eastwards. The Great Plain here faded into a hilly, sparse woodland. Walking the road would have made their going faster, but Laurel had apparently no intention of doing so.

Laurel led the file, moving rapidly through the tall grass. Brix came after her, easily keeping pace, and then Grim, who kept glancing over his shoulder to make sure Emery was not left behind. The old man was wheezing a little, but he moved briskly, leaning on a lance that Brix had found somewhere for him, which he was using as a staff. Tanner closed the file. He had picked up a long leaf of grass, and was sucking on it, like a shepherd on a day out.

"But then," Grim mumbled to himself, "what do I know about shepherds?" Brix heard and glanced at him, and he grinned at her.

When they came to the woods, it was like a wall in front of them. The trees stood close to each other, their roots intertwined, emerging from a thick undergrowth of thorny bushes and ferns, shrouded in thin, ghostly mist.

"We'll have to hack our way through," Grim murmured, and glanced at Tanner's axe.

But they did not.

Laurel walked to where the trees and shrubs were thicker, and she seemed to disappear.

"What now?" Emery huffed, voicing their surprise.

They hastened after her, and soon Tanner found a gap in the vegetation that Laurel had gone through. Now the elf was advancing briskly, and she seemed to follow a path none of them were able to see. Through a clearing and then into the trees again, weaving around the tall oaks and stepping past the bushes, barely leaving a trace. They tried to keep her pace, and follow in her steps, and it was like the woodland opened to let them pass, and then closed again at their back.

Laurel did not turn to check whether they were following .

She marched on, along a creek, and then over a fallen tree up to a cleaved rock, where she turned sharply south and walked along a chalky rock crest for the rest of the morning. Brix and the others followed, and dared not look back. Soon the ground began to rise, and they slowed, the distance between them shortening. The sun climbed as steadily as they did, and reached its peak. A cold breeze blew from the east, pushing the low clouds together, making the light patchy. Thunder sounded in the distance, and they could see the gray draperies of rain as autumn showers swept the fields and vineyards, coming in from the east.

"We could stop for a bite when we reach the top," Grim said in a thin voice. Nobody replied. He shrugged, and looked back. The hills were closing in, shrouded in ghostly fog, the shadows of the clouds running along their sides. The trees were a patchwork of green, copper and gold, standing in line where the fields ended. Like a bastion, a defensive wall. From halfway up the slope they could not see the road anymore.

"Are you fine, old man?" he asked.

Emery harrumphed.

"Save your breath for the climb," Tanner said.

Grim sighed. He fanned his face with his hat. "Shouldn't there be birds out here?" he asked.

"You're scaring them off," the orc replied.

Grim pushed his hat more firmly on his head, and pressed on.

Then, without a warning, the land seemed to run away in every direction, and they were at the top of the next hill. A copse of gnarled trees guarded the summit, the windswept sentry-post of the forest that now surrounded them. Laurel stopped, and with a happy sigh Grim sat down on a large rock, in the shade of a small tree.

"Resist the temptation," Tanner told him.

"What?"

"Right now you feel like pulling your boots off. Don't, or you won't be able to put them back on."

Grim sighed, wriggled his toes in his boots, but followed Tanner's suggestion and tried to forget his aching feet. Try and enjoy the sights instead. They were in a place of austere beauty. All around them, the landscape was silent, wave after wave of land and deep woods. Blades of light cut through the cloudy cover like sunlight through a high temple's windows. A thin mist clung to the trees in the distance.

Brix handed him a water-skin. Grim nodded a thank you, but before he could drink, a flurry of wings broke from the top of the trees, and a flight of birds took to the air above them. Sparrows, he thought. Or rooks. Or something.

They stood watchful for a moment, but nothing came. Brix

sighed, and Grim looked at her. She realized that she too had been holding her breath. Laurel was right: they were a bunch of city-dwellers, and knew nothing of the wild.

"I wonder what happened to Aerendor Keep," Emery said, looking east. He was leaning heavily on his lance.

"Nothing good, I fear," Tanner said. He glanced at Laurel, but she did not say anything. "The Uthuk came through the plains," he went on. "The least that happened is they laid siege to the Keep."

"The Keep can withstand a siege," Emery said. "One hundred and twenty-seven years ago–"

"If the Lady Harriet had any sense," Grim said, cutting him short, "they did not wait for the Locusts to get there, and now they're on their way to the mountains. Better for them to chance the passes and the early snows than the Uthuk Y'llan."

They all fell silent again, looking at the smear of green and blue that was the horizon. Then the orc pointed. "There's Mayvale," he said. "See that smoke?"

They watched. Halfway to the horizon, a large column of black rose in the air, its source hidden in the thick of the trees.

"That's no chimney," Grim said, his voice cracking. The Blight had put its mark on the land, and there was no way to ignore it. Without turning, he handed the water back to Brix.

"No," the orc replied. "Not a chimney."

A deer emerged from the ferns, antlers branching proudly over its head. It shook the rain from its back. A cloud of mist-like spray surrounded it for a moment. It turned and looked in their direction, fear and curiosity in its dark, quiet eyes. Then something moved in the undergrowth, and the deer leaped away, and soon disappeared amongst the trees.

Laurel had stopped, her eyes on the big buck. Now she started moving again, and again the others followed in the waning light. An owl called from the trees, welcoming sunset and the beginning of its hunting night.

Tanner took a deep breath, savoring the fresh, clean air and the smell of the moist ground under his feet. He did not care about the rain that much, the hood of his short cloak protecting him enough. Memories of youthful mischief came back to him, when he would leave behind the city walls and with his brother and their friends spend a night out in the wild, looking for hare trails and pheasant nests. Away from the smell of smoke and chemicals of his father's tannery. Most days, the boys would spend time shooting their slings against piled rocks, or following the course of solitary creeks, looking for trout to catch bare-handed and cook on small fires.

He liked the quiet of the wild, and time passed swiftly as his legs did the walking and his heart pumped blood into his limbs. It was like waking up after a long sleep. When he looked around again, the sun was setting and the elf was gone. He stopped, and cursed under his breath. He had been stupid, and reckless, and got lost in his reveries instead of paying attention.

Brix caught his eye, and silently pointed up a tree. Laurel was settling at the fork of a large branch, about ten feet in the air. She had her bow in her lap, and was loosening the straps of her armor.

"Looks like we are stopping for the night," he said.

"Are we going to climb up a tree?" Brix asked.

Tanner laughed. "If you feel like it, Mistress Brixida, by all means go ahead. I will not try to stop you. Me, I'm no squirrel, and I think I'd rather look for a sheltered spot on the ground."

She grinned, and bowed. "Make way."

The spot turned out to be a jutting spur of rock on which the roots of a large ash tree hung like a skeletal hand. By stretching a blanket over these finger-like appendages, Tanner was able to build a shelter large enough for the four of them. Wrapped tightly in their cloaks and coats, they sat down and passed around a skin of wine and some cheese.

"We could light a candle," Grim said. "And enjoy its warmth. A small flame would be enough."

"A little warmth is not worth the risk," Tanner grunted. "The light might attract unwanted attention."

"In this drizzle?" But then Grim shrugged. "Better safe than sorry," he conceded. He rummaged in his bag and came up with a small metal flask. He unstopped it and took a gulp.

"Here, for warmth," he said, handing it to Emery.

The doctor smelled at it. "Brandy?"

"Strictly for medicinal use." Grim winked.

The doctor took a gulp and handed the flask to Brix, who shook her head, as did Tanner.

With a shrug, Grim put it back in his bag. Then, with a satisfied grunt, he removed his boots and started massaging his feet.

"Won't she get cold out there?" Doctor Emery asked. He sounded honestly worried about the comfort of their silent guide.

"This is her life," Tanner said. "Contrary to all of us, Mistress Laurel is a creature of the woodlands."

"I thought you were supposed to be an expert woodsman yourself," Brix said.

"But I am no Bloodwood elf," he replied. She was needling him, but Tanner recognized the attitude as something so many used to strengthen their bonds in a group. It had been this way with his friends, when they ran the fields and the woods, and it had been this way with his companions in the militia. Not hostility but camaraderie, if somewhat awkward coming from a slim, elegant creature like Brix.

A loud screech rent through the night.

"What's that?!" Brix asked. She sat up, her ears flattened.

Grim shook his head. "Some kind of night bird."

"It did not sound like a night bird to me," she replied. Her fingers found the hilt of her sword.

"A fox, going about its business," Tanner said, easily.

Brix pulled her coat closer. "What business?"

The screech repeated. Tanner shrugged. "You know, its business. Fox night business."

Her eyes widened as the fox screeched a third time. "Oh, I see."

"Not all things that go about in the woods are monsters," Tanner said. But she was a city creature, much more than himself, and he could understand her fear.

Sometime later, Brix stretched out her legs and laid back against the gray rock. "I wonder if what they say about the Bloodwood is true. About the Aymhelin, really, and the Latari elves. I read a lot of stories about elven princesses and such, but usually they dressed in fine silks and were courted by brave knights. There was a lot of poetry involved. None of them was as silent and bloodthirsty as our friend out there."

"Makes you glad she's on our side," Grim chuckled.

"I guess it depends on which sources you trust," Doctor Emery said, adjusting the collar of his cloak. "About the Aymhelin and the Bloodwood and all that, I mean. The elves themselves have been less than forthcoming, in the ages past, about their history and their politics. For all that we fought side by side against the darkness, they are a private and aloof people, and seem to perceive us as upstarts and bounders. Maybe with some reason. And from what I read, I am not even sure that princesses exist in the Bloodwood."

"It was not about the politics of the elves I was thinking," Brix said. "But more about the dark legends that surround the wild in which they live. Everyone seems to agree the Bloodwood is a dangerous place."

"Mostly because the Latari live there," Grim said.

"You don't like the Latari?" She gave him a sharp look. "And yet here you are with us, seeking sanctuary in their domain."

"In all honesty," Grim said, brushing some crumbs from his shirt, "I wouldn't be here had we not an elf with us. No disrespect intended to you people, of course. And it is not an issue of disliking the Latari – and I have nothing against them, mind you. It's just that the Bloodwood was never renowned for being a cheerful, welcoming place."

"Certainly with a name like Bloodwood it does not sound cheerful at all," Brix said.

"While often mentioned in stories, there is not much known about the Bloodwood," Emery intoned, ignoring his companion's glances. But Tanner was curious to hear what the old man had to say. He knew the Latari only from rumors and stories, and as an orc he had learned young that rumors and stories were often worthless, and wrong. And yet Emery was a book learned man, and he did seem possessed of a sharp mind, despite his age. He waved a hand, motioning the old teacher to go on.

"The region," Emery said, "as we all probably know, is

said to derive its name from the red color of the foliage of its trees, according to legend and fable due to the spilled blood of ten thousand enemies that soaked the earth of an ancient battleground. Which is preposterous, of course, if certainly fascinating in its own grim way, and somewhat off-putting."

"Especially so if you think the blood in question was ours," Grim said. He pulled his boots to the side, and sat cross-legged. "Or the orcs'. Invading barbarians, right?"

"I do not believe that the story has to be taken literally," Emery said, skeptical. "It is likely a romanticized memory of a much more mundane historical fact, handed down through the generations."

"If the elves are as long lived as they say they are," Tanner ventured, "maybe it's not a matter of generations."

"But the message the story conveys is pretty straightforward anyway," Grin replied. He pushed his bag against the rock and used it as a pillow, interlacing his hands behind his head. "As I said, I'm glad we have someone vouching for us, even if she does not fit Mistress Brix's idea of an elven princess."

"I do not believe," Emery said, dryly, "that one should give too much thought to what is found in romances."

Brix's ears flattened against her skull. "I've been told that already."

The old man blushed. "I did not mean–"

"Of course not."

She curled up and wrapped herself more tightly in her coat. Her eyes were lost in the distance, and she gently shook her head. "Had I known my choice of pastime was so important, I would have kept it more private."

Tanner and Grim traded a look. The short man shook his head and shrugged. There was something there, Tanner thought, something that Brix and Emery shared. He understood they had worked in the same grand house in Vynelvale.

"The girl was scared," the old teacher said, with a sigh, and Tanner suddenly saw they were talking about the blonde girl that had been with them. "People often lash out at others when they fail to confront their own fear. And they use words they do not really believe. Léa had no right to say what she said, and you should not take her words to heart."

Brix propped herself up on one arm. "But we left her behind. That's what hurts."

"It could be argued," Emery said in a soft, reasonable tone, "that it was us that she left behind."

Brix took a deep breath, and nodded. "And then again."

"The hurt does not change what's been," Grim said. He yawned. "And I am as sorry as you are young Léa made that choice, though I barely knew her. She looked like a nice girl and all that–"

"Really, now," Brix snapped.

Grim paused, and looked down at his hands. "Sorry. I did not mean to sound patronizing." She just snorted. "But what I meant," he went on, "is that it's not like we could knock her out and carry her along. She made her own choice."

"You should not carry the responsibility for your friend's decision," Tanner said, the words of Ventner echoing in his mind. "Although I guess it's not easy to let go."

"She was not my friend," Brix replied, her voice sour. Then she sighed. "We better try and rest."

She rolled on her side, turning her back to them, thus signaling the question was closed.

"Good idea," Grim said, and he pulled his hat over his face.

"We should take turns and keep watch," Tanner said.

"What about the elf?" Grim said from underneath his hat. "They don't sleep, right? Isn't it what they say? Sleepless and immortal."

None of them answered him. It remained unspoken that none of them quite trusted Laurel.

Tanner groaned. "Fine, I'll take the first turn."

"You go on and rest," Emery told him. The orc looked him over. The old man was so thin, he could have lifted him with one hand. Yet he did not seem as tired as he had been along the path.

"When one gets old," the doctor said, as if reading the question in his eyes, "one needs less sleep than in one's youth. Maybe it's because little time remains, and soon a long sleep will come, and body and mind react accordingly. So you sleep, and I will keep watch until the moon goes down, or the rain stops. Tomorrow the road will be long again to reach Mayvale, and whatever we'll find there. Rest, young man."

At the foot of the hill a narrow brook ran by, singing. Laurel stopped and washed her hands in the cold water, and then ran a wet fingers on her neck. She glanced uphill behind her. The four refugees were still negotiating the last part of the descent, careful on the steep goats' path down.

They were not as quick or as silent as her people would have been, but she was impressed by their persistence. The one in the hat, Grim, was helping the old one, the doctor, who was clearly afraid of stumbling. The others were scanning the trees, sniffing the air. It was like they were trying to outrun their fear, she thought, and every time their going became slow, they grew nervous.

"Here's some cool water," Tanner said as they approached.

Grim accompanied the doctor to the creek. The old man took a long breath and then bent, his back creaking like dry branches, and dipped his fingertips in the water. He straightened up and ran his thumb on his lips. He nodded, and signaled to the short man that he could leave his side.

"We have therefore come to a border of sorts," Emery said. He might be short of breath, but still had words aplenty. "Here we see perfectly where the countryside ends and the wild, as it were, begins."

It was an interesting idea – that the world was not one whole, but a mosaic of different parts and pieces. They were very fond of building boxes, these people. And yet it did not seem to make their lives any easier. It would be good, Laurel thought, to have the leisure to discuss philosophy, but this was not the time.

"It's still a long way to the Bloodwood," she said.

A single fat raindrop plopped on the brim of Grim's hat. Another followed, and another.

"Come," Laurel said, and sauntered across the stream. When they did not follow suit, she turned, expectant.

"Uphill, and soon under the rain," Grim said. He looked at the sky and scowled, but Laurel knew it was just the wind, carrying raindrops from the east.

"At least we're in good company," Tanner said, and slapped the other man on the shoulder.

Grim made a face, but then laughed. "Yeah, I guess so."

Laurel watched the woman, Brix, help the doctor cross the river, while the orc picked up the rearguard again.

They were strange, these four, but whether it was the strangeness of all the city dwellers, or something more personal, more about them in particular, Laurel could not say. She had traveled a lot, but her experience with the people of the Free Cities was limited. And although they were slowing her down, just as she had predicted, they were also intriguing in their own way.

She could learn about them, if not from them. The world was changing fast around them, and Laurel felt learning about other people was a good thing if both Latari and humankind wanted to weather the passing of the Locust Swarms. That had been one of the reasons she had left the Bloodwood in the first place, together with Redstar.

The previous night she had listened to them chatter as they huddled under a rock. The bitter Brixida, the falsely cheerful Grimald, soft-spoken Tharadax and the old man Emery, so full of words. The intertwining of their voices had sounded like a dawn chorus. Maybe she had spent too much time alone, Laurel thought, tracking her enemies. A worthy pursuit, but there were higher things too. She pulled up her cloak's hood, and wondered what she would learn from these strange companions.

Behind her there was a brief scream, a curse, and then a splash. She turned to watch as Tanner, standing with one foot on the creek's edge and one in the water, pulled Grim, dripping, to his feet.

"You fine?" the orc asked.

"Swell," the man grumbled. He squeezed water out of a corner of his cloak. "At least getting rain-soaked won't be a problem anymore."

The next time they stopped, Brix saw Emery collect a leaf from the ground. After turning it this way and that, he took a book from his bag and placed the leaf between the pages. She moved closer, and noticed there were already a number of other leaves sticking through the pages. It was the same book he had been reading on the coach.

"Do you collect leaves?" she asked. Their former master, Galter Petremol, had collected books he did not read, and coins. His whole life, she reflected grimly, was about collecting coins.

Leaves made more sense to her, and it was a side of the old man she had never suspected.

"Not as such," he replied. "You see, I realized I do not know the names of many of the trees we are seeing. I spent too long in a city, surrounded by walls and cobbled streets, I suppose."

Brix nodded. "I was thinking something similar. I know enough to see there are different trees around us, but not enough to put a name on them."

"Isn't that irritating?" He put his book back in his bag. "I have asked our young friend," he said, nodding towards Tanner, who was busy picking blackberries from a bramble bush, "but his knowledge of the wild is eminently practical. He can't name trees, but he will tell you which is the likeliest to carry edible fruits or be associated with palatable mushrooms. Our master Grimald, on the other hand, knows a lot about herbs used for cooking or, somewhat less surprisingly, in potions and infusions, but is otherwise quite unable to put a name on a tree unless he has a use for its bark as a cough remedy. So I decided to collect along the way samples of the trees I find more interesting, and plan to learn their names later, either from a book, or by talking with someone more botanically inclined."

"Have you tried asking Laurel?"

The elf was within earshot and turned to them. "Ask what?"

"Do you know the names of the trees?" Brix asked.

Laurel frowned. "Not all of them," she said slowly. "But many of them don't know mine."

And she started along the path again, leaving Brix standing there, open mouthed.

"So you are a schoolteacher," Tanner said.

Emery looked up from where he was sitting, and gave him what he hoped what was a reassuring look. "I'm fine," he said. "A little short of breath, but I'm fine."

"It's all right. But that's not what I asked."

Emery chuckled. "You sought an excuse to wait for me, and make sure my heart is still beating. Which is much appreciated."

Tanner just shrugged.

Along the path they were following, the golden leaves on the ground were like a carpet on the forest floor. The others were moving on. With a groan, Emery stood.

"Yes, a teacher," he said. "Private tutor, to be exact. That is, a teacher to the rich."

Tanner helped him along, and soon they were catching up with the rest of the band. Emery was tiring easily, increasingly so as they went. He could see the others were worried. The young orc was just the one that showed it more openly. And Emery shared some of their worry. He had never planned on becoming a burden to the young.

"The rich do things differently, isn't that what they say?" Tanner said.

Surprising himself, Emery laughed out loud. The others along the path stopped and turned.

"Mostly," he said, placing a hand on Tanner's shoulder, "they can afford to pay someone for doing it for them. But in my experience, they are not as different as they like to think."

"That's a reassuring thought, don't you think, doctor?"

Emery thought seriously about it.

"Maybe so, yes. Maybe."

Part Two

SHADOWS OF THE BLOODWOOD

CHAPTER SEVEN

In the gray light of the late morning, Mayvale was a score of stone and timber houses huddled around a well, the mud of the streets churned by feet long gone. The forest surrounded the buildings, cuddling them in a protective embrace that had not been enough to defend the hamlet. The rain had washed away the smell of smoke from the air. Only the physical signs of the fires remained. Thatched roofs had been set aflame, and two of the cottages were burned-out husks, the stone walls smeared in black, the timbers blackened and consumed. No wall protected the houses, but orchards and gardens, bare now for the coming autumn.

They watched from among the trees, looking for any sign of life, any possible menace. The hamlet was silent and still. A lone crow sat on top of the roof of the well, the only living thing they could see or hear.

"Let's go," Grim said. He was not one for sleeping rough, and the three nights they had spent wrapped in their cloaks, under the rain, had left dark circles under his eyes, his round face sallow.

"Not so fast," Tanner said. He was crouching behind a thorny bush, trying to hide his bulk.

"Whatever was here," Emery said, "seems to be long gone."

Grim snorted. "And maybe it's better this way."

"Probably the same warbands that attacked us on the road," Tanner said, tightening his grip on his axe.

"Where are the bodies?" Brix asked.

"There are some old stories, from the time of the First Darkness–"

"Maybe we're better not knowing," Tanner said, shutting Emery off.

"Not knowing won't do us any good," Grim said. The only knowledge that had ever hurt him had been not having enough.

"I agree," Emery said in turn. "Ignorance is bliss only to the ignorant, and what you don't know will hurt you all the same, no matter what some dubious popular wisdom holds to the contrary. Usually such maxims are expounded by those that have a vested interest in other people's ignorance."

Grim agreed. "Forewarned is forearmed."

"Fine," Brix hissed. "I'll go and check."

They all turned to her.

"What?" Grim spat.

"This is a soldier's job," Tanner said.

Brix stifled a chuckle. "Really? Did you tell her?"

They all watched where she was pointing. It took some effort to spot Laurel, perched on a branch of a large oak overlooking the village. She was so perfectly still that she seemed to merge with the autumn leaves and the shadows. Her tunic was another patch of light, her green and brown armor another clump of fading greenery. She was holding her bow, one arrow ready.

"I should be the one going," Tanner said.

"You're not a squirrel, remember? Nor a Bloodwood elf. I'm lighter on my feet than you'll ever be, and I'm used to moving silently." With a snap, Brix undid the clasps of her coat, shrugged it off and handed it to Grim. "I'll go and check," she repeated. Her tail whipped her hips, betraying her nervousness. "If something happens–"

"We'll run the other way," Grim replied, and winked.

Tanner made to speak, but she cut him short. "You keep your eyes and ears open, I'll give you a sign if the coast is clear."

Brix went lightly through the back yard of the first house. She skirted around the abandoned chicken coop, its gate open, the birds gone. Eggs trampled on the ground. Not a fox, the cause of this destruction. A single feather laid in the mud, so white it seemed to burn in the uncertain sunlight.

She leaned gently against the wall of the burned-out house and scanned the dirt road going into the village, and the square surrounding the well. The stone was warm through her shirt. The crow was still perched over the well. She squinted at the trees and tried to locate Laurel. It would have been nice of her to acknowledge their presence, and maybe plan a common strategy. It would be good to have the archer covering her. But the elf was nowhere to be seen.

Brix loosened the sword in its scabbard and slid along the wall. By a window, she looked in. The roof had collapsed, everything was blackened timber and ash, pale graying embers still live, if fading. A lone metal plate, dented and stained, was half-buried in the still smoldering remains. She moved on.

As she crossed the street, the crow spotted her and cawed. It flapped its wings, as if challenging her to come closer, but did not fly away. She kept an eye on it and moved on, soft on her feet. Years spent moving as a shadow in the corridors of the Petremol house had made her adept at being stealthy.

Yet she had to agree with Léa. This was not like one of her romances. The stories had lacked the foul smell, the mournful sense of oppression. The fear knotting her guts and, yes, also the excitement. She could feel her heart beating in her ears.

A door dangled from leather hinges, beyond it a common room, wrecked. She went in, careful where she put her feet. Not so much a sign of violence, as of a sudden, frantic escape. Yet the planks of the floor were stained the color of rust, the smell of blood sharp in her sensitive nostrils. The place had been savaged but not looted. A single field mouse looked at her from the top of a grain sack, and ran.

She went out at the back and continued on, moving from shadow to shadow. As she approached the well, she could see the houses were in better shape, untouched by the fire. The doors had been crashed through, and the interiors devastated, but the roofs were still standing, and there were no soot smears on the walls. Whoever had attacked the village had set only the outermost houses on fire. To scare the people, to push them in a certain direction. She waited for a moment in front of the small shrine to Kurnos. The god of the druids had not done much to protect this village and its people. She wondered passingly if the gods of the land had grown tired of humans and their petty squabbles, and welcomed the Blight.

She pushed aside such morbid reflections and looked inside another abandoned building. How many had lived here, she wondered, and where were they now?

She heard something and froze.

Brix looked at the crow, who looked back at her. A donkey brayed, and someone cursed. A door slammed.

She glanced at the bushes where her friends were hiding. She could not see them, but was sure they were there, staring at her. She lifted a hand, pointed at her ears, then at her eyes, then at the next corner. She tiptoed there, and carefully peeked around the house.

A donkey loaded with wicker panniers stood in a small, cobbled courtyard, its long ears turning this way and that, scared. A man came out of the nearest building, carrying a big burlap sack. He was tall and broad-shouldered, a thick handlebar mustache his most prominent feature. He was wearing trousers with a knotted rope as a belt, and a loose tunic, stained with grease. He dropped the sack in one of the panniers, and rubbed his hands together.

"Come on!" he called in a hushed voice as he turned.

A dwarf with a bald head emerged from a nearby shack, a long beard tucked in his belt. He had two small barrels, one under each arm. "Look what I found!" he chuckled, not caring to keep his voice low.

"This will make us a nice bundle," the man said.

Brix pulled back, breathing slowly. Looters. The fear of the Blight had been so strong, so present, she had forgotten the common rapacity of the good people of the land.

The two thieves were arguing now, in hushed tones. Not here for some fabled treasure of legend, but just to steal food and provisions, and whatever else had been left behind. Warm clothes, thick blankets, tools, and weapons. Money, too. Brix caressed the hilt of her sword. She dared look again. The two looters were standing by the donkey, and trying with much hand-waving and head-shaking to find a way to load the two casks onto the animal.

Finally, the man gave an exasperated huff and announced

he would go in and look for a rope. In he went, his companion looking at him go. The donkey brayed again.

Brix took a step back, then another.

She never knew where the Uthuk came from. One moment the dwarf was commanding the donkey to stop his noise, the next he was holding his throat, the spiked fist of an Uthuk raider buried in his beard. The dwarf spluttered and spat blood. Stepping aside, the Uthuk turned to the donkey, and a second punch cut the animal's braying short.

The donkey staggered and collapsed on the paving just as the man came out of the house, carrying a rolled-up rope. His face was blank for a moment. He dropped the rope. The Uthuk stepped over the dead dwarf.

Brix suppressed a gasp and took another step back. She should run. She should warn the others. Seek refuge in the wood. She took a deep breath, ready to sprint.

A hand grasped her shoulder. "Where do you think you are going, uh?"

She turned and stared at the rough-faced woman standing in front of her. She had a long knife with a triangular blade in one hand, and a sack in the other. She gave Brix a mean frown.

"Run!" Brix hissed. The clash of weapons echoed behind them.

The woman smirked. "What the–?"

The crow croaked, loud, and flew away, its wings flapping. A lance punched through the woman's back and jutted out of her sternum. A surprised expression passed over her features, and she looked down, incredulous. Her legs failed her, the light faded from her eyes. A second Uthuk warrior had gone around the house and caught them as they squabbled.

Brix cursed in a very unladylike fashion and dove through

the nearest window, the sound of steps and a bloodthirsty growl drawing closer as she did.

Brix landed on a floor strewn with broken pottery and dried up foodstuff. She rolled behind an upturned table just as one of the Uthuk raiders came in through the door. He screamed and charged at the table head first, like a raging bull. Hissing, Brix was pushed back until the table legs hit the wall and boxed her in. She looked up as the bone axe of the Uthuk descended towards her head. She dove to the side, between the table legs. The jagged blade bit into the wood, and she ran for the door.

A hand as big as a ham grabbed her tail and pulled her back, painfully. She screeched as the Uthuk lifted her bodily. He reeked of fresh blood, old dirt and decay. Her claws left grooves on the floorboards. He tossed her against the wall. She turned in midair and landed in a crouch, the short sword glinting in her hand. Her adversary took a moment to free his axe, and she lunged and cut at his leg. The blade slid over a bony spur and cut through the thick skin and muscle, two inches above the knee. The monster screamed, and Brix jumped out of the path of his weapon, the blade hissing by her ear. The floor shuddered under the impact.

He was still between her and the door. And there was another one, out there.

Brix glanced at the nearby window, measuring the distance. Large enough for her to get out, not for an Uthuk to get in. The voice of her father sounded in her head. Deep, warm, the words clipped. "Against a larger opponent, you should always use your size and speed to your advantage."

She could almost remember the smell of the waxed floors of the gymnasium, the warmth of the air, and the motes of dust in the sunbeams. Her mother had not approved of Hatoz teaching their daughter his trade, but he had always good-naturedly ignored her.

The Uthuk punched through her reverie, and she barely dodged his fist. Her breathing slowed down.

"Dance on those feet, girl!" her father had said. "Keep moving, keep avoiding their blows. They will tire, or make a mistake. That's when you strike."

But the Uthuk did not seem to be the sort that tired easily.

He swung his axe again, and when she ducked to avoid it, he hit her with his free hand. Brix crashed into the wall and went down on her knees, winded. Her sword rattled in a corner of the room. Pain spread in her side and her chest.

"Only amateurs lose their weapon," her father had said.

She grabbed the edge of a sideboard and pulled it down. The wooden frame crashed on the floor, scattering pots and dishes around. The Uthuk was forced back for a moment, to avoid being crushed.

"It's a dance, I tell you, girl," her father had insisted, "A dance, and your adversary makes the music. Feel their rhythm, and use it."

Again the axe fell. Then a step closer, and a punch. Brix dodged, crouched, danced away. He was swinging with his axe with his right hand, and when he pulled the weapon back, he lunged with his free left hand. He would step forward when he stretched his left, his weight on the right foot.

She flexed her fingers, showing her claws.

The Uthuk laughed and reached for her, his left hand barbed with bone spikes. She kicked a stool in his way, aiming at his right leg. She jumped, grabbing one of the wooden beams above and vaulting under the roof. The Uthuk was unbalanced.

He stumbled and fell, crushing the stool. He was momentarily entangled in the wreck of the sideboard.

Brix stepped lightly on the beam, looking for a way out. Keep moving, she thought, make him tire. Ignore the cobwebs and the dust. Don't sneeze, keep your eyes open. The beam creaked.

The axe slammed into the wood under her feet, splinters flying, and she vaulted through the air. Her stretched claws sank into the wood of the next beam. She kicked, let her weight carry her, and dove out of a window feet first. The light of the day blinded her as she rolled in the mud and scrambled to her feet.

She stumbled on a body lying in the street. She had but a moment to see the arrow stuck in the prone body's left eye socket. Then arms grabbed her, and she was again rolling on the ground, thrashing to get free. She caught a glimpse of the dead donkey, and the dead looters, and screamed, the smell of blood choking her.

"It's me, Brix, it's me!"

Her brain recognized the man's voice just as she rammed her elbow into Grim's face. He cursed and let go. She turned in time to see the first Uthuk shamble out of the house, limping, and get caught in the gut by the shining crescent of Tanner's axe. The silver blade bit deep, and Tanner let go of the handle. His momentum carried the dying Uthuk forward and he landed in the mud, pushing the axe blade deeper.

Brix looked up, and saw Laurel perched on the top of the roof, her bow at the ready. The elf nodded at her.

For a long moment everything was perfectly still. Then the Uthuk on the ground kicked, shuddered, and died.

The wrecked village was silent again, and Brix could only

hear the roaring of the blood in her ears. Her hands were as cold as ice.

"I thought you were supposed to run the other way," she said to Grim. The man was massaging his jaw, but grinned at her anyway. "Maybe I should have," he groaned. "But you seemed to be having such a good time–"

She was not sure if he winked at her or if it was the eye where she had punched him.

"Sorry for that," she said.

"No good deed goes unpunished, huh?" He grinned.

With a grunt, Tanner turned to the dead Uthuk and freed the silver axe. "Are you all right?" he asked, looking up at her.

Brix nodded.

Both men were panting. They had run through the undergrowth. They were mud-splattered and dirty. There was a brown leaf in Tanner's hair, and Grim's pants were riddled with brambles, and his shirt was torn. How long had she been fighting? Ages, it seemed.

The crow came back to perch on the well, and cawed at her.

"Who were they?" Tanner asked.

Brix glanced at the bodies and shuddered. "Looters, I guess."

She remembered the surprised look on the woman's face, the strange blank expression of the man as he walked into the Uthuk's arms.

Grim shook his head, and cursed under his breath.

"You were lucky," Tanner said.

Brix was shaking as she heard her father's mocking laugh. "You can't count on luck, girl. You're a fighter, not a gambler."

She stood straight, and wiped the mud off her face.

"I am Brixida Tanith Lovell," she said, pride giving her voice an edge. "I am the daughter of Hatoz Lovell, first swordmaster to the duke of Reviere. Luck has nothing to do with what I do. I am not a gambler."

The orc's eyes widened. Then he lowered his gaze. "I stand corrected, Mistress Lovell. Peace."

"Peace, yes," Grim said. A bruise was spreading under his eye.

Brix limped past the dead Uthuk and towards the abandoned house. "Now if you please, I'll retrieve my sword."

She did not want them to see her cry. She had been lucky, and she knew it.

"Do you think she'll be all right?" Tanner asked. "Who's this Hatoz she speaks of?"

Grim shrugged. Together with Tanner, they were dragging the bodies into one of the burned-out houses. "They might attract carrion eaters," the orc had said. "Or worse."

They had buried the three looters the same way. Emery had said a few words, and wondered briefly about their story, about where they had come from. The donkey had been heavy, and it had taken all three men to drag it into the shed, after they had taken away its panniers. Now they were taking care of the raiders.

"There is, or there was, a duke of Reviere," Emery said. "Very minor aristocracy, had an estate outside of Riverwatch. Never amounted to anything in local affairs, but–"

"She certainly can handle herself in a fight," Grim said, a new respect in his voice.

"This is quite interesting," Emery said suddenly, tapping the body with the end of his lance.

Grim let go of the dead Uthuk's ankle and stretched his back, groaning.

"You might lend a hand," Grim said, with a sly look at the old doctor. "This thing weighs a ton of rocks."

"And it looks like it's going to be raining again soon," Tanner added.

The old man arched his eyebrows. "A ton of anything weighs just that, a ton, rock or whatever."

The orc gave Grim a glance. The man pushed his hat back and sighed. "Fine, then. What is so interesting about this brute?"

Emery used the end of his lance to pull aside the crimson rags the creature had worn, and pointed. "Look at the pattern of scars on the creature's chest. Over his heart, notice how the lines seem to form a clear geometric design. A circle cut by three slashes, from the left to the right."

Grim looked down at the body. Bone spurs pierced the creature's ashen skin, over the shoulders and along the arms, giving it a jagged profile. There were bone plates under the epidermis. Ugly marks crisscrossed its body, telling a story of violence and brutality. "This guy's kept together by scars and bruises."

The old man snorted. "Yes, I imagine that life in the desolation of the Ru Darklands is not conductive to an accident-free existence. And yet, if you will only apply your powers of observation, you will notice that these are not like the rest of the signs on his body, and his companion has exactly the same design, in the same position. Over his heart, which I daresay cannot be a coincidence. And this, to answer your question, is what I find interesting about them. They are marked, they carry a brand of some kind."

Grim clicked his tongue. The old man was right. The sign on the chest was different. It was geometric, deliberate, like a lord's crest, or a strange glyph from an ancient language. A language he did not recognize. He crouched down, and ran his fingers over the lines. He grimaced at the cold of the creature's flesh. The scars were in relief, like ridged grooves. They had rubbed some kind of alkaline salt in the cuts to make them stand out. The old man was right. It was a sign of some sort.

Grim's long dormant curiosity stirred. "This must have hurt," he said.

He turned. Laurel was perfunctorily searching the other body. He went to her, careful not to step in the pooled black blood, and she looked up at him. She was holding a rough leather pouch. She tossed it away in disgust.

"Do you have any idea what that is, on his chest?" he asked the elf.

The other dead body showed the same design. Everything else was different, the shape and position of his bony crests, the network of cut, puncture, and laceration marks. But they carried the same sign.

Laurel frowned, and shook her head.

Grim looked back at Tanner, who was still holding the dead Uthuk by the ankle. "Do you remember any of this on the ones that attacked us on the road?"

Tanner let go of the body. "I was not paying attention–"

"I don't remember anything like that," Doctor Emery said. "Just in case anyone is wondering."

Brix came out of the house, cleaning her sword on a piece of rag. She leaned on Grim's shoulder and peeked at the dead Uthuk. "It looks like a crest," she said. She glanced at Laurel. "You know anything about it?"

Again the elf shook her head. Grim thought she looked

worried, the first time any emotion other than curiosity or silent contempt had been painted on her face.

Thunder rumbled in the distance.

"Let's save the mysteries for later," Tanner said. He picked up the legs of the Uthuk again. "Come give us a hand, Grim."

CHAPTER EIGHT

They camped on the second floor of one of the village's largest houses, a single candle throwing a bubble of light. Grim had found some hard cheese and even harder bread in one of the looters' panniers, and had also retrieved a cask of wine. The house pantry had provided more food.

"They did us a courtesy rounding up this stuff for us," Grim said.

"This makes us no better than those poor guys out there," Tanner observed. "Robbers."

Sitting on her own, Brix listened in silence, surprised at how everyone felt like talking.

"I never claimed to be better than them," Grim replied. "I'm just alive, and they are not. It is a crime to leave this stuff for the crows and the wild dogs when there are people with empty bellies."

Tanner's stomach rumbled, and that was all the answer the other man needed. Once settled in one of the houses, Grim had lit a small fire inside of a pan, and had boiled some oats, seasoning them with some spices he had in his bag. Brix wondered what else he was carrying in his precious satchel.

She would have imagined parchments and alchemist supplies, but not food seasoning.

"Just like my mother used to make it when I was a kid," he said, as they all took some. Offered a bowl of the sticky mixture, Laurel had sniffed suspiciously at the food, and then nodded appreciatively after tasting a spoonful. Outside, the evening had brought more cold rain, and it was good to be dry and safe. They had shielded the fire as best as they could, and locked the night outside.

"She'd cook for us, and then for the guests at the inn," Grim said. "And back in the day I did not really appreciate what a bowl of warm gruel can mean in the life of a man." He eyed Brix. "Or a woman, of course."

"The young often overlook the simple things of life," Emery said, wisely. He was the only one sitting on a stool. "A warm dinner and a dry place to sleep is often all that we need to feel content."

He held the steaming bowl in his hands and stared at Brix. "You never hinted at your skill with a sword," he said.

She sighed. There was no escaping this conversation.

"One does not have much opportunity for swordplay when caring for brats," she said. She shifted where she sat, and wrapped her tail around her right leg. "But believe me, there were days…"

Then she sighed again, and laughed a brief laugh.

"My mother did not approve of her daughter becoming a sell-sword," Brix said. "Not the proper occupation for a good girl, she said. I stopped practicing when I was," she shrugged, "fifteen."

After her father's death. But she did not say that. She sat on the floor, her red coat spread beneath her, her legs crossed.

"Not that long ago, then," Grim said. Food and wine had

brought back his cheer. With his round face and a black eye, he looked like a bulldog. She chuckled, and looked at where Laurel was perched on the window sill. She was peering into the darkness outside. She had shared food, but was not sharing stories with them. She listened.

"My mother had been a dancer when she met my father. They met somewhere on the coast of Lorimor. And when I was born she became the governess to the Reviere children, of which there was a whole army, given their habit of raising all their little ones together. My father trained their men, my mother looked after their children. It seemed normal for me to follow her path when I became of age."

"A sword-wielding schoolmarm," Tanner said. He had shoveled the oats into his mouth faster than any of them. Now he munched a piece of bread, and shook his head. "Next we'll learn that Doctor Emery is a runemaster from the Halls of Greyhaven."

The orc was becoming more confident and open towards the doctor, who did not seem to resent his simple humor or his frequent questions.

"Or you are the son of a chieftain of the wild." Grim laughed, but Brix caught the ghost of a frown passing over his face at the mention of the Academy.

"I am afraid I have no mystical powers whatsoever," Doctor Emery said, spreading his hands, "hailing as I do from a different sort of academia." He stretched his hands towards the candle flame, and then rubbed them together.

"And what about you, Master Grimald?" Tanner asked. "What secrets do you hide under your merchant's clothes?"

Grim drank a gulp of wine before he spoke. "A pair of aching feet, and an empty belly."

"Well, that last part at least we'll take care of," Tanner said, handing him a piece of cheese.

They laughed, but Brix still saw something there, under the surface. She was sure the doctor had sensed it too. For all his long-winded affectation, and despite his body's frailty, his mind was as sharp as a diamond, and untouched by old age. And there was something the shopkeeper was not telling them, something that weighed upon his soul that he strove to keep well hidden under his hat.

The conversation lagged, and they listened to the rain falling on the thatched roof, and through the branches of the surrounding forest.

"We can't stay here," the doctor said suddenly.

It was something they had discussed, along the road, their original plan to go to ground in Mayvale and weather the storm. Let the elf go on to her people, and try to spend the winter in the village. That felt like wishful thinking now.

"Those two were no stragglers," Tanner agreed. "Scouts, probably. More of them could come, and next time we might not be so lucky," he nodded at Brix, "or skilled."

"It would be nice to know whence those three robbers came, too," Emery said.

"If for no other reason, to avoid the place like the plague," Grim nodded.

"Maybe they have a safe haven of some sort," the old man said. "A sanctuary we might want to join."

Grim grunted. "A sanctuary that needs food."

"We could buy our way in with food."

"A sanctuary of looters and robbers." Brix remembered the eyes of the woman that had faced her, and hissed. "I am not sure I'd like to spend time with any friends of those three."

"And any sanctuary remains such only as long as it is secret," Grim added. "They would not welcome us."

"We continue south, then," Brix said, and looked at Laurel. "Away from the plains and towards the heart of the Bloodwood."

The elf looked back at her.

"My people will not turn you away," Laurel said finally. She did not sound very convinced. Brix wished she could read the elf better.

"Which means we should call this an early night," the doctor announced, pulling his cloak about him. He stood from his stool and walked to a bench along the wall, eyeing it with suspicion. "Tomorrow will be here soon, and bring more miles through the woods."

"And more aching feet," Grim grunted. "And more rain."

The others mumbled in agreement.

Brix stood and walked to the window. She had slung her sword on her shoulder, the golden sash like a baldric. Laurel looked at her, questioningly.

"Go take some rest," Brix said. "I'll take the next shift."

Laurel nodded. "They won't come tonight," she said.

"But I'll be on the lookout anyway." Brix smiled.

The elf stood.

"We never thanked you properly," Brix said.

Laurel's frown deepened, a question in her clear eyes.

"For helping us out there," Brix went on, feeling a growing awkwardness. "On the road. And for taking us along."

The elf shrugged. "It was the right thing to do."

Brix shifted her weight from one leg to the other, and ran a hand through her hair. "Not everyone does the right thing. And–"

Laurel placed her right hand on her shoulder. "It's fine," she said. "You're worried they will come in our sleep. Which ones? The ones with the sign on their chest? Or more looters?"

Brix sighed. "I worry about a whole lot of things."

A single tapering stone stood upright in the middle of a small clearing. The grass grew around its base. The breeze had piled the brown leaves of autumn at is foot, and it pointed to the sky like an accusing finger. Swirls and grooves were etched on its smooth surface, and Grim found it difficult to focus on the pattern. The thing gave him a topsy-turvy feeling he did not like one bit.

"Here your woods end," Laurel said.

Grim took a deep breath, and looked at his companions. The air had been cool for most of the morning, but they were warm from the long walk. They had packed and divided among themselves all the food they had been able to find in the ruins of Mayvale, and had added a few blankets and a bunch of tools to their kit.

"And yours begin?" he asked. "The Latari's?"

The trees looked closer around them. Older. There was a vague sense of menace in the air. Like being watched by some invisible foe, hiding between the branches. Grim wondered if the others could feel it too.

Laurel looked at him, puzzled. "They are not ours," she said.

"I did not think your people built with stone," Doctor Emery said, coming closer. He peered at the design on the stone from underneath his bushy eyebrows, and sniffed. He ran a finger along one of the grooves, following it. He pulled his hand back, rubbing his fingers together. He shook his head and tapped the stone with the staff of his lance.

"Not in the Bloodwood," Laurel said.

"Who put this up, then?" Tanner asked.

Laurel shrugged. "It's always been here."

The old man blinked, for once lost for words.

Brix brushed her hand across the surface. "But what does it mean, exactly?"

"Your woods end here. From here on your rules don't work anymore," Laurel said. "Your people should stay out."

"It tickles," Brix said, under her breath. Her tail swung from side to side.

"Tickles?" Grim turned sharply, but the others were not listening. The longer they stood here, the less he liked it. But Brix just lifted her shoulders and walked away from the stone.

Tanner looked around. "And whose rules work, then?"

"The woodland's."

The travelers looked at each other.

"No wood can be gathered without first asking for leave," Laurel said. "No tree must be harmed, or animal hunted without asking for permission."

"Whose permission?" the doctor asked.

"The woodland's," Laurel said again. And then, "Take care from here on in. Stay on the path, and do not stray. Don't heed voices you hear, no matter how familiar they sound."

And she started off again.

"Well, that's disturbing," Tanner mumbled.

"We've been careful so far," Brix called after her.

The elven woman stopped and looked at her over her shoulder. "Then be more careful."

Slowly, they picked up their packs and followed her.

Grim nodded to Tanner to go on, and fanned his face with his hat. He watched the stone with open curiosity.

"Always been here," he mumbled.

He rubbed his right hand on the front of his shirt, and then placed it on the rough surface. Whatever tingling Brix had perceived, he failed to register, but a faint blue glow flooded the grooves, like poured quicksilver, its brightness growing in intensity.

Grim pulled his hand back, like the stone was burning, and cursed under his breath. The glow faded and died.

Putting his hat back on, Grim hastened to follow the others.

At first the woodlands did not look different to Arnost Emery, but he admitted to himself he was more familiar with bookshelves and writing desks than with trees and bushes. Now that they were, formally, in the Bloodwood, there were still tall trees and thick canopies of leaves, the green fading from them as the browns and the golds advanced with the autumn. He caught the sight of a fox, standing so still by a bramble bush that it was almost invisible. Only when it moved its tail at their passage did the old teacher spot it. He half expected it to screech, like they had heard before, but it just decided the travelers were not worth its time. With one final look, it turned and disappeared in the shadows.

There were other sounds. There were birds in the trees, chirping softly, and they crossed a singing brook, the water dripping on rocks in a small, melodious waterfall.

He looked around in wonder as they walked in single file behind Laurel. The elf moved through the bushes like they were a mist, barely touching them. She led them easily through thickets that to Emery's eyes seemed impenetrable. She was also warming to them, or at least to Brix. He had seen the two women talk together when they stopped along the way.

But gradually, as the day advanced, Emery noticed the

colors begin to change. The tree canopies shifted from the dark gold of autumn to ten shades of vibrant red. It was easy to see how these woods had gotten their name. But it was not just the trees. As they marched on, the bushes in the undergrowth acquired hues of copper and purple, with occasional patches of green-black ferns. Soon, the woodland was a mosaic of red leaves and dark, almost black tree trunks, like ink sketches. Mosses and fungi hung to the tree bark, soft pink and violent red, and acidic orange. It was like watching the world through a wine glass. But the air was clean, heavy with the smell of the wild, and solitary birds sang in the branches.

It was beautiful, and quiet.

"Maybe keeping humans out of here was not a bad idea," he said. He stopped and stretched his back.

"Are you all right?" Tanner asked.

Emery waved a hand, motioning him onward. "Of course, young man, of course. I was just enjoying the sight, and the peace. It makes it easy to forget what is happening out there."

He gestured vaguely at the distance.

"The armies of the barons will face the Uthuk," Tanner said. He lingered back, and it did not escape the old man that the young orc was matching his pace with his. "We fought them back once already."

"Nobody ever dreamed a new Darkness would befall us," Emery sighed. "And out of complacence comes weakness. Much as I want to believe our aristocracy will be able to muster its forces and withstand the onslaught, I still can't forget that at the time of the First Darkness the world was different. Less fragmented. Less, if you pardon my word, selfish. Our nations have honed their fighting skills by confronting each other. We have grown distant, and distrustful. This makes us an easier prey, maybe, than we were in the past." He stopped, and took a deep breath. "But maybe it's just an old man's pessimism talking."

The wolves cowered and wailed.

The bone whip cracked, and the animals retreated further, their tails tucked between their legs, their heads close to the ground.

Beastmaster Th'Uk Tar was unimpressed. He was sure in two or three generations he would be able to bring forth the violence and aggression in these creatures, but as they were, the wolves of Terrinoth were a poor excuse for a predator.

The pack had been attracted by the remains of two men and a pack mule that the Uthuk had surprised in the woods. They must have strayed from the great road, or maybe they were seeking someplace to hide. The Beastmaster's scouts had crossed their path as the Uthuk marched deeper into the woods, heading for the Latari's lair. The men had put up a decent fight, and had been awarded a quick death.

And their carcasses had served as a lure for these black and gray animals, that now trembled in the Beastmaster's shadow. In their fear of their new master, at least, the wolves proved their good instinct.

But he had no time, now, to breed and mold them to his purposes, so he just fed them to the caecilians.

CHAPTER NINE

That night, some creature of the wild called in the darkness, waking them where they had settled at the foot of a big chestnut tree.

"What was that?" Grim asked, in a croak. He was a bundle of cloak and blankets, barely moving, only his nose peeking out.

"I don't know," Tanner replied. "That's a call I've never heard before."

He had taken watch duty, relieving Laurel. Now he saw the elf woman was gone. A low mist hung through the trees, and dripped down the leaves of the thorny bushes they had used as a screen.

"I had a strange dream," Brix said, yawning.

"Oh, my goodness," Grim mumbled.

Tanner turned to where her eyes glowed faintly in the dark. "What sort of dream?"

The cat-woman shrugged and yawned again, covering her mouth with her wrist. She pulled up the collar of her coat. "Something moved in the darkness," she said. She pointed at a gap between two nearby trees. "It stood there and it looked down at me with glowing red eyes–"

Doctor Emery coughed and shifted.

"It was like a piece of the forest had come alive and moved," Brix went on.

The call resounded again in the darkness. Halfway between a roar and a howl, ending in a long, overdrawn squeal. This time Tanner was able to pinpoint a direction. As he squinted through the mist, Laurel appeared, walking on tiptoes, her bow ready.

"Something moves in the woods," she said.

"Something?" Tanner asked.

She just shook her head.

"A tall thing made of branches and vines, threading like a shadow through the trees," Brix said. Laurel turned to look at her. "Like a strange puppet, with an elongated head like a gourd, brushing the lower branches as it went. I saw it. It was uncanny. I thought I was dreaming."

For the third time, the strange call echoed through the trees, this time farther away, fainter.

"No," the elf said. "This is something I've never heard of before."

Emery stopped, almost bumping into Tanner. The orc had frozen, his eyes two slits. He lifted a hand, asking Emery to be silent. They had been marching most of the morning, and the doctor welcomed a pause, but something was clearly off.

Emery looked around. He spotted Brix, Grim and Laurel crouching behind a low ridge, like a natural wall of gray rock and dark moss. The ground was becoming more varied as they went deeper into the Bloodwood. There were boulders and troughs, creeks and small cliffs. What most in the Baronies and the Free Cities considered a flat wooded plain was in fact a rugged stretch of land.

Tanner's hand was on his shoulder, and the orc half-dragged, half-pushed him in the direction of the place where the others were hiding. Grim turned to them, as they walked swiftly on the moss carpet, and lifted a finger to his lips.

Emery pushed back the questions that were crowding his mind. He closed his eyes and heard the approaching shuffle of feet, and then the grunting, guttural sound of barbaric voices.

Slowly, carefully, Laurel looked over the rock spur. Brix did the same, and her ears flattened out as her tail wrapped itself around her leg. Then Tanner. Only Grim sat with his back against the rock, his hands clenched into fists. He was breathing through his mouth, his eyes closed.

Leaning with his hands on the rough surface of the rock, Emery joined the others and looked beyond the barrier. He spotted a dozen pale shapes, walking through the undergrowth. He recognized the crimson scarves and britches they were wearing, the jagged shapes of their grotesque bodies, the twisted weapons they carried. They marched to the east and south, pushing through the vegetation, cutting a path of broken branches and trampled bushes. Emery squinted when a single beam of pale sunlight caught one of them as it stopped and scanned the shadows in the trees. The three scars in the circle were there, on the warrior's chest. His red eyes turned to the rock ridge.

Emery stood perfectly motionless, remembering the fox he had seen. The Uthuk turned and rejoined his companions. The cold hand of fear pressing on his chest, Emery closed his eyes, wishing the Uthuk away, praying to a nameless deity he had not been spotted.

They huddled in their hideout until the sounds of the Locusts faded and were gone, and then they waited some more.

"Uthuk Y'llan in the Bloodwood," Laurel said, anger and disbelief creeping into her voice. "This cannot be."

"Looks like your standing stones are not that effective," Grim said. She did not even look at him.

"I need to go," she said. "Warn my people."

"And leave us here?" the shopkeeper hissed.

"I need to go to Methras. They must know what is happening. They need to know now."

"Well, how fortunate, we are going there too," Grim replied.

"You will slow me down."

"We will not," Brix said.

"They wear the same sign," Emery said. "Have you noticed? On their chest. These are the same we met in Mayvale, but not on the road. Something strange is afoot."

"He's right." Tanner nodded. "They're all branded in the same way."

"Some tribal sign, or a protective mark of some kind," Grim said. "Do Uthuk champions brand their warriors?"

"Whatever it is," Emery said, authority rising in his quiet tones, "it is something that makes them different from the ones that attacked us on the road. Just as the fact that they are here makes them different."

Grim frowned. "A seal to protect them from whatever the Latari have up for defense?"

He turned a questioning look at Laurel.

"We don't have time for this now," she said. "We need to go. If you slow me down, I will leave you behind."

"Fortuna's Eyes, whatever happened in this place?"

Laurel heard Emery's voice but the question did not register with her. She only had eyes for the destruction surrounding them. She felt a pressure in her chest, like her lungs were being squeezed, and the tips of her fingers were like ice. A whimper escaped her lips.

The others joined her at the center of the clearing, exclaiming in surprise. It was like a giant plough had cut through the forest, a colossal hand had crushed the trees, snapping the trunks like twigs, scattering broken branches around. Laurel's head reeled. She was familiar with the way in which humans and the orcs harvested the wood for their buildings, and to make fire. She had walked among the stumps that were all that remained of a once luscious forest, chips and sawdust under her feet.

But this was different.

Here, the very earth had been churned and upturned. In places, pools of some revolting goo boiled and breathed bubbles of greenish mist. The trees had been broken and savaged, as if by a raging beast. There was a hollow sound ringing in Laurel's ears, and it took her a moment to understand it was her blood, pumped by her heart beating faster. She shuddered, her feet taking her closer to the smashed remains of a centuries-old oak. The ground creaked under her feet, covered in wood debris, dead leaves, and more wreckage. She spotted a solitary nest, crushed on the ground. Her eyes became tangled in the exposed roots of an uprooted beech, the hole like a dark pit, a wound in the earth. The ground had been trampled and churned, the dirt mixed with the ashes. Five yards away, another tree had been set to fire, its blackened branches stretching to the sky like it was asking for help from the sun. But the sun had hidden behind thick gray clouds, indifferent.

"It's a good thing it's been rainy these last two days," Grim said. He patted the blackened bark of a gnarled old oak, and then clapped his hands together to clean away the soot. “In a drier season, the fire would have spread to the whole valley.”

He shook his head.

Another charred tree stood alone in a circle of ashes and burned grasses. It was old and bent, like a man with arms outstretched, its back bent against a strong wind. It was like it was invoking the sky, one branch like a human limb with an imploring hand. Hot air bubbles crackled through its trunk.

Brix touched the charred bark. “It’s still warm. Barely.”

Emery used the blunt end of his lance to dig in a pile of burned branches. His face paled, and he looked away. Then, covering his face with his cloak, he collected a fistful of charred bones.

“Squirrel?” Brix asked.

The old man looked at her, and then at Laurel. The expression on his face forced her to draw near. She looked at the blackened palm of the old man’s hand, over which rested a bundle of twisted, deformed bones. An owl, maybe, or some other night bird, by the boxlike skull and large eye sockets. But it was hard to say. The bones were elongated and bent, and long, delicate spines branched from them. A saw-toothed crest of spikes rose across the length of the skull. She was reminded of the bone spurs that pierced the Uthuks’ skin, their heads misshapen and their arms and legs too long and thin.

“What sorcery is this?” Emery asked.

Laurel just shook her head. Her alertness was quickly dissipating, replaced by a growing fear. Her mind was running wild, and she fought to keep it under control. She, who had never run away from a battlefield, now wanted to leave this cursed place behind, and fast.

At the other end of the clearing, Tanner fell to his knees. His movement was so sudden, it brought Laurel back to reality. She was present again, her breath under control, her heart slowing, an arrow ready.

But the orc was just looking at the ground, crunching the earth between his fingers, searching for tracks in the churned mixture of mud and ash.

She felt a sudden respect for his dedication. He had not been distracted. He had remained focused. Tanner was acting as a warrior, as she should too. Emotion was not a good counsel on the battlefield.

Tanner turned to her. "Ever seen anything like this?"

She was by his side in three strides. A path had been cut through the wreckage, a wide swath of forest floor scrubbed clean and marked by the passing of a large body.

"They dragged a tree away," Grim said, coming closer.

"Why?" Brix asked. He shrugged.

But Tanner shook his head. "Look at the way the track snakes around the larger stumps. This is not something being dragged. It's something alive, moving like a snake. Some kind of huge beast did this. Something as big as a dragon."

"Something not of the Bloodwood," Laurel said. The thought alone made her furious. She pushed her anger back once again.

"A large snake or worm," Doctor Emery said, pensively. "One wonders–"

"You know what did this?" Tanner asked.

"There are creatures in the Ru Darklands," the teacher said, "described in the old chronicles. Things that came with the Locust Swarms during the First Darkness, hungry for the flesh of men. They inhabit the lands from which the Blight comes, and the Uthuk Y'llan live with them, and sometimes form a sort of companionship, like a carrion eater does with a large predator. Some, we have seen. The beasts we met on the road. But there are others, mentioned in obscure sentences in the chronicles of the First Darkness, and never properly described, if not like gargantuan nightmares."

"But the destruction?" Tanner said. "Could such a beast do all of this?"

The old man took a deep breath. "Possibly. These are old stories I am talking about."

"And why here?"

"What do you mean?"

"If this First Darkness monster is roaming these woods," the orc said, "it did not fall from the sky, but marched or crawled here from the wilderness of the Ru Wastelands. Why did it choose this spot and not another to cause such destruction?"

"I seriously doubt such a creature came here alone," Emery said.

"I wonder what whoever put up that standing stone will do about this," Brix wondered.

"And I suggest we don't stay to find out," Grim added.

Laurel was moving already. She needed to get to her people and warn them. She had to hope someone knew what this thing was. And how she could kill it.

To Brix, the woods were no longer the same. There had been a certain sense of relief, before, like the red-topped surrounding trees were somehow protecting them. It felt like a day out, fun and carefree despite the bad weather. The Uthuk were behind them, a fading nightmare that was easy to forget.

That she had wanted to forget.

It had felt safe.

But not anymore. The Uthuk were here, and other strange beasts too, and the Bloodwood was no longer protecting them. The wood itself, it seemed to Brix, needed protection. And that was a disquieting thought.

Now every step of the way was carefully placed. They walked in silence, and she soon noticed that Laurel seemed to move like a ghost, barely disturbing the bushes and the ferns, lighter than the mist. She tried to imitate her, and she noticed the elf chose mossy patches or rocks, and carpets of dead leaves, where they could go without a sound, and leave no trace. Sometimes she stopped and raised a hand, and they all froze where they were.

Brix followed suit, and Grim and Emery came after her. Tanner, his weapon balanced over a shoulder, closed the file. They all looked around, and walked hunched, almost unconsciously. The fear they had felt on the road was back, more intense, as every shadow and every bush seemed to hide a possible menace, a fight-hungry enemy.

They stopped at bird calls, or when a twig snapped.

They were not just careful. They were afraid.

But they were keeping up with Laurel, and that was good. Brix suspected, for all her talk of leaving them behind, the elf was waiting for them, allowing for pauses so that Emery and Grim could get their breath back. If that was the truth, it also was good. It meant the elf cared for them, and wanted to have them along.

Or maybe it was just pity.

When they stopped for rest, they always looked for cover. In those moments, as they passed around a skin of cold water, Brix could see that both Doctor Emery and Grim were having a hard time. It was not the rhythm of their walk, she believed, even if Emery was short of breath for his age, and Grim for his idle lifestyle. It was much more the silence, she was sure, that was getting at them. Both men were enamored of their own voices, and full of opinions. Walking in silence was pressing down on them as much as the menace of the Uthuk Y'llan.

Tanner, on the other hand, seemed not to care, and Brix herself had learned long ago to keep her counsel. Back in the old house in Vynelvale it would have been by knitting, or burying her nose in a book, or going for a walk; here in the Bloodwood it was by keeping her eyes and ears open, and trying to follow in the footsteps of Laurel.

"Why don't we see the defenders of the city, I wonder?" Emery asked one night, as they sought some warmth in their cloaks and coats, not daring to light a fire.

"I guess we wouldn't see them unless we had to," Tanner said.

Laurel nodded. She was no longer staying away from them when they rested. "They are hunters," she said.

"And not only them," Grim said.

"What do you mean?" Brix asked.

The merchant shrugged, and rubbed his hands on his arms under his cloak. "There is something on the move," he said finally. "Something watching through the branches, shadowing us. It's like the whole forest is looking, and waiting for something."

Brix traded a glance with Tanner. This was no time for playing games.

"I saw nothing," the orc said.

"Just like you said, these are things we will not see, if we are lucky."

"The woods do feel that way," Tanner said, "especially to city people. They baffle our senses, confound our sight and hearing. We become fearful for what is not there. We jump at shadows."

"Until the shadows come for us, with claws and fangs," Grim retorted. Then he chuckled. "But you of course are right, and I am just a city-grown man, lost in the wild. Forget what I said. We have enough to worry without giving thought to will o' the wisps."

But his tone betrayed his words, and Brix caught Laurel looking strangely at him.

Yet on they moved, swift, silent, careful. And as the fabled Methras grew nearer, Brix strove to push her fear back. There were Uthuk in the Bloodwood, but they were not here, not now.

She should strive to be more like Laurel, more focused, and unhindered by unnecessary preoccupations. Everything would be good, she told herself.

Until it wasn't.

CHAPTER TEN

The Uthuk Y'llan broke through the undergrowth, screaming. There were five of them, one a mountain-like monster with a dribbling mouth, and folds upon folds of gray skin hanging from his frame. He was wearing an animal skull as a helmet, and had antlers strapped to his arms, to compound the bone spikes that pierced his skin. He advanced slowly on stumpy legs, preceded by his companions.

Brix and the others were following a rocky ledge that ran like a causeway through the forest, the slick stone covered in soft, soggy red leaves. The stratified rocks formed a short, wide staircase between two sides of a crack in the world. A braided waterfall ran down the rock wall, its thunder smothering every other sound. Because of it they did not hear the Uthuk Y'llan until they were upon them. The attackers came from the topmost side of the gorge, and Laurel saw them too late.

She cried out a warning, and managed to slam two arrows in the chest of one of the runners. The stricken Uthuk staggered back just as the one by his side jumped over the ledge, letting out a bellowing scream, the bone claws tied to his wrists outstretched. Tanner intercepted him with his axe, and the weight of the incoming body pushed him off the rock path and down into the bushes.

Brix freed her sword and her dagger from its scabbard. With a scream, Grim tried to pull Emery away from the course of a third incoming brute, armed with a twisted blade of black metal.

The old man slipped on the wet leaves and waved his arms about to try and keep his balance. The tip of the lance in his right hand struck the assailant under the ribs. The Uthuk gurgled and twisted, and pulled the weapon out of the old man's grasp. Emery tottered, and Grim put an arm around his waist to hold him steady. He gasped as Brix rushed to meet the next foe.

She flew through the air, her coat flapping behind her, sword and dagger in hand. She landed so close to the next assailant that the sour smell of sick skin caused her to choke. The warrior had long sharp crests of bone running down the length of his arms, and claws like black obsidian on his oversized hands.

He made to grasp Brix and she lunged, aiming for his neck, where his skin was soft. The warrior slapped her in the face, and she rolled on the grass, her cheek throbbing, her neck in pain. By her side, a warrior with blood pouring through his mouth was trying to stand, a broken lance in his side. She flipped the dagger in her hand and stabbed him in one eye just as a streak of fire ran down her back. She turned, the claws of her first adversary dripping red. Twisting out from under him, she tried to push her blade up through his ribs, but he grabbed her sword and laughed.

The trampled grass and soil rubbed in Brix's wounded back, and she hissed in pain. An arrow hit the Uthuk through the cheek, and he turned, his jaw dislodged by the projectile. Brix gritted her teeth and slashed at his leg, severing the tendon in the heel. The monster roared, caught between two adversaries.

Tanner heaved the dead Uthuk off his chest and stood as Grim ran along the ledge, keeping his head down and dragging Doctor Emery along. One of the incoming Uthuk made a grab for the cloak of the doctor, and Tanner lunged, swinging his axe, severing his arm at the elbow. Brix limped up and skewered the warrior from behind before ducking down among the ferns. She crouched there, her back aching, her dagger lost.

Laurel shot the wounded Uthuk in the neck, and then jumped down where the others were. Grim was helping Emery negotiate the last of the great stone steps as Brix joined them.

The last of the Uthuk opened his mouth and let out a long, gurgling roar, and then hurled himself down the steps, like an avalanche of homicidal fury. He was seven feet tall: a mountain of flesh with long arms and a great expanse of belly. The crimson rags his people favored barely covered his body, flapping like torn banners as he lurched forward. A chain of sharp, teeth-like bone spikes ran down his left arm. His features were masked by the animal cranium he wore for protection, and a single human skull hung on his neck from a string.

"Now is the time to run," Grim said.

"There's five of us," Brix snapped back, standing at his side. She pulled off the rags of her coat.

"And a lot of him."

Laurel's bow creaked as she pulled her arrow back, waited for a heartbeat, and let fly. By the time the arrow hit the Uthuk in the chest, two more had followed. The monster ignored them. With a sweep of his spiky arm he broke the shafts, and then with a mighty backhand slap, tossed the elf out of his way.

Tanner shouted and stood in the giant's way. He brandished his axe. The giant stopped it with his right hand. The blade bit deep into his palm. Black blood dripped on the silver. The Uthuk ignored it, and punched the orc in the gut, pushing him back.

Grim cursed.

Brix sprinted, keeping low. Then she stopped and stretched, the sword a steel arch as she cut at the creature's arm. The blade bit into the tangle of ropes holding the deer antlers in place. The colossus caught Brix with his free hand. His fingers closed on her neck and he lifted her up, shaking her like a rag doll.

With dead fingers, Grim opened his satchel, trying to coax his blank mind to think, and remember. Was there something useful in there?

Tanner came back with another swing of his axe. He was screaming, like a berserker. The Uthuk turned his eyes from Brix and lifted his left arm for another backhanded slap.

With a wheezing curse, Doctor Emery pushed his broken lance under the giant's arm, the sharp end of the broken pole biting into the soft flesh of the armpit. The monster turned, his surprise echoing Grim's. The tangle of deer antlers caught Emery in the chest. The damaged ropes holding the makeshift weapon in place snapped, but the strength of the impact tossed the old man like a broken puppet.

Brix stabbed upward through the wrist, and then turned the blade viciously. The hand that gripped her went limp and she fell to the ground and rolled away from under the giant's feet.

An arrow hissed one inch from Tanner's head, and plunged into the cut he had opened with his axe. The monster roared and started flailing his arms around, Brix's blade still stuck in his wrist, Emery's broken spear in his side.

Laurel stuck one more arrow, the last, in his body, and watched powerless as he charged Tanner and steamrolled him. Brix was by Emery's side, trying to get him out of the way.

And the giant exploded.

With a loud plop, like a gourd dropped from a tower, the colossal body was torn from the inside, and bits and pieces were scattered all around, painting the clearing with the dark blood of the monster. It was at the same time gruesome and comical. In the moment of perfect stillness that followed, everybody turned to where Grim stood, a fire-juice ampule in his fingers, his mouth open in surprise.

"What have you done?" Brix asked.

Grim shook his head. He felt a coppery taste in his mouth and shuddered at the thought it could be from the dead Uthuk. "I did nothing."

His ears were buzzing.

There was a spike of hot iron slowly plunging into his brain.

"Run," Laurel said, her voice cracking. They turned to her. They had never heard fear in her voice, until now.

"Run!" she screamed again.

Then Chaos was upon them.

Chaos walked into the clearing on long legs that bent in a strange way. Chaos was wreathed in a cloud of rainbows and lightning, its feet barely touching the ground. A path of pale flowers and white, long-stemmed mushrooms sprouted where it passed, and the trees whispered and swayed, but there was no wind.

Brix tried to retrieve her sword, but Tanner pulled her back.

Chaos wore a billowing cloak of ancient stars and rippling light, and clothes that flowed like a clear creek, sparkling in the sun. Its hands were long-fingered and delicate like an embroiderer's, and a long mane of fire hair fell around its face like a frozen flame.

And it screamed, soundlessly.

Just like Laurel, Grim knew what this was, and just like her, he shouted for them all to run. Run now. Run fast.

But it was useless.

His fingers grew cold and limp, and the vial of fire-juice he had intended to use against the giant dropped, slowly, to the ground. It twirled as it fell, and it seemed it was taking forever. When it hit the stones, it broke and erupted into a plume of green and blue fire. The flame rose like a fountain and froze, a tall and ragged flower of alchemical fire that gave no heat.

Horns like tall spiraling seashells adorned the forehead of Chaos, and Chaos had no eyes. Its perfectly oval face as smooth as an eggshell, as white as porcelain. As it came closer, its mouth manifested above its chin, a red-lipped black pit filled with row upon row of sharp, triangular metal teeth.

Laurel was on her knees, her face in her hands, the longbow forgotten. Taking a step away from the frozen fire, Grim could not tell if she was sobbing, or just trying to unsee what stood in front of them.

It was useless. Even if he closed his eyes, Grim could still see the Chaos as it advanced through his thoughts like a curse.

But he did not close his eyes for long. It was not his nature.

More curious than was advisable, that had always been Grimald of Guyot. His gaze met Emery's, and the old man spoke, and gave a name to Chaos.

"Fae."

The creature stopped and the air rippled and crackled in front of it.

Brix hissed and swayed. Doctor Emery brought a hand to his forehead, and Laurel finally looked up. Tanner groaned, and gripped his axe until his knuckles were white.

Grim felt the burning spike go in deep through his forehead, searing his brain. It turned, like a surgeon's lancet probing a wound.

The trees that enclosed the clearing were sighing, and heaving, their branches stretching like rapacious claws, their canopies shivering, strange faces emerging from the patterns on the scarred bark. The whole of Bloodwood was coming to life in the presence of Chaos.

"What do you want from us?" Grim said out loud. His words sounded strange to his ears. The others looked at him, shock and fear on their faces, their pain momentarily forgotten.

Chaos, the Fae, bent its head on one side, like a bird observing a flower swinging in the breeze. Or maybe an insect that would make a nice meal. Its hair burned like the sun itself. Chaos took one more step forward, and stretched a hand to caress the frozen blue flame Grim had made.

Images flooded Grim's mind, pushing abruptly along the burned path the spike of anguish had dug in his thoughts. The others screamed. Emery put his hands on his head. Brix crouched on the ground and hissed. A storm of images, fluttering like light through tree branches. Sounds. Smells.

Grim's old discipline kicked in, and he tried to sort through the storm, to impose order on the chaos. Fire. Pain. Gray-skinned demons. Something cold and deep and powerful, twisting and distorting what was, into what should not be.

Grim's fists unclenched. "We mean no harm," he shouted.

He knew words were superfluous, but they helped him focus and channel his thoughts. Some things are never forgotten, he recalled. Some things will stay with you forever, whether you want it or not.

He clenched his jaw. Let's use them, then, he thought.

The storm receded and thoughts took shape, like a crystal sculpture from a glass-blower's pipe. His thoughts, fueled by spite, anger and, yes, irony. It did not escape him how a strong undercurrent of comedy ran through this whole affair. It was the excess and the flamboyance of the Fae, of course, its overwhelming display of power. But there was more.

Grimald of Guyot chuckled.

In his youth he had known people that would have given an arm and a leg to be here, now, in his place. To meet the Fae face to face, to see what all the stories and the ballads were about. To learn, to probe, to take measurements. To talk, to strike deals. Fools. He had met so many self-centered fools in his youth.

But it was him here, and not them. Grimald of Guyot. The son of a poor man. Honest Grim the shopkeeper. Curiosity and ambition were the bread and butter in Greyhaven, and not a single one of his old mates would hesitate to sell their soul to be here in his place. His old teachers would damn themselves to the eternal flames of the Ynfernael to be here in his place. And he would gladly be elsewhere.

What a joke.

What a frightful, deadly joke.

Grimald of Guyot burst out laughing.

The others stared at him, eyes wide, pain and panic twisting their features. A thin stream of blood was dripping from Doctor Emery's left nostril. Brix's tail cracked like a whip. And Laurel, the frost maiden, the silent warrior, was trembling in fear. Tanner was breathing hard, like after a long run, and holding on to his axe like a drowning man holds to a chunk of driftwood.

The Fae raged in the middle of the clearing, its presence burning a hole right through reality, and at the edge of that hole stood a lone man in a black slouch hat.

Grim pulled his sleeves back and stood, legs planted on the ground, arms akimbo.

"What. Do. You. Need. From. Us?"

One by one the others fell to the ground, and were still.

Brix felt like she was waking from a long fever. Her body ached, her bones creaked like old timber, and her head was abuzz. She coughed and spat, and then water poured into her mouth, cold and sweet. She opened her eyes and blinked in the glare. She grabbed the hand that held the water-skin, and sucked more water.

"Easy," Grim said, holding her up. "You're bleeding. Take it easy."

Brix let go and sighed, and propped herself up on one elbow. The movement caused her back to go up in flames. She was laying on her side in the grass, the blood-hued leaves of the forest canopy arching over her. "What happened?"

"It's all right," he said. "Can you come give us a hand with the others?"

With a long groan, Brix sat up and then climbed to her feet. Her torn back burned with every move she made, but she ignored the pain. The clearing was still and silent. She took a tentative step, feeling lightheaded. She remembered the Uthuk slashing at her shoulders.

Grim was helping Laurel up. "Take a look at the doctor," he said.

The old man was propped against a tree, his hands on his chest, and for a moment Brix feared the worse. Then she saw he was breathing.

Walking to where Doctor Emery lay, she passed a wide circle of burned grass, and caught sight of a sparkle. Her sword. She carefully bent down to pick it up. It felt good in her hand. She turned to where Tanner was lying face down in the ferns, stirring, and saw a path of pale yellow withering flowers and white rotting mushrooms. It was three feet wide, and it proceeded from the edge of the trees to the burning circle in the grass.

It was like a punch in the gut. Cold sweat broke on her brow, and she went down on her knees, her stomach churning.

"Are you all right?" Tanner croaked.

Laurel's voice flared up. She was speaking in her own language, and her eyes were wide with fear and anger.

With a sigh and a curse, Brix pulled herself together.

"Mother of Kurnos, woman, put that pig-sticker down!"

Grim was sitting on the ground, hands up, and was talking slowly and soft as he pushed back with his heels, trying to put some distance between himself and the elf murderously advancing on him. Laurel spat some angry words. Brix thought they were not as musical and fluid as the storytellers would have her believe.

"I can explain," Grim said.

Tanner had helped Emery to his feet, and now he took a step forward. Laurel turned to him and hissed more angular words. Brix walked between them, raised a hand, and stopped the orc. "Easy," she said.

Laurel glanced sideways at her, and then turned again to Grim. A solitary beam of sunlight caught the edge of the knife in her hand.

"There's no need to be angry," Brix said, and wondered if it was true. But she put conviction in her voice. Like when she used to pacify capricious children. "Look at me, Laurel!"

The elf turned her eyes on her. Her red warpaint was stark on her pale face, like blood. Grim pushed himself back to his feet.

"There is no need to be angry," Brix repeated. In her disappointment, she could understand the feeling. "He is a mage."

Laurel's eyes widened.

"What?" Tanner blurted.

"A wizard. A warlock. Something like that. A spellcaster. He's from Greyhaven, I reckon."

Grim's shoulders fell. "I always said you're the brains of this company."

"It does make sense." Doctor Emery nodded. "Mind you, it is extremely unusual, but really not unexpected. There were hints, you see–"

"And he's on our side," Brix said, and gave Grim a hard stare, defying him to say the contrary. He took a deep breath.

Laurel was still holding her knife up. Brix put her hand on her shoulder. "Let him explain," she said softly. "Then if you want you can kill him."

They patched up Brix and Emery, and then built a fire, and as the darkness advanced, sat around it and shared some food. Grim cooked some beans and lard from the ruins of Mayvale, and some eggs from the abandoned hen coops. They watched in silence as he worked. Tanner had retrieved a long straight branch from the wood, and was cleaning it of saplings with a knife, making a new walking staff for Doctor Emery.

When the meal was ready, Laurel sat herself across from Grim, and kept staring at him with eyes like daggers.

"So, how was Greyhaven?" Tanner asked around a piece of toasted bread he had dipped in the beans.

"Full of opportunities for the right people," Grim replied, his voice bitter. He used a twig to push a log into the fire.

"I think I know where this is going," the orc said with some warmth, nodding. "How come we're never the right people, I wonder?"

Grim chuckled. "Beats me."

"So you studied magic," Brix said, cautiously.

"Or pretended to."

A night bird called in the distance. Doctor Emery pulled the poor rags of his cloak closer. "I think it would be a good thing if you told us what this is all about," he said, quietly.

Grim cleared up the last of his food and set his bowl down.

"I had shown a certain penchant for spirit-speaking, as a kid. Family and teachers noticed." He shrugged. "I picked up bits and pieces of gossip nobody should know. Found lost items. Knew things I should not have known. Nothing that made me very popular. But enough to pass the first admission test into Greyhaven. And, I don't know, maybe the second. And the third."

Tanner whistled softly. "You're what – a warlock?"

"Warlocks are somewhat different, I reckon," Emery said. Grim nodded.

"And you passed those tests? Just like that?" Brix asked. "From what I heard, the selection to get into the Academy at Greyhaven is quite hard."

"Not all of Greyhaven is like in the stories," Grim said. Brix felt a pang of irritation, but then saw the look in his eyes. He was not being smug, he was just being honest. "And even a tavern owner's son can hope to find his way in those marble halls. Maybe. Sometimes. Just keep your head down and play by the rules."

"I didn't mean to offend you."

He grinned at her. "I'm not the kind that gets offended easily, girl."

Her ears flattened. She did not like being patronized. "What went wrong?"

Grim took a sip of water. "It was just not my place. And the things I did – better suited for a hedge wizard than a member of academia, they said. Too many interests and not enough discipline. Or something like that. I was good, but I was not, I dunno, adequate." He chuckled. "Also, in all honesty, I was a young smart aleck and I rubbed a lot of people the wrong way."

"How long were you in Greyhaven?" Doctor Emery asked.

"More than enough, believe me. Certainly longer than my welcome."

"You left?" Emery was incredulous. "Or did they throw you out?"

Brix gave him a hard stare, but Grim just shrugged. "Does it make that much of a difference?"

Emery chewed for a moment. "No, I guess not. Sorry for prying."

Grim waved a hand.

"And so you left and you opened a shop in Vynelvale," Brix said, "selling magic supplies."

"And counterfeit spellbooks," Emery added.

"Hey, I never said–!"

The old teacher was stern. "Please, Master Grimald. I was not born yesterday."

"Oh, whatever." The man shrugged. "It's a living. A fool and his gold, right?"

Brix laughed despite herself. She found it hard to remain angry at the man.

"Why did not the Fae kill us all?"

They all turned to Laurel, startled by the sound of her voice. She was staring at Grim like she was trying to strangle him with her eyes. Never a soft person, she now looked as hard as a steel blade.

"Because we are too beautiful." Grim grinned at her. She blinked, twice, surprised. He threw his twig in the fire. "And because they want something from us."

"From us?" Tanner said, incredulous. "The Fae?"

Grim chuckled. "Believe me, my friend, it is not as good as it sounds."

He looked at Laurel. "What is the Well of Tears?"

The elf stared at him.

Emery looked deep into the fire. "There is a Well of Tears, if I remember correctly, in the old legend of Ayrar and Mehllibo."

"Never heard of it," Tanner said.

Brix shook her head. Mysteries were piling upon mysteries. "Me neither."

"I don't believe it's anything out of an old ballad," Grim said. He leaned towards the elf. "Am I right?"

Laurel looked him in the eye, defiant. "It's a place, here in the Bloodwood. I know nothing else."

"It's a place south and east of here. By a stone tower, and a thorny rose bush," Grim nodded. "The Fae want us to go there."

"Really?" Tanner blurted. "What for?"

"They want *us*?" Brix asked, stressing that last word. "Why us?"

Before Grim could say anything, Laurel spoke. "We don't go there," she said. "Nobody goes there. Ever."

Grim arched his eyebrows.

"We go to Methras," Laurel said. Her tone was final. "To speak with Dareine."

CHAPTER ELEVEN

It was like a heart, beating.

It sounded deep, and hollow, and it never stopped.

It drowned the other voices, like a drum.

A thousand warriors had joined his army, and now Th'Uk Tar could feel the Well drawing closer, calling to him, promising him all he ever wanted.

Crush the hated Latari.

Burn their forest, turn their kingdom into the training pits for his new warriors.

Become the master of the Scions of Aymhelin, and unleash them over the whole of Terrinoth.

The promise was there, and he would fulfill it.

And now it was drawing near.

No longer a thing of dreams, but a reality.

No longer a prod, pushing him forward, against all odds.

A place, here, in these woods.

A place he would conquer.

Followed by Gorgemaw and his increasing menagerie of creatures, he pushed forward into the Bloodwood, opening a swath of smashed trees and churned earth.

This was what the world would look like once he remade it.

And fires. Fires would burn everywhere.

He cracked his bone whips, and ordered his followers on.

Beastmaster Th'Uk Tar never slept, nor would his warriors.

Grim took a long gulp of water. He was sitting on a flat rock, his black hat perched on his knee. They had stopped for a moment, taking advantage of a bright shaft of golden sunlight that filtered through the trees and warmed a widening in the path. Ever since the meeting with the Fae, Laurel had been marching at the double, and they all were spent and shattered for running behind her. He had an impression that she was torn between leaving them behind and bringing them to Methras, the city of the elves. Bringing him there, in particular.

Dareine was the name of the Latari leader they would see there. Or maybe Dareine was a title, Grim was not sure. But they were what passed for authority among the Bloodwood elves. Laurel insisted they be informed of everything they had seen as soon as possible, and Grim could see her point. But he was not too keen on meeting elven royalty. He did not like attracting too much attention. Grim sighed and shook his head. It was a bit late for that.

He put down the water bottle and watched Doctor Emery. He wondered how long the old man could keep up.

"We need to rest," Grim said, his voice broken. He did not know how long he himself would be able to keep up. Sleeping was difficult, as bright, aggressive dreams visited his slumber. He saw glimpses of what the Fae had shown him, and he was having a hard time telling apart the true visions and whatever his tired mind was adding to the stew.

Laurel looked at him and frowned.

"We really need to rest," he said again. The elf lifted a hand and angled her head, like she was sniffing the air.

Grim would not be shut up. "Listen–" he said.

A soft purring sound to his right caused him to turn. He croaked, staggered, lost his footing, screamed. Two large yellow eyes drew closer through the undergrowth, and the purring turned into a growl.

Tanner grabbed him by the collar and helped him up and dragged him away as a mighty beast emerged from the bushes. It gazed at Grim with big, glowing eyes, and then at the others. Silent like a shadow, it came forward, its long striped body rippling with supple muscles. Its low growl grew louder.

Other voices replied to the call.

The travelers drew closer. Emery leveled his walking staff, his hands shaking, and Brix half-pulled her short sword.

Laurel moved in front of them and clicked her tongue. The big cat opened its mouth in a long yawn, and arched its back, stretching its claws. Its teeth were like knives. Laurel rubbed it behind an ear. The beast purred, and then sneezed.

"She's a friend," she said.

Grim cursed under his breath. Laurel's friend had just robbed him of ten years of life. It was not like he needed more to fear.

"Is that a leonx?" Doctor Emery asked, taking a tentative step forward. The elf nodded.

"You were long gone, Laurel."

A tall Latari in leather and chainmail stood in the middle of the path. His chestnut hair was long and streaked with gray, and there was a star-shaped scar on his chin. He leaned on a straight-bladed lance, the sort used to hunt boars, with two short barbs at the side. His belt held a quiver and a horn made of a large seashell, finished in silver.

Laurel stopped petting the great cat, and bowed to the newcomer.

As she did so, another great cat jumped on top of a nearby rock. An elven warrior was riding it, but the great beast moved with elegant ease, like it did not feel the elf's weight.

"It's been a long time, Cillian," Laurel said.

The others were huddling together. Grim took a step forward and picked up his hat from where it had fallen. "Friend of yours?" he asked out of the corner of his mouth.

Laurel glanced at him.

"I was about to ask the same question," the elf Cillian said, arching an eyebrow. "Who are they?"

"We come from Vynelvale," Brix said.

"Along the Old Road," Tanner added.

"We need to reach the city of Methras," Emery said. "With a certain urgency, in fact."

"You have been walking in Methras since dawn, old man," the elf chuckled. "If only you had eyes to see it."

The doctor's eyes widened. Grim decided he liked Cillian a lot less than he liked Laurel.

"We seek audience with Dareine, urgently," Laurel said.

Cillian gave her a questioning stare, then glanced at the others. "We?"

"The Uthuk Y'llan are in the Bloodwood," Laurel said.

He scoffed. "You think, mayhaps," he told her, "we are out here hunting for rabbits?"

Another leonx rider appeared behind them, this one armed with a long bow.

"We need to see Dareine," Laurel repeated.

Cillian moved closer to Grim, and passed between him and Emery. He gave a long stare at Brix, and then he looked up at

Tanner. The orc crossed his arms and held his gaze, defiantly. Grim saw he was not the only one the elven hunter was rubbing the wrong way.

"We will escort you to Ledish Schall," Cillian said finally.

There were seven hunters, including Cillian, armed with bows and lances, and eight leonx. The one that had first approached them through the bushes did not carry a rider and wore no harness. It walked close to Laurel.

"This is Hewma," Laurel said to Brix. She rubbed the big cat between the shoulders, and it turned its head, glancing at her. "She used to hunt with me and my cousin, Redstar, when we were younger."

They were following a path of broken rocks, like stepping stones in the undergrowth. The mist was thickening around them, turning trees and bushes into black silhouettes. The refugees scanned through the shadows, and looked overhead, trying to catch a glimpse of the mysterious city of Methras. But the Bloodwood looked even wilder and untamed than before, and they could not spot any sign of life.

"I came back to seek Redstar," Laurel said. "But if Hewma is here, Redstar is not."

"And the gray-haired one?" Brix asked.

"He is Cillian, the master huntsman to Dareine, the lord of Ledish Schall and magistrate of the Bloodwood. Cillian is the leader of the Hunt, and his scouts patrol the Bloodwood."

"A sheriff." Grim smirked. "A thief-catcher. A scufter."

Hewma growled softly at the sound of his voice, and Grim took one step aside, keeping his distance from the big cat. "A poacher-hunter," he said, in a lower voice.

"A mutton shunter," Tanner said.

"A bullyman." Grim nodded.

"And he doesn't like orcs," Tanner said.

Grim chuckled. "He's not exactly keen on humans, either. And he doesn't seem to care for cat-folks, with all due respect to Mistress Brixida."

"If he truly hated you, he would have killed you," Laurel said, her voice level, without turning.

Grim and Tanner traded a look. Brix thought they made a fine jester act.

"I guess we're lucky," the short man said. He looked at Emery. "Everything fine, doctor?"

The old man had stopped along the way to collect a pebble from the ground. "What? Yes, yes. I am fine," he said. He squinted at the rock, and then he slipped it in his bag. "This place is very different from what I thought from reading the old chronicles. The books speak of a large plain, which leads one to imagine a featureless bowl, filled with red-topped trees. But look around you and you'll see the signs of great natural upheavals, shaping the land in strange configurations."

Brix caught Grim rolling his eyes, but as usual Tanner was interested. "And you can see that from a pebble?"

The old man laughed, and arched his back, his bones cracking. "From the pebbles and the rocks, the way certain trees grow, the rising and falling of the ground. There is a story written in the landscape, if you have eyes to see it."

"Well," Grim said, "keep your eyes open, or you'll fall in."

They had come to the ledge of a steep gorge, the trees bending over it as if to look in its depths. At the bottom, Brix saw a narrow strip of water flowing around sharp rocks.

Cillian rode his leonx to where they stood.

"Do they always talk this much, and this loud?" he asked Laurel.

She glanced at Brix. "Today they are unusually quiet."

Brix chuckled, but Cillian was not amused. "We must keep quiet now, until we're past the bridge. See that you keep your pets in line."

Brix's eyes widened. "Pets?" she hissed. Maybe Tanner and Grim were not wrong. Cillian stared at her expectantly. She turned her head. "Gentlemen," she said over her shoulder, in her best governess tones, "Hunt Master Cillian wishes us to be silent from now on."

Grim clicked his tongue and nudged Tanner. "And we were just about to burst into song."

"A pity," the orc admitted.

Brix stared Cillian in the eye. "Lead on."

The elf turned his beast and was gone.

The path of broken stones continued along the margin of the gorge to a place where two tall oaks stood side by side at the very edge, in the shape of a gate. Their canopies intertwined to form a gallery of blood-red leaves over the chasm, and met the branches of two similar trees on the other side. Beyond the trees, a bridge stretched over the river, a length of fifty yards of what looked at first like a wicker lattice.

It took Arnost Emery a closer look to realize what the bridge actually was. He went down on one knee, his joints creaking, and ran his fingers along the long tendrils of wood that emerged from the dirt and stretched across the gorge. Halfway, he saw, they met similar offshoots, and they intertwined, like fingers of clasping hands.

Tanner was by his side, his voice but a whisper. "Doctor–?"

Emery waved a hand, reassuring him. "Have you seen this?" he asked.

The leaves rustled above them.

Tanner looked up into the flint-like eyes of an elven archer. He was perched on a low branch, an arrow pointing at the old man.

"Come," he whispered, as he forced Emery up.

They hastened across the bridge, the structure gently giving under their weight, like a thick, soft carpet.

"It's the tree's roots!" Emery said, so low Tanner was sure he was talking to himself. He looked down at the interwoven twigs that supported him and the others over the jagged rocks below. He slowed his pace, allowing Emery to go on, and then turned. The doctor was right. The bridge was a complex braid of twigs and tendrils, an offshoot of the roots of the four oaks standing guard at the two sides of the gorge. Looking closer it was easy to see where the offshoots had been tied or pruned, shaped and trained to acquire a certain shape, a certain structure.

The last of the elven hunters passed by and looked at him. She was thin and pale and unsympathetic like all her companions.

Tanner turned and walked briskly back to Emery's side.

Soon they passed between the two oaks on the southern side of the river.

"They made it!" Emery told him in an excited breath. "Can you imagine that? The patience, and the skill, to nurture and groom the trees so? And no one ever imagined such a wonder!"

Tanner nodded, hurrying him on.

About half a mile from the river, they finally stopped by a stone slab, a stratified table of rock that laid by the pathway like a gigantic, discarded playing card. Cillian dismounted, and stood staring at Emery and Tanner as they approached, the doctor a-bubble with wonder.

"The sheer amount of time!" Emery was saying, "And I am sure you appreciate how the pattern of the trees is the same as the columns in the Great Library at Vynelvale. Or, I should rather say, how the architecture of the library does emulate the natural world…"

He stopped, and looked at Cillian. He suddenly remembered where he was, and lowered his gaze.

"Uh-oh," Grim mumbled to Brix. "Now we'll go to bed without dinner."

"Master Cillian," Emery burst out, walking right up to the elf, "I had heard wonders, as one does, and yet I must say I am impressed and, yes, humbled by the mastery shown by your people…"

He fell silent, and his cheeks reddened.

Cillian took a deep breath. "Welcome to Methras, doctor," he said, with a weary smile. He raised his voice. "We'll rest here for half an hour."

It was like a catch was released. His hunters relaxed. They started talking among themselves. One of them loosened the straps of her armor, and another handed a small treat to his leonx. For the first time, they showed open curiosity for their wards. One of them offered a water bottle to Brix.

"What does this mean?" Emery whispered.

"It means discipline, doctor," Tanner replied. "These guys have discipline."

"It also means they are more scared than they let show," Grim added. "Which is not good news."

Brix sighed. "At least they will take us seriously."

Cillian took a few steps to ease the muscles of his legs after the long ride. A leonx was a beautiful creature, but its feline moves made for a hard travels sometimes. He walked to the edge of the clearing, pacing the grass carefully. He wished to be away from the incessant chattering of the humans. He whispered a thanks to the brambles, and picked some berries from a bush.

He turned, and there was Laurel.

"I am surprised you made it so far with them tagging along," he said, not without sympathy.

"They are better than they look," she replied.

"I will take your word for that."

They looked at the three men and the woman where they sat in a shaft of sunlight, Hewma sprawled on one side, the cat-woman rubbing its belly. The short man said something, and the orc laughed. Those two were troublemakers, Cillian thought, and he did not like the man's bad manners and mocking smirk. He did not know what a "scufter" or a "mutton shunter" could be, but he was sure those were not compliments.

Cillian sighed. He should not allow emotion to color his judgment. "Hewma seems to like them," he said.

"You trust her instinct more than my judgment."

"One should always heed a leonx's instincts."

He turned his back on the refugees, and Laurel took a deep breath. "I seek news of my cousin, Redstar," she said.

Cillian frowned. "She was out hunting with you–"

"That was weeks ago. We went our separate ways, but were to meet again in Applewood Forest, in two tendays. Or if we could not meet there, Redstar said she would send word."

He shook his head. "I have no news for you," he said. He saw her expression darken. "But we have been on the hunt at the outskirts of the Bloodwood for over a month now. You should ask Dareine about your cousin. If word came from Redstar, as I am sure it did, it will have been heard in Ledish Schall." He put his hand on her shoulder and squeezed it gently. "By tomorrow night you will know."

She just nodded, still frowning. Knowing Redstar, he could see why Laurel was worried.

"How was your hunt?" she asked after a moment.

Cillian rested his hand on the hilt of his sword. "Long, and strange. There have been warnings about the Uthuk Y'llan bringing their torches to the Aymhelin, their demon witches summoning seven kinds of hell for the Latari. But so far, we have seen little of that in the Bloodwood. A few bands of stragglers, and what look like scouts for a larger force. But no witches."

"Now that's strange."

They turned. The short man in a black hat was leaning on a nearby tree, using his pinky fingernail to clean his teeth. "Sorry to intrude, but that oversize cat was getting a little too chummy for my tastes."

"One should always trust the instinct of the leonx," Laurel said, with a sideways glance at Cillian.

"But this thing you said about the blood witches is strange indeed," the man went on, ignoring her. "The harridans are never far behind when the Locust come, or that's what the chronicles say. They are supposed to do unholy things and thus enlarge the horde of the Uthuk Y'llan. And they are the smart ones anyway, right?"

Cillian felt a spike of irritation surge through his chest. This surprised him, as he was not used to feeling such strong emotions towards strangers, and this only increased his distaste for the human. He asked too many questions, and he lacked the grace the old man had shown.

"You know more about the old chronicles than I do," he said, pushing back his fury.

"Ah, no, that's Doctor Emery. He's the book-learned one in our little band. Maybe we should ask him?"

Cillian exhaled slowly. "Later, maybe. Now we must move if we want to get to Ledish Schall."

Grim bowed and made way for him, a genial smile on his rotund face.

CHAPTER TWLEVE

"This is a city!"

Tanner glanced at Doctor Emery. For over an hour now he had been leading the old man by the hand, like someone drunk. And in a way he was, Tanner thought: drunk with wonder. The doctor walked with his nose in the air, squinting at shadows among the leaves. Tanner had grabbed him by an elbow and helped him over surfacing roots and under low branches, pointing out rocks on the path, and when his warnings were ignored, pulling the old man forcibly away from the obstacles.

Now Emery raised a hand and pointed. "Look!"

With a sigh, Tanner glanced at the rest of the column and stopped. They were being left behind.

"What now?" he asked, trying not to sound too impatient.

"Over there," the old man said, pointing. "See that patch of yellow and green?"

Tanner squinted. The sunlight through the leaves played with colors like one of the tall glass windows in the temple of Kellos.

He had been to the temple only once, soon after he had left home.

"What is there to see?" he asked.

He had asked the same thing in the temple, before the colored pattern had resolved in front of his eyes into a scene with characters in it, like a story in pictures.

The column of soft-footed leonx was merging with the shadows of the undergrowth. A bird fluttered by. A woodpecker, its chirping song like laughter.

And Tanner saw it, just as it had happened in the temple, all those years ago. High in the trees, all around them, a web of bridges and causeways connected tree-houses and hanging platforms. Hidden in plain sight, fifty feet above the ground, a maze of flying walkways connected the aerial houses of Methras.

He gasped in disbelief.

"You can see it, right?"

Tanner nodded, and finally remembered to shut his mouth. "I do, doctor."

"And just like the bridge we crossed," the old man said, "the majority of the flying streets of this city are just the trees, shaped and bent to fulfill a purpose. The houses too, I believe."

Tanner did a slow turn, craning his neck. It was like standing at the bottom of a lake, looking up through the surface. The city of Methras was up there, hanging on branches and hugging tree trunks, the trees intertwined to form the structure that supported it all. As he watched, a slight shape, he could not tell if an adult or a child, ran along a latticed branch bridge that connected a box-like building to a platform under a large, umbrella-like marquee.

A whistle made him turn.

Grim was standing in the path, waving his hat.

"Come," Tanner said, and again he half-supported, half-dragged Emery along. "We can't stay behind."

"But you see it, don't you?"

Tanner nodded, and glanced up. "Yes, doctor. I see it."

He looked in wonder at the city in the trees, and shuddered at the idea of climbing up there.

Unexpectedly, now that they were in Methras, the Bloodwood thickened.

The undergrowth became more tangled, the path less clear. Larches and birches appeared side by side with oaks and chestnuts. Doctor Emery could tell one from the other by the shape of their leaves, and the grain of their bark. All had the same blood-red foliage, though, and the same black texture to their trunks.

As the sun settled, Emery's wonderment grew. There were lights now in the canopy. They lined the footbridges and flying catwalks of the aerial city, marked the suspended plazas like moonlight halos, and burned with amber warmth in the houses of the elves. Some lights were isolated, little more than a trembling spark in the deepest shadows of the leafy canopy. Others were clusters, hanging together like the chandeliers that had burned in the Petremol house in Vynelvale, when the Master entertained guests.

It seemed so far away now.

There were also floating lights, like will-o'-the-wisps, burning in the branches and moving slowly along with the breeze.

They stopped all of a sudden, and he bumped into Tanner, who fretted to make sure he would not fall.

The elves were dismounting from their leonxes. A few of the animals had already left the clearing to disappear in the undergrowth. Only Hewma seemed in no hurry to leave the travelers behind. Cillian stood, flanked by two of his hunters, a man and a woman.

"I will have to ask you," Cillian said, "to hand over your weapons."

Tanner and Brix looked at each other.

"Why?" the cat-woman asked.

"These are the gates of Ledish Schall," the elf said. "No one goes beyond this point carrying a weapon but the Hunt."

"I see no gate," Grim said.

Cillian ignored him. The hunter on his left took a step forward and bowed. "We will hold them for you," Cillian said.

Tanner snorted. He held the shaft of his axe, and weighed the weapon for a moment. He gave a long look at Cillian, and then grinned. He handed it to the elven guard. "This was given me by my captain," he said. "And he wants it back."

The elf looked at him. By his side, Brixida slipped her sword and her dagger from her sash, and let the hunter take them from her.

Cillian turned to Grim and Emery. He took the staff in both hands, and offered it to the elf. No reason to make any fuss about it.

"Would you deny an old man his walking staff?" Grim asked.

The elf scoffed. "And what about you, Master Grimald?"

The short man spread his arms. "I do not carry any weapon. I do not believe in that sort of thing."

"He tells the truth," Laurel said. "He is better at running than at fighting."

Grim gasped. "Well, now!"

Cillian nodded.

"Do you want these, too?" Laurel asked. She offered Cillian her quiver and her scabbarded sword.

The two elves looked in each other's eye for the time of ten heartbeats. Then Cillian turned on his heels. "You wait here," he said. "Kestrel will take care of you," he nodded at the female hunter on his right. "I will go forth with Gadan and break news of your coming to Dareine."

Laurel watched him go. Then she shrugged, and hooked her quiver to her belt again.

"What now?" Emery asked Kestrel.

She was, he saw, different from Laurel or Cillian. Her features were sharper, her chin more pronounced, and her cheekbones were angular and high. Her skin was the color of pale ivory, and her hair had a blue hue peeking through her black tresses.

She gestured for them to follow her.

"What is this place?" Tanner asked. He had been on edge ever since his axe had been taken away. Now he sniffed at the faint mist that extended its tendrils towards them. The air was warmer than before, despite the sun being very low on the horizon and lost in the shadows of the Bloodwood.

Kestrel laughed, and then composed herself. They had left the disbanding hunting party behind, and only Kestrel and the leonx Hewma were still with them.

"Before we meet Dareine," Laurel said, "we will be brought to the guest quarters to rest. And before that, you need… we need to bathe."

Tanner looked down at his stained, grimy leather jerkin and frowned. "Uh."

"I guess we do not smell exactly like field violets," Grim said. He sniffed at the sleeve of his shirt and grimaced. "Especially to our hosts' sensitive noses."

They walked between two large larches, their branches intertwined to form an arch. Brix gasped.

In front of them was a pool, maybe twenty yards across,

roughly circular in shape and with a pathway of stepping stones going down the middle. The water was a deep, piercing blue color, and it was gently bubbling. A mist hung heavy over the surface, that was strewn with the crimson leaves of the Bloodwood. They took a few steps closer as Kestrel hung back.

"What's the eggy smell?" Tanner asked.

"Sulphur, in the water," Grim explained. He crouched down and dipped his fingers in the pool. "It's a thermal spring."

There were lamps, hanging over the pool, casting a light the color of warm honey.

"In you go," their guard said. "We will bring fresh clothes for you. Make sure you scrub yourself thoroughly."

"All together?" Emery asked. "In there? At the same time?"

Laurel put her hand on Brix's elbow. "We go to that side." She pointed. "The men go to the other. Come."

Brix cast a glance at her companions, and followed her. They walked slowly around the shore of the pool. The ground was covered in soft moss. "Do you people bathe together? I mean, men and women, young and old?" she asked, a note of unease creeping into her voice.

"The pool is large enough to allow for privacy," Laurel said. "For those that need it."

They heard the voices of the men from the other side, too low to understand what they were saying. Then Grim guffawed.

They stopped in a place where wooden buckets were piled in a small pyramid by a stone bench. "To wash away the dirt before we get in," Laurel explained.

"I did not grow up in a cave," Brix replied. "We do have bath houses where I come from."

"Of course, yes. I beg your pardon."

With quick efficient moves, Laurel undid her belt and untied the straps of her armor. She stood in her tunic and pants, and laid the armor gently on a bench.

Brix was staring at her with her eyes wide. Laurel kicked off her boots and pulled off her pants. She shivered despite the warm mist. With quick efficient moves she selected a bucket, dipped it in the pool, and then upturned it over her head. The water was warm enough to let off steam. She then slipped hastily into the pool, barely causing a ripple on the surface.

Once in, she undid the ribbon that kept her brown tresses together, and threw it on her bunched clothes. The warmth was seeping through her skin. She rolled her head, making her neck pop. She pushed a strand of hair back with a wet hand, and took a deep breath. She let the stillness wrap around her like a shroud. Her mind was restless. She needed to see Dareine and tell them what she had learned, about the enemies in the Bloodwood, and the Fae. She needed to ask them about Redstar. The world was going up in flames around them, and time was of the essence. But despite this, the rest of her mind was telling her to enjoy this brief moment of peace. Collect her thoughts, take good care of her body. Time was of no consequence. There was no time here.

Brix was standing at the edge of the water, staring at her.

"Come in," Laurel said.

Brix dipped the tip of her foot in the pool.

"You are shy," Laurel said. "I understand that." She turned her back. "I will not watch."

But she did.

Through the mist, she looked over her shoulder, giving in to curiosity. Brix dropped her ragged coat, and then her bloodied shirt and her torn trousers. She unwound the stained bandages, pulling where they had stuck to her wounds, and let them fall to the ground. Laurel had seen the cat-woman's back when she had helped wrap her wounds. The cut was not deep, but its edges had been inflamed. She knew the hot water would hurt, but it would help clean and heal the scar. Now she could see Brix wore three silver rings at the base of her tail. Laurel turned as the cat-woman collected a bucketful of warm water and poured it over her body, hissing. Then Brix took a deep breath and entered the pool. She huffed and clicked her tongue.

"It does feel good," she admitted.

She waved her hands in the water, pushing some of the floating leaves away. Behind them, a pale form in blue came over and collected their clothes. From the other side of the pool came a big splash, followed by the sound of laughter.

"Men," Brix scoffed. She undid the strap that held her ponytail, and her red hair fell over her face like a curtain, hiding her from Laurel's gaze.

"I guess I'll have to sit down," Tanner chuckled. He was standing with water up to his waist, his hands on his hips.

"Or walk where the water's deeper," Grim replied, nodding towards the middle of the pool. They could hear the gentle splashing of Laurel and Brix in the shadows on the other side.

"I could get used to this," he said. He splashed water over his face, and rubbed it until his cheeks were warm. "Mind you, I get the beauty of the woodlands and all that, but a hot bath and a fine dinner make life worth living."

Tanner sniffed again at the water, and then crouched down, splashing his shoulders.

Grim dipped under the surface, to reappear after a moment.

He ran a hand through his hair, and smacked his lips. "It's slightly salty," he said.

"This is disgusting," Tanner blurted.

"It is in the nature of hot spring water," Emery said. Tanner thought the old man was trying to change the subject of the discussion. "Heated by the primeval fires, the water rises through the rocks and acquires the properties of the salts and the metals it encounters. Hot spring water is good for blood circulation and as a pain relief, and a dip in a hot spring pool grants an easy sleep, and takes the mind off the worries that weigh it down. It is greatly conducive to a sound night of sleep."

Grim rubbed his face. "You should have worked as a street crier for my father's inn," he said. "You would have brought customers in by the dozen."

"Did your parents' inn feature a hot spring?" Emery asked.

"If needed." Then he turned to Tanner again. "What?"

The orc shook his head. "I was just thinking–"

"What?"

Tanner shrugged. "I'm tired." He ran a hand over the back of his neck. "It would be nice to wash away the miles. And what we went through. The fear, the worry."

Silence was suddenly heavy.

"I wish we could," Grim said seriously. "I really do."

When they finally got out of the water, they found a stack of aromatic leaves to use for drying themselves, and plain white tunics with simple green sashes to use as belts.

Kestrel was waiting for them at the gates, and Hewma too. The great cat purred and rubbed herself against Grim, who patted her with caution, and then she gave a sound between a roar and a mewl when Laurel and Brix appeared, also wearing white shifts. “Dareine will sit at court tomorrow morning,” Kestrel said. “They have been informed of your coming, and are eager to meet you. Now I will see you to your apartments, where there is food and refreshments. You will sleep safely in Ledish Schall tonight, and meet Dareine with the new day. Come, follow me.”

Tanner hesitated, but Brix shrugged. “There is not much else we can do.”

“I thought our companion was in a hurry to see this Dareine,” Grim said.

“I am,” Laurel replied, without turning. “But things are as they are. Tonight, we rest.”

“And you better never underestimate an elf’s hearing again,” Tanner chuckled.

Grim mumbled something and hung at the back of their file.

Moving like ghosts, Hewma picking up the rear, they followed Kestrel past a cluster of brambles, and took a narrow ramp that wound around the trunk of an oak, climbing up. Emery went down on one knee and tried pushing his fingers through the latticework of the ramp. “Wonderful,” he said. “Is the whole city built like this?”

“Not built, but grown,” Kestrel replied.

“Of course, of course.”

“We second the natural growth,” she added. “Guide it, sometimes. But we try not to interfere.”

“Gardeners, rather than city builders,” Emery observed.

“In a way, yes.”

Thirty feet up, the ramp branched and joined a narrow gangway that led them to a circular platform. A single rope disappeared in the shadows overhead, and maintained the wooden disk suspended over the floor of the forest. The platform swung gently, and Tanner grabbed the cable for support. With mild surprise, Emery realized the big orc was afraid of heights. He patted him on the shoulder, trying to reassure him.

"This way," Kestrel said, and stepped onto a large branch that rose gently to join a wider footbridge.

"I believed Ledish Schall to be Dareine's mansion," Emery said.

Kestrel stopped and looked at him, and then at Laurel.

"The place where they live," Laurel explained.

Kestrel frowned. "It is."

Emery cleared his voice. "I mean, I imagined Ledish Schall to be a place. In Methras. Like a building, a castle, a villa."

"It is not," Kestrel replied. But Laurel nodded. "Our languages are different," she said. "This is something I learned in my travels: we see the world differently. What you call house and what we call house are not the same thing. As for Ledish Schall, it is the ancestral stretch of forest whence Dareine's line originated."

"Like a neighborhood," Emery offered. "A part of the larger whole that you call Methras."

"Yes, I guess so."

"Ledish Schall was here before Methras," Kestrel said. "Methras grew around it, as more people came to live in the Bloodwood."

They walked in line behind her, balancing along the next branch.

What looked like clusters of silk lanterns hung from the higher limbs of the tree on which they found themselves. Kestrel led them past a fork in the trunk and along a path consisting of two interlaced branches.

"This is where you will stay," she said, stepping inside one of the red silk structures. Emery hung back for a moment, and smiled when a rag-pale Tanner tiptoed past him and through the doorway.

CHAPTER THIRTEEN

"It looks like festival night," Brix said.

Through the silk screen of the window, the city of Methras was a cluster of lamp-like pavilions hanging from the tallest branches of millenarian trees, and connected by sweeping rope bridges and causeways. Some burned solitary, high in the trees, while others were grouped in flocks of a dozen, suspended in the void and huddled together around a central deck. Brix felt like she was adrift in a sea of stars. The earth was but a memory, lost in the darkness down below. Fireflies danced between the branches, and the rustling of the scarlet leaves was like a distant sea. There was faint music in the air, but she was unable to pinpoint its origin.

Tanner walked carefully to the window and stood by her side. He smelled of soap and clean clothes. The elves had provided them with clothes that resembled, in shape and color, the ones they had discarded. They had found the new garments in their rooms, together with their bags and satchels.

"They probably burned all of our rags," Grim had said.

Now Brix was wearing a red silk shirt over abundant blue pantaloons, and Tanner had been fitted with tan leather trousers and a silk jacket.

Silk seemed to be ubiquitous. The pavilion in which they were right now was made of strong silk. The fabric was stretched over a light wooden frame, and shaped like a five-petaled flower. Each petal was a room, accessed by a door closed by a curtain, and the rooms were arranged around a central space, where the braided rope that supported the platform was hooked to the floor of polished wood. A circular couch sat around the point of connection, and a platform-like shelf hung from the support cable, and served as a table. There was a faint oscillation that Brix found soothing and Tanner, evidently, found unnerving. He avoided looking down.

Kestrel had showed them their quarters, and explained they would spend the night there.

"You are our welcome guests," she had said, but when she had gone, they had seen that two hunters were discreetly stationed on the walkway to their pavilion.

"Less than guests and more than prisoners," Brix had quipped. It was obvious that their presence in the Latari city was an exception to a tradition the elves found hard to break.

Each one of them had picked a room, leaving the fifth empty. Brix felt a pang of guilt thinking about Léa for the first time in many days. As she tested the bed, which she had found pleasantly hard, Brix had wondered whatever happened to the girl, and the people on the road. Everything seemed so far in the past, but it had been less than ten days.

Emery was sitting on the circular couch at the center of the hall when the door opened, and he turned eagerly. He had asked for writing tools and paper, but through the door walked Laurel, and behind her the long, slick form of a leonx. The elf had shed her green metal armor, and was wearing a simple tunic in green and russet. She moved a little stiffly, as if she was not used to wearing anything different from her armor.

From a fold in her dress she extracted a roll of cream-colored paper, and a tube containing a pen and an inkpot. "Here you are," she said, handing them to Emery. He looked quite dignified in a black gown with green and gold embroidery.

"What are you going to write?" Tanner asked, backing slowly away from the window.

"We are the first humans in Methras in a very long time," the old man said. "Or maybe we should call it Ledish Schall, I am not sure. From what I understand, Ledish Schall is Dareine's seat of power, and one of the boroughs of Methras, that feels to me more like a confederation of loose communities than a city proper as imagined by the people of Terrinoth. This is in itself a fascinating insight. Anyway, previous accounts are tinged with awe and romantic nonsense, wasting a lot of time on details of no consequence derived by ballads and stories penned, I am sure, by people that never set foot in these places. Any accurate note or factual observation will be a precious tool to historians and philosophers, and might help improve the relations between our peoples."

"And will make you a nice bundle," Grim said, as he came out of his room pulling at the cuffs of his new white shirt. The leonx turned sharply towards him and made a loud purring sound. She pushed her head against Grim's side and pressed firmly, her eyes closed. Grim staggered and made a face.

"She likes you," Laurel said.

"For dinner?"

Brix snorted. "Don't be silly. She's the nicest girl in the world, aren't you, dear?" She scratched the leonx between the ears, down its muscular neck, and under the chin, inches away from the long, knife-sharp fangs. The beast purred and seconded her movements, enjoying the attentions of the cat-woman.

"A nice girl, yes," Grim said. "Those jaws could snap an Uthuk in half like a twig."

"But we have nothing to fear from her, have we?" Brix cooed, and kept scratching the war beast. "Of course we have not."

The leonx stretched, yawned, and then followed Grim as he went to sit on the couch. With total abandon, the beast sat on the floor by his legs, and laid her head on the short man's lap. He breathed in sharply, as if expecting she'd try and bite one of his legs off.

"If this is not love…" Tanner chuckled.

"Looks more like appetite to me," Grim said. But he scratched the cat tentatively under the chin, and she seemed to appreciate it, purring loudly.

"Have you heard from your cousin?" Brix asked in a low voice.

Laurel turned sharply, her eyes meeting Brix's.

"You mentioned a cousin of yours. Brightstar?"

"Redstar," Laurel replied.

"You said you were coming to Methras for her. Is she all right?"

Laurel shook her head. "There is no news from her, at least not from Cillian."

Servants came in, carrying trays of food, and they all moved to the hanging table. "It is not unusual," the elf went on. "We often fail to hear from each other for weeks when we are out hunting."

Brix sat by her side.

"But this time," the elf took a deep breath, "something is not right. I can feel it."

Brix placed her hand on top of Laurel's and pressed gently. "I am sure you will hear from her soon."

Laurel nodded.

"Mind if I sit here with these ladies?" Grim asked out loud, approaching the table. The leonx by Brix's side stared at him and sneezed.

"I'll take that for a yes."

He sat on Brix's other side, and she quickly pulled her hand back, releasing Laurel. Tanner picked a bright red apple from one of the dishes and polished it on his sleeve.

"You should eat the soup first," Brix said, in her best governess voice, before he could bite into the fruit. The orc looked at her guiltily.

"You better do as she says," Grim said, "or she'll challenge you to a duel."

"Or assign you some extra homework," Emery added, sitting down with a grateful sigh. "Old habits die hard, don't they, Mistress Brixida?"

"Oh, please!" Brix said, but she chuckled. "Eat what you please, Tanner, and do not mind me."

It was strange, she thought, to feel so at ease with these people. And yet she felt a stronger kinship with them than she had ever felt in the Petremol household, where she had spent ten years.

"But still," she added, "soup would do you good."

"Yeah, you're so skinny," Grim winked, "some soup would do you good indeed."

"And you, conversely, should stick to salad," Brix retorted, causing more laughter. Grim gave her a hurt look, and then turned to the great feline squatting at his side. "You're the only one that understands me," he said with a dramatic sigh, and scratched her between the ears. "We shall share some stew." He picked up a bowl of what looked like fruit salad. "And some of this too, whatever it may be."

There were a number of dishes on the table they could not place. The elves clearly enjoyed game, and that was familiar indeed, but some of their fruits and vegetables were a mystery to the travelers. Now Grim tried some of the fruit salad, and nodded appreciatively.

"This is very good," he said.

"Don't sound so surprised," Tanner replied, "or you will offend our hosts."

Laurel was looking at them in silence. Brix thought she maybe felt somehow left out of the conversation. She offered her a bowl of soup. The elf accepted it with a nod, and started eating with swift efficiency.

The others served themselves, and for a moment they just ate and exchanged some comments about the food.

"What will happen now?" Tanner asked, pouring more soup in his bowl, and grabbing a loaf of bread.

The others looked at each other, and then they turned to Laurel.

"Cillian is seeing Dareine as we speak," she finally said. "He has arranged for a meeting, and is reporting on what he saw in the Bloodwood during his tour. It is most unusual for people from the Baronies or the Free Cities to be admitted to the Council Hall of Ledish Schall, but we made a strong case–"

"Or a strong impression," Grim smirked.

She looked at him, and went on. "Tomorrow, we will be admitted to the presence of Dareine, and we will talk then. We will relate what happened. Then they will decide."

"Decide what?" Tanner asked.

"What will come next."

"And this means Master Grimald will be at the center of the stage," Emery said.

"And he will have to refrain from being his abrasive self," Brix added.

"I'd rather do without it," Grim said, seriously. He turned to Brix. "You are the smart one, and I say you should be the one to speak for all of us."

"But you are the one who spoke with the Fae," she replied.

"That's a way of putting it," he grunted.

Brix shook her head. "It's you they want to question," she said, softly. "In their eyes, we are just along for the ride. But we will be there, and we will stand by you."

He did not seem to find that much of a consolation.

Two pairs of glowing eyes were staring at Grim when he gasped awake and sat up in bed. There was a pressure in his chest, and his breath was ragged. His sweaty hand went to his pillow, and slipped under it just as he remembered where he was, and how long it had been since he had last slept with a dagger under his pillow.

"Are you all right?" Brixida asked from the darkness.

The leonx moved closer to the bed, and leaned its head by Grim's side. He distractedly scratched its chin. "Yes," he breathed. "Yes, I think so."

"Another bad dream?"

He frowned. "How do you know?"

In different circumstances, both the presence of the cat-woman and the leonx would have stirred different emotions, but Grim was too tired for that, too weighed down by what had visited him again in his dreams.

"It is a governess' job to know if her charges sleep peacefully."

Grim chuckled. "Is that what we are? Your charges? We are a bit long in the tooth, don't you think?"

She moved in the darkness, and he imagined she was shrugging.

"Like Doctor Emery said, old habits die hard. I have spent many a night walking the corridors of the Petremol house, listening for the children. What is making your sleep so uneasy?"

"It's the Fae," Grim said. Speaking like this, without seeing her face, made things easier.

She made a little gasp. "Are they still talking to you?"

"No," he said. "I do not believe so. It is just the memories and–"

"What?"

"It is like when you eat too substantial a meal, and have a hard time digesting it. I believe the Fae poured so much in my mind, it takes time for me to go through it and make any sense. It's like there are many layers, and the deeper ones come to the surface only when I'm asleep."

"What is it that you see?"

He sighed, and ran a hand through his hair. "There is a creature. Man-like, but different. One of the Uthuk Y'llan, but not like them. They fear him. The Uthuk, that is. And also, in some way, the Fae fear him. He screams in my dreams, a creature of dread and anger. It's not a pleasant thing."

Brix took a long breath.

"Maybe you should have eaten just a salad," she said then.

"But I did," he groaned.

They were silent for a moment, then they both laughed, keeping their voices as low as possible. Hewma looked up, startled.

"I better be going. Our talking might wake our companions," she said.

"I wouldn't worry," Grim said, "I can hear Tanner snoring from here, and Emery was almost collapsing from tiredness at dinner."

"You try to sleep too, and rest," she said. "I'm sure Hewma will stand guard over you. Have a good night."

Grim caressed the head of Hewma, who purred happily.

"I will try," he said, but Brix was already gone, silent and invisible.

"This looks more like a marketplace than a council hall," Emery mumbled. Both Brix and Laurel cast a glance at him, and he sniffed and was silent. The elf walked first, and the other four followed, huddled together.

They had seen Ledish Schall from a distance, hanging in the soft mist of the deep wood. A treehouse, as they had expected, but of colossal proportions, it would have been impossible not to see it. Three ancient oaks, so large that fifteen men could not have embraced them, rose up to the sky like towers. Under their blood-red canopy, rooms and platforms hung from the branches, and suspension bridges and stepladders connected the different sections. There were pavilions like the one in which they had slept, and hanging gardens that looked like birds' nests, the intertwined twigs carrying autumnal flowers and fruits. Birds did make their home here, and flew in chirping flocks as the strangers approached, scared by their strange voices. Guards manned the gangways at the periphery of the structure, and light came through the foliage in rich golden beams, and was supplemented with flying lanterns and reflecting mirrors.

There was music in the air, and the scents of nature were too refined and pleasant not to be by design.

The leonx riders were escorting them. They had left the hanging pavilion and followed a wide causeway, suspended underneath the red canopy of the Bloodwood. The guards had left their beasts at the foot of another access ramp, and now walked by the side of the group, holding their lances. Up through the palace they climbed, soon lost in its maze-like structure.

There were causeways instead of corridors, ramps instead of staircases, and as they moved along, the travelers had spotted refined elven lords and ladies sitting in conversation in cozy nooks, and scruffy elven children playing hide and seek in large chambers filled with greenery. Looking down, they saw that a brook ran between the three oaks, and they passed contraptions designed to lift the clear water to the higher levels and others designed to channel the rainfall to the ground. Brix compared what they were seeing to a music box. She was the only one still able to speak in front of such wonder.

As they entered the hall, Grim whistled softly. This was not a room, but more of an open courtyard, a large wooden platform, about fifty yards across, with the red canopy of the Bloodwood for a ceiling. Cables as thick as a man's arm, four in number, held it in position, but it was impossible to ignore the faint oscillation as they set foot on it. It was like stepping on a barge on a quiet lake, still but not perfectly so.

The elves of Methras sat and stood all around: along the margin, under the arching branches and the canopy of the pillar-like trees. They were talking among themselves, their voices mingling in a quiet cacophony. To one side, some were playing flutes and harps, or picking long-necked lutes, in harmonious anarchy. One was declaiming what, by its rhythm, sounded like a poem. Others were playing a game on a six-sided board, surrounded by a small crowd. Tokens changed hands as the game progressed, the pieces clicked on the polished wood. Their attire was strange and diverse, from the most utilitarian woodsman's leather to layers of silk and colored feathers. Their features were different too, their hair and skin color, and if most were human-like in size and shape, a few were so tall and lanky they topped all those around them. Only the guards, in their green and silver chainmail, the same that Laurel had worn, were at all familiar to the refugees.

There was an overall attitude of casual intimacy that it was hard to associate with a council meeting. Light filtered through the canopy of crimson leaves, and was supplemented by floating globes of pale paper that hung in the air by no apparent means, and cast an amber light over the polished floor while they bobbed gently.

Slowly, as the travelers advanced, eyes turned to them, and the talk quietened. One by one the instruments went silent, and only the clicking of the pieces on the board and the rise and fall of soft whispers remained.

"Friendly crowd, huh?" Grim mumbled. Tanner dug his elbow into his side.

In front of them, sitting on a pile of cushions, was an elf of unspecified age or gender, their elongated features framed by long dark hair, and a single teardrop earring on their right ear. They dressed in a layered coat of many shades of brown, copper and gold, the colors of autumn, over a simple tunic the color of moss. Felt slippers were at their feet, and a thin coronet sat on their forehead, a single blue stone sparkling. They looked up as the band approached, surprise replacing ennui.

The beast riders stopped, and crossed their spears in front of Emery and Brix, who opened the file. The four refugees stopped, and Laurel walked on alone.

"We are happy to see you well, Laurel of Bloodwood," the sitting elf said. Like their looks, their voice was impossible to define. Laurel stopped, still five steps from the low dais on which the cushions and the elf rested. "Cillian brought news of your coming, and we welcome you back."

There was a silver ring on their hand, another blue stone sparkling in it.

"I am happy to be here, Dareine. I come seeking quarter, for me and my companions. We bring dark tidings."

Dareine turned a languid eye on the refugees. "You travel far and wide, Laurel. And you come back with strange companions."

"These are my friends," Laurel said. The crowd's whispers rose, like waves on a distant sea. The game players stopped playing, and turned towards the newcomers, finally showing interest.

"Friends, indeed. Yet they carried weapons in our woods."

Cillian came forward, flanked by Kestrel and Gadan. The latter was holding Tanner's silver-bladed axe, and the former Brix's sword and poignard.

Laurel half turned. "These are Brixida Lovell, cognate of the cat-people, and Tharadax Tanner of the stone-dweller orcs. They come from Vynelvale, the great city in the west, that was laid waste by the Uthuk Y'llan. We met in the wild, and shared companionship on the road. Together we fought the Uthuk Y'llan on the Old Road of the Kings, and later in the hills, and lastly into the Bloodwood. Would you deny these warriors the right to carry arms, and their right to vengeance?"

The chattering from the watchers rose in volume some more. A few of them moved closer, as if to take a better look at the newcomers.

"Well played," Emery breathed, and Grim nodded.

"Uthuk Y'llan in the Bloodwood?" Dareine said. All of their softness was gone, a sharp edge revealed in their voice. One of their thin eyebrows arched as they turned questioningly to the leader of the hunters.

"She tells the truth," Cillian said. "The Locust Swarm has entered our woods. Small warbands, scatterings of the main force that coursed through the Great Plains to the Free Cities of men. Raiders looking for loot. Our riders are seeking these stragglers out. A strange occurrence in these strange times, but not something worth worrying about."

"Not simple warbands, and not strays," Laurel said. "And reason enough to worry and be prepared."

"I can see you are worried, cousin," Dareine said. "It is good you brought more blades to defend the Bloodwood against the Swarm."

Chuckles came from the crowd. Both Laurel and Dareine ignored them. "What about the other two?" they asked. "They do not look like warriors."

"They do not carry weapons," Cillian said, but Dareine waved a hand, and looked at Laurel, expectantly. "What of them, cousin?"

"The old man is Doctor Arnost Emery, a wise scholar and a man of good counsel, a teacher of children. And the other is called Grimald, from the hamlet of Guyot, by way of Greyhaven. He is a powerful spirit talker." She made a pause, her eyes gazing into Dareine's. "He is intimate of the Fae."

Grim cursed under his breath, just as the hall of Ledish

Schall was completely still for three heartbeats, and then everybody started talking at the same time.

"Here we go," he said, softly. Laurel had set the noose, now he only had to pull his head through it.

Dareine looked around, frowning, but the din did not subside. The crowd was wavering, as if pulled by the curiosity to look closer at the strangers, while repulsed by the danger they now represented. The platform swayed in sympathy, like a raft on a choppy sea.

"What is this talk of the Fae?" Dareine finally asked. The tone of their voice imposed silence in the hall. All eyes were on the travelers, and Laurel spoke.

"The Fae came to us, on the Grey Steps not far from Fletchers' Hollow, where we were facing the Swarms," she said. "They joined the fight, and did away with the last of the Uthuk Y'llan. They caused great havoc, and overwhelmed us all but Grimald. He stood his ground and they spoke with him, and spared us. They had a message they wanted us to deliver."

"Speak? With a human? And what of this message?"

"A warning," Laurel said.

Grim took a step forward. "It's about the Well of Tears."

The absolute silence was deafening. The elves were a host of long pale faces, their expressions impossible to fathom. They huddled together, keeping back from the center of the hall. It was as if even the breeze through the leaves above them had stopped. Everything was very still.

Dareine stood. "Leave us alone," they commanded. "Only Laurel and the spirit talker Grimald shall stay."

"We are not going anywhere," Brix said, causing a new flurry of chatter from the crowd. "With all due respect, my liege. We do not leave one of ours behind."

Dareine looked at her. Tanner took a step closer, standing behind her, and crossed his arms. The elf smiled. "So be it. Our guests will stay."

They waved a hand. "Leave us alone now."

CHAPTER FOURTEEN

While the courtiers filed out of the hall, Dareine had cushions and food brought over by some servants. Shortbread, cake and fruits, light wine and sweet juices. They invited the refugees to sit down and eat. Dareine was courteous and yet distant, and the refugees did not wait for more invitation. Tanner grabbed a piece of shortbread and a cup of juice, and passed it to Emery. Brix sniffed at a fluffy cake, and took a slice. Only Laurel and Grim did not touch any food, but stood waiting, exchanging worried looks.

Then, from one of the winding ramps came Cillian of the Hunt and Kestrel, followed by two more elves, a tall male with dark hair and a thin, silver-haired female in a complicated dress. They moved with the slow deliberation of someone that is used to power. They looked at the travelers with open curiosity, and then they spoke to Dareine in the singsong tones of the elven language. Grim did not catch any of what they were saying, but heard the word Dimora, repeated twice.

Grim remembered from his days in the Academy. The Dimora were the ancient spirits that were said to haunt the Aymhelin and the Bloodwood, and were possibly even more sinister and mysterious than the Fae. The differences and similarities between the two were much debated by old men that knew very little about either of them, as was the habit in academia. Soon afterward his name, somewhat oddly accented, followed. He glanced at Laurel, but she was not looking at him. She certainly understood what was being said, and it did not seem to make her any happier.

The two newcomers turned their eyes towards him, and Grim straightened his back. Everything about them spelled magic users, and it stood to reason that Dareine wanted to have some mystical support in what was to come, since the Fae had been mentioned.

The last time Grim had faced an elven mage had been in Greyhaven, a lifetime before, and two days before they kicked him out. He had felt the same back then as he felt now under the steady gaze of the two newcomers. Like his own life depended on what the elves would say, and his life was the last of their cares. He braced himself for what was to come.

Now the three Latari came forward, walking side by side, and spread out around Grim. Cillian remained behind, standing by one of the support cables, looking on. Kestrel was by his side, one step behind, as silent and still as a shadow, Dareine and their two companions settled at the three corners of a triangle around Grim, at a distance of about two yards. Like they were getting ready to attack him, three against one. This too was like his time back in school. He had hoped to leave all of it behind, but now he tossed his head, defiantly.

"These are Travaran and Delsanra," Dareine said. Their voice was soft but authoritative. "They are of Ledish Schall, and wish to question you."

Grim gave a nod. The geography and politics of the

Bloodwood was too fluid and strange for him to grasp completely. He'd have to discuss this with Doctor Emery. The old owl was writing an essay on the subject, after all. But for the moment, he would simply accept that these two were of Dareine's house, and powerful in more ways than one.

The elves started slowly walking around him, and Grim tried to remain focused on them as they moved. By the way she looked at him, it seemed that the Delsanra woman would have rather kicked him out of Ledish Schall, out of the Bloodwood and, if possible, out of Terrinoth. Travaran was harder to read, but his penetrating gaze spoke of a sharp mind just as his plain clothes spoke of a practical man. Dareine remained distant and alien.

"You are the one that is intimate with the Fae?" the silver-haired woman asked. Her eyes were so pale blue they looked white, and there was disbelief verging on mockery in her icy-cold voice.

"Intimate is a big word, my lady," Grim said, and cast a glance at Laurel. The elf stood outside of the interrogators' circle, a worried expression on her face. The others had left the food and wine behind when the questioning had begun, and were now standing by Laurel, waiting. "But I had communication with one of them," he went on, "after a fashion. It was one-sided, and came not out of my skill, or by my own decision, but just out of their benevolence."

"Benevolence?" Travaran scoffed, his voice like the crack of a whip. He was rougher around the edges than Delsanra or Dareine. A mage for sure, but one of the people, so to speak. He was direct and straightforward, while around Delsanra hung an air of nobility, of implicit superiority, a sense of great age and power, and a habit for command.

"Benevolence from a Fae?" Delsanra echoed her companion, a mocking note again in her voice.

"Your mirth is giving voice to my terror, mistress," Grim replied.

This *was* like a Greyhaven exam. Bullying, but under a coating of good grace and dignity. He had walked away from all that, because he hated these sorts of games. But he knew how to go about it, if needed, as long as these mages would play by the rules.

"The Fae must not be trifled with," Travaran agreed. "It's good that you feel terror."

"You should not be alive," Delsanra said, coldly. She turned her pale blue gaze to the other travelers. "None of you should be, after meeting the Fae."

Sorry to disappoint you, Grim thought.

"What did the Fae tell you?" Dareine asked. They shifted their weight from one foot to the other. Reasserting their authority. Were they growing impatient with their friends' approach to the inquiry? Dareine was not a wizard, Grim thought, but a politician. They had decisions to make, not papers to write.

"How did they speak to you?" Travaran asked, acknowledging Dareine's question.

Grim sighed, and shook his head. "It's complicated. It's not like they talked to me, the way we are doing now. It wasn't so straightforward."

"How was it, then?" Travaran asked. He seemed genuinely interested.

"It was like..." Like trying to read a book, Grim thought, while somebody hits you in the face with it. Hard. Repeatedly. He took a deep breath, searching for another way to say it. If there was one thing he had learned in Greyhaven, it was never to be too clever in front of your betters.

"Have you ever walked with a small child, holding hands?" he said. He looked from Delsanra to Travaran and finally to Dareine, who nodded imperceptibly. "Your legs are longer," he went on, "and your hand is so much stronger than hers, but because you want to walk with her, and not just drag her along, you take short careful steps, slow down to match her short-legged pace, and you hold her hand without crushing it. It requires effort, and care, adapting your way to what is natural for her. That is how it was. I was able to understand what the Fae was projecting my way, because they slowed it down, and restrained their strength. They made it easy for me. They made it simple. As simple as they could." He looked at Delsanra. "And that is the reason I'm alive. Why we all are. They simply held back their full power, and strove not to kill us. Because they had something more urgent in mind." He paused. "And that is what should make us all scared."

The three interrogators stopped their walking, and the two elven mages looked at each other, and then at Dareine. Travaran nodded.

"What was the message?" Dareine asked.

"There is a place you call the Well of Tears," Grim said. Images flashed in his mind, pale memories that still carried the pain of what he had witnessed. Faint memories of nightmares, too. He pressed on. "A stone tower surrounded by rose bushes. It is a place of power, revered by the Fae. Ancient."

There had always been something between the Fae and water. It was thanks to the rivers flowing by that Greyhaven was clean of them. It was the first thing one learned when he got there. The pattern of the rivers made Greyhaven safe from the Fae. He had never got around to learning why. Nobody really knew, probably. But this well was somehow different.

"And there is something – someone, roaming the Bloodwood, seeking the Well. One of the Uthuk Y'llan, I believe. Some sort of creature the Fae themselves never knew. A champion of some kind, maybe a demon-speaker. They showed me–"

"What?" Delsanra asked, suddenly impatient.

Images pounded on Grim's memory. He shuddered, and sweat shone on his brow.

"A tall and lanky thing," he said. "Pale like the belly of a fish, with spikes like a sea urchin, and evil. Not human, nor human-like. A thing of nightmares, burning with hatred, and violence."

"And the ones he commands are not common Uthuks," Emery said. His voice came out of nowhere and echoed under the leafy canopy. Everybody turned to him, and he took a tentative step forward. Dareine glanced sideways at the two mages, and then nodded for him to get closer.

"I contend," the old man said, "that the Uthuk who have invaded your woods are not the same as the ones that are putting the lands of men and orcs to the torch." He pulled at the lapels of his coat, and sucked the side of his cheek. "What prompts this hypothesis is the strange sign we have seen, etched on the living skin of the warriors we have met ever since we left the Old Road. The use of banners and insignia is not unheard of, and it is in fact mentioned in the chronicles of the First Darkness. But what we have witnessed? Such a cruel branding is unheard of, even among the Uthuk Y'llan." He arched his eyebrows. "Or is it?"

"Can you describe this sign?" Travaran asked, suddenly interested.

"A circle, as ample as a stretched hand, from the tip of the thumb to the tip of the little finger. And across it three oblique gashes, like by the claws of a wild beast. The scars were treated with a mixture, I believe, of ash and lye, to make them permanent and make them stand out on the skin, blacken them, and give them hard burned ridges. But I am no alchemist, and I could be wrong. All the Uthuk we met in the woods carried the same sign over their heart. It has to mean something."

"Men often attribute a secret meaning to what they do not understand," Delsanra said.

"And elves do not?" Emery asked, only to bow his head at her stare.

"And there are no blood witches," Grim said, almost to himself. Then he turned to Cillian. "Now that is weird, isn't it? No blood witches with these warbands. Your hunters saw this, too. Which is strange because it is commonly accepted that the witches are the ones that wield real power within the Uthuk Y'llan, and the warriors do their bidding, out of fear if not out of respect."

The master of the hunt nodded in response to Dareine's questioning look.

"It is true. We found and killed warriors, but no witches."

Delsanra and Travaran looked at each other. Unsurprisingly, it was Delsanra who spoke. "And what does this inhuman champion of yours want? Did the Fae care to explain it to you?"

Grim pressed his lips together, and exhaled through his nose. "To interfere with the Well of Tears in some way. To take possession of it. To poison it, somehow. That was what I perceived, their strongest suggestion. Something like a gangrene, poisoning the Well of Tears, and then all of the Bloodwood."

The Fae's projected images had grown hectic and confused

on that point. Like the creature of chaos was in panic, like too much needed to be conveyed, and Grim's mind had not been up to it.

"The Bloodwood and all of the Aymhelin," Travaran said. Delsanra gave him a long look. Grim shuddered at the thought that something could scare these two. Yet their stance had changed subtly, and their questions had lost their arrogant edge. They were no longer circling him like hungry wolves, and looked at each other more often than they looked at him. They were worried, and that worried Grim too.

"Why would the Fae tell you all of this?" Travaran asked, frowning.

Grim caught the cold intelligence in the elf's eyes, and saw he had misjudged the man. For all his growing preoccupation, Travaran was level-headed and focused, showing the same attitude Grim had so often observed in Laurel. A warrior. This was not a simple woodland mage, but rather a tactician.

"I think they want somebody – they want us to do something about it. About this Uthuk champion and his warriors. About the Well."

And he had no idea of how they would ever do it. Grim closed his eyes and wished he was somewhere else. He heard his companions shuffle their feet, and strained not to turn.

"Why don't they do something themselves?" Delsanra asked.

Grim gave her a look. The attitude that had contributed to make him an outcast in Greyhaven reared its snarky head. "You should ask them, mistress, and kindly. As I said before, I'm not as intimate of the Fae as some would believe. I was just the tool they had at hand to deliver their message. Someone who could listen to them, and not go completely mad with it."

Delsanra stared daggers at him.

"But if you want my opinion," he went on, "I'm under the impression they can't do anything, because they are too scared at the idea of getting close to whatever is walking your woods right now."

"The Fae?" Delsanra asked, again with a mocking lilt in her voice. "Scared of the Uthuk Y'llan?"

Grim tasted again the copper bitterness of the panic that had radiated from the Fae, and saw it reflected in both Travaran and Dareine's eyes. Only her arrogance, he thought, was stopping Delsanra from being just as scared. "Scared of what they might do."

"How so?" Delsanra asked, in a dead voice.

Grim shrugged. He felt incredibly tired. "Your guess is as good as mine, my lady. Better, in fact, because you know what this Well of Tears is, and what its taking by the Uthuk Y'llan could mean."

Silence weighed on the hall. The three elves looked at each other. Delsanra shook her head, but Travaran nodded and crossed his arms. By the access ramp, Cillian was frowning, and Kestrel's face betrayed her utter bafflement. It came down to Dareine, then, to make a decision. As was fit.

"Margath the Unkind," Dareine said, slowly. "Levirax, Baalesh, Zir the Black, Avox, and Gehennor."

They looked at the travelers, who in turn looked at each other.

"The Dragons of the Third Darkness," Doctor Emery said like he was answering a school test. His voice eased in the rolling cadences of his classroom manners. "They came in from the north in the time of the Elder Kings, each of them leading a horde of their ilk, descending on the Fair Kingdoms to steal the Stars of Timmoran. The Wyrm Queen and her hybrid offspring were their allies, and the Bloodguard Knights rose again from whatever darkness had held them, and placed their blades in the service of the dragons. For five years they set the land asunder, causing much pain to humans and dwarves and, yes, to elves too, until they joined in council–"

"With the orcs, too," Tanner added.

Emery cast him a glance, but nodded. "Indeed, young man, this was the time when the orcs joined the commonwealth of peace-loving peoples, and together the four races faced what was to be called the Third Darkness. In Sudanya, on the river Ru–"

"We are not here for a history lesson," Delsanra said, cutting the old man short.

"And yet we are," Dareine said in turn, "because we owe our guests the part of the story they were never told."

Delsanra turned her gaze away, and Grim got the impression she was none too keen on revealing the secrets of the Latari to a bunch of strangers. But the role of the elves in the history of Terrinoth had been shrouded in mystery and hearsay, and he was curious to learn more. He eyed Emery, and saw the eagerness in his face.

"Many believe the Latari were the least touched by the Third Darkness," Dareine said. "They believe the silver halls of Caelcira were left untouched, and never did the dragons and their kin invade our forests. And though others suffered more than our people, in truth the Third Darkness poisoned our lands just as it did the rest of Terrinoth. We fought just as any other kingdom of Mennara. We mourned our dead, and suffered the devastation of our homes. And when the darkness receded and the dragons were pushed back into the mountains, the Latari looked for a way to heal their dominions, and thus turned their eyes to the Fountain of Purity."

Delsanra whispered something, her expression dark. Dareine glanced at her, and went on. "The Fountain is a natural spring in the woodland by the Thalian Gates. I have been there, I have seen it. The forest grows rich and lush because of the Fountain's waters. Its water has a rare power, it nourishes the pure of heart, and it devours the wicked from within. It was by the virtue of the Fountain that the beauty of the Aymhelin was restored. The water from the Fountain cleansed the forests of the shadow-touched, healing the wounds of the land, regrowing the trees to their fullest. The Fountain is the heart of our land, and the mere sight of it is forbidden to all but the elves, and is but a legend to the people of Mennara. Even speaking of it, as I am doing now, is a breaching of our laws. Yet, for all the secrecy that surrounds the Fountain, over the centuries a number of individuals have attempted to take control of the mystical waters by force, because commanding the Fountain means commanding the heart of our people. But the Fountain is guarded, and well defended, with weapons and magic. None have succeeded in taking it, so far."

"What has the Fountain to do with the Well?" Grim asked. He felt foolish for the wording of his question, but he didn't like where all of this was going. Just like he wasn't comfortable being at the very heart of this riddle. He felt suddenly very tired, and sick, and wished he could just sit down for a moment.

"Your people," Dareine said, and they looked into Grim's eyes. Grim wondered if they meant the people of Terrinoth, or the humans, or the mages and wise men at Greyhaven. "Your people believe the world is made of many separate things, that chance or fate have put together, like baubles collected in a box. But we know that the world is like a forest, in which everything is connected and intertwined, and different elements balance each other and are bound by invisible ties."

They stretched a hand, the blue stone on the silver ring sparkling, and encompassed the trees surrounding the hall with an ample gesture. "The sun and the moon, the wind and the rain, the roots and the branches of each tree – is not each of these a part of the forest? To the unwary they appear to be independent of each other, and yet are but parts of a whole. A single tree, a whole forest, the world at large, are connected into a single larger living entity."

"I am familiar with such theories," Grim said. He could hear his companions shift and fidget behind him, tired just like him of all the philosophizing.

"Then you will understand when I say that what we call the Well of Tears is part of this larger whole, and connected with every other part."

"Including the Fountain of Purity," Emery whispered.

Grim cursed under his breath. This was worse than he had imagined. And yet, as fearful as this was turning out, at least they were coming to an end.

"The two are like weights hanging at the opposite ends of a stick. Like the sun and the moon, they balance each other, and are connected while being separate," Dareine said.

"You believe…" Brix started. Every eye was on her now. Grim had to admire her elegant stance. Only her tail, endlessly twisting, betrayed her nervousness. "You believe," she said slowly, "this strange creature, this Uthuk champion the Fae have warned us about, is making a bid for the Well as a way to take control of the Fountain? Like a thief entering a house through a back window when the front door is too guarded."

"Isn't the Well protected?" Tanner asked.

"There is a guardian," Dareine said.

Delsanra scoffed. There was something there, but Grim could not tell what exactly. There was too much happening too fast, and he was starting to feel lost.

"Then," Grim said, "I guess it is high time we alert them something's coming for them."

Dareine took a deep breath. "This council is dismissed."

Kestrel and her hunters led them back to their quarters, high in the cluster of silken pavilions. It was late afternoon, and the realization surprised Brix. She had lost all sense of time during the audience with Dareine.

Along the way they did not talk among themselves. Elves watched them go by, lords and ladies, and a few children, all equally curious. The news of their coming was spreading, and curiosity was rife in the elven community. A very young elven child ran along the flying causeway and looked intently at Brix. She smiled and waved at them, and they stopped and stared. Their mother called them back, and then pulled them away by an arm.

So human, Brix thought. After the many strange things Dareine had revealed, it was almost underwhelming, witnessing such simple behavior. And for a fleeting moment, she wondered what had become of the two little Petremol monsters, and it all felt so distant, like a lifetime before. She hastened to follow the others.

Once they were in their rooms, they looked at each other.

"That was unexpected," Brix said.

"And abrupt," Grim nodded.

Hewma purred her welcome, and rubbed herself against Brix's side, and then against Grim's. By the door, Laurel was talking with Kestrel, their voices so low they were but a whisper.

"Dinner will be served presently," Laurel said, walking into the central room.

"That is good news, but not what we were worrying about," Grim said.

"Although food is always welcome," Tanner added.

"What's happening?" Brix asked.

Laurel lifted her shoulders, slowly, and let them sink again.

"Dareine will consult with Travaran and Delsanra," she said. "That's the way it is done. The magistrate cannot take a decision without consulting two councilors."

"Sounds like a wise way of doing things," Emery said.

"Wise but slow," Grim said.

"I thought the Latari were under a prince's rule–" the old doctor continued.

"The Bloodwood is different," Laurel said. "Authority is… distributed. We do not put such a great stock in the traditional ways as our people in the Aymhelin."

"Dareine called you cousin," Brix said. "Are you really related?"

"We come from close lines. But my people fought in the battle that made the Bloodwood. Dareine's came later to Ledish Schall."

"So we've been brushing shoulders with royalty and we did not know."

Laurel looked at Grim, and frowned. "There is no royalty in the Bloodwood," she said, seriously. "Your people have stories about us," she went on, "but as I said, those are about the Latari in the Aymhelin, not those of the Bloodwood. About us you only rightly know we do not love your people, and your people do not love us. But we that live here have even less love for rigid politics. We rely on ourselves, and on the wisdom of our community, more than on the blood right of a king. This is the reason why now a larger council will be called. Speakers will convene from all the smaller enclaves in Methras, and further afield. A strategy will be defined. Commands assigned, to organize the defense of the Bloodwood. Scouts have already been dispatched, to trace the movements of the Uthuk Y'llan, and to warn the other communities in the Bloodwood. Then a general plan of action will be drawn, warbands formed…" She nodded at the leonx asleep at Grim's side, her powerful chest slowly rising and falling with every breath. "Your friend will be soon called to fight the Locusts."

Grim looked somberly at the animal, and ran a hand along her side.

"Will all of this take long?" Brix asked. Much as she was impressed by the Latari's organization, she was feeling a growing urgency, like they could not keep pace with all that was happening.

"What about this guardian at the Well?" Grim asked.

Laurel shook her head. "That is something I have no knowledge of. I am a warrior, not a mage. But it is likely they will be alerted. That is a decision Dareine can take without convening a quorum." She looked at Brix. "A decision I'm sure they've already taken."

"Will you allow volunteers to join your forces?" Tanner asked.

Laurel arched her eyebrows.

"My friends will be safe here," the orc said. "This is, after all, why we came here in the first place. To find safe haven. I planned to rejoin my captain when they settled, but now... maybe you'll welcome one more blade in the fight to come."

"Or maybe two more blades," Brix said. She felt a strange chill along her spine, but yes, she thought, this was what she should do. She looked at Emery, his face turning as red as a beet and then as pale as a rag.

"Are you out of your mind?" the old man asked, in a thin voice.

"These people helped us," Brix replied. "Now it's our time to help them."

The old master shook his head. "Of course we shall pay our debt, of course, in some way, yes. They welcomed us, gave us shelter, food–"

"A bath," Grim smirked.

Emery glanced at him, and continued. "But you, my dear, are hardly a warrior–"

"It will be more a matter of willingness than of finesse, I believe," she replied. "And you know I can hold my own with a sword."

"She has a point," Tanner admitted.

Doctor Emery huffed, and shook his head. "This is not what we planned. We were supposed to find a quiet place and weather this storm–"

"Storms rarely follow people's plans," Grim said. He sat by the table, and the leonx placed its head in his lap.

"We need ideas, Master Grimald, not platitudes," Emery snapped.

Grim shrugged, and scratched Hewma between the ears. They remained silent for a long moment, avoiding each other's eyes. Brix understood Emery's misgivings, but she had made her decision. She was tired of being carried along by the flow of events. She was tired of being afraid.

Servants came, and brought food and drink. Kestrel walked in with them. "Dine, and rest," she said. "Tomorrow morning you will be in council again."

Tanner thanked the serving elves, and approached the table. "Do you mind if I have an apple?" he asked Brix.

She clicked her tongue, but appreciated the orc's attempt at lightening the mood. "It's good for your health. Isn't that what they say, doctor?"

The old man looked at her, frowning. He emerged from his thoughts, glanced at the red apple the orc was holding, and allowed himself a smile. "Yes, of course–"

The leonx looked up and growled, a low menacing sound. The cups and dishes clicked, and one of Tanner's red apples rolled off the table. The pavilion swayed from side to side, the suspension cable creaking sinisterly.

Tanner was already up on his feet. "This thing is moving!"

But Brix was no longer listening. She was looking at the dancing light that filtered through the gauze of the window. Her nose wrinkled at the smell of smoke.

A cold ghostly hand squeezed her throat, robbing her of her voice.

Methras was burning.

CHAPTER FIFTEEN

A sea of flame was spreading under the hanging pavilions and the tree houses of Methras. It consumed the underbrush, fed on the sere grasses, and attacked the bark of the red-topped oaks that were the backbone of the city. Fluid red and yellow light illuminated the treetops from below, casting snakelike shadows that mingled with the thick black smoke that rose from the wet materials the flames were feeding on.

Never had such a catastrophe hit the elves of the Bloodwood. Not even in the time of darkness, when dragons flew low over the trees, belching red fire from their maws. Those attacks had been stayed by magic and personal sacrifice, preparedness and courage. But this… this was unheard of. Not during the rainy season, when much of the dry autumnal brushes were soaked wet.

As the fires crackled and hissed, a chorus of animal calls rose in the forest, and was soon joined by the screams of the citizens of Methras, as they called to each other, or vented their terror. Nothing was worse for the city in the trees than a widespread fire. The citizens reacted in panic. Some tried to smother the flames, or pour water on them. Others were busy running away from danger or, in many cases, towards it, in the hopes of helping a loved one, retrieving some keepsake, or to bring relief to their neighbors.

The fire attacked the walkways and the pillars, bit into the cables supporting the structures of the elven city. Elven-made structures, taxed by the weight of the fleeing crowds, groaned and creaked under the weight. Clouds of flying embers were carried by the evening breeze, like swarms of fireflies. Dry autumn leaves burst aflame when touched, and the fire spread, ever faster.

Behind the flames, the Uthuk Y'llan came.

After killing the sentries, the Uthuk had piled dry branches along the perimeter. Th'Uk Tar had struck the flint personally, and his warriors had shared the flame, lighting their torches. A spark, and the wind had done the rest of the work.

At the start, Th'Uk Tar had to use his whip to keep the frenzied raiders in line. The warriors had smelled the reek of the Latari, and were hungry for death. His army had grown since the sack of the city of temples, and now he commanded a horde that would strike fear not only into the rag and bone forces of the Bloodwood, but also into the very heart of the Aymhelin.

The fire spread slowly at first, eating the wet bushes and caressing the massive trunks of the tallest trees. Black billows of smoke rose in the air. In the grip of impatience, Th'Uk Tar scanned the shadows of the forest. Would the fire cause the scions to manifest? He hoped so. He was eager to get his hands on one of the fabled guardians of the Bloodwood, and see what he would make of it. But he would not let hope be a distraction.

A shrill call resounded through the burning trees. Horns

sounding the alarm. The hated Latari had caught the scent of what was coming to their den. But it was too late.

"Go," Th'Uk Tar said, in a measured voice.

But now the flames were rising, and the warriors had lost their bloodlust. Remembering the bite of his whips, those closest to him took a few tentative paces towards the red and yellow hell bursting in front of them. None of them was eager to be devoured by one of the beastmaster's pets, but the prospect of being consumed by fire was holding them back.

The mass of red-clad warriors wavered, and crept forward. They leaned into the scorching heat, but instinct kept them from entering it.

Th'Uk Tar bared his fangs and spread his arms, his clawed fingers cutting through the smoke-thick air.

"GO!" he screamed at the top of his lungs. He cracked his whips over the heads of the warriors. "Let not a single elf live to see the light of day!"

Behind him, Gorgemaw rose and screeched its hunger at the sky. The smaller caecilians that writhed around his colossal shape coiled and bawled in response. The flesh rippers screeched in answer, and with a thunderous howl of blood frenzy, the Uthuk Y'llan marauders ran into the flames, disregarding personal safety, frenzied by the prospect of killing elves and spurred by the fear of their own leader. They rushed up the ramps and the gangways, jumped across fiery gaps brandishing their misshapen weapons. A new note entered the screams of the people of Methras. The clash of blades and shields mixed with the roar of the fires, and war cries replaced the screeching of the Latari fleeing their homes.

The battle of Methras had begun.

•••

Squinting in the uncertain light and smoke, Brix watched as one of the onion-shaped, red silk pavilions hanging from the branches of a nearby tree fell into the roaring inferno fifty feet below. She averted her eyes, gasping.

"Keep running!" Kestrel shouted in her ear, and pushed her on.

They were following a narrow gangway that ran over a large branch and bridged the space between two oaks. Brix was helping Arnost Emery, holding him up. The old man had trouble breathing, and was looking around like he was lost.

"Such a wonder," Emery mumbled. "Destroyed."

"They'll build it anew," she hissed, dragging him along.

They had left their quarters and were trying to make their way to safety. Brix had no idea what had become of Tanner and Grim, and the last she had seen Laurel, the elf was running to join a band of defenders. Dropping down on the ground was impossible, it would be like ducking into an oven. Their only hope was to get far enough from the front of the fire they'd be able to reach the forest floor and continue on.

A whole tree burst into flame with a loud bang, the flames engulfing its canopy, running along its branches. Brix heard screaming. The hot air was burning in her lungs. Emery slipped again, and she clutched him tighter.

Then she saw them coming.

Three tall gangly warriors, armed with bone axes, red rags hanging across their bare bodies. The fires from below painted dreadful masks on their grotesque faces, and blood-red smears on their weapons.

"Watch out!" she shouted, too shocked to stop and reflect what the presence of the Uthuk Y'llan could mean. She pushed Emery away, and he stumbled, cursing under his breath, as a bone blade cut through the space where he had been but a moment before. The old man stared wide eyed at the grinning warrior just as Brix skewered him with her sword. The blade slipped easily under one of the bone plates protecting the warrior's heart. The edge grated on a rib, the vibration reaching Brix's hand. The Uthuk growled and half turned, but Brix held on to her hilt, and the movement only made his wound worse. She put her foot on his midriff and pushed, freeing her weapon and tossing the Uthuk over the parapet.

Kestrel pushed against her side and lifted her shield, intercepting the blades of the two remaining attackers. Brix took a deep breath, the tang of the smoke gagging her, and struck blindly with her blade around the rim of the shield. Behind them, Gadan let out a warlike shout. His spear passed between Brix and Kestrel. With a metallic sound, the shaft brushed the edge of Kestrel's shield, and pierced one of the Uthuk Y'llan just under the collarbone.

As they pushed back together, Brix wondered what had become of the others.

Tanner wanted to descend from the hanging platforms and the suspended bridges. He was not keen on heights, and rickety contraptions, and for this reason he had not followed Kestrel and the others as they climbed up and away from the flames. He was no squirrel. A hot wind rose from beneath, alimented by the roaring flames, but the orc was sure he'd be a lot safer with firm ground under his feet. Balancing precariously at the fork of a massive branch, he looked down, squinting in the glare of the flames. He watched the Uthuk warriors climb the stepladder-like ramp to a tree house, a tangle of box-like rooms and open balconies. A woman screamed. One of the Uthuk fell back, and was swallowed by the flames.

A monster looked up at him, red eyes burning, a gaping maw filled with triangular teeth.

Tanner pulled back, panting. Fear was a flash, followed by the need to survive.

The snakelike creature curled around the tree trunk, and from there slithered onto a nearby branch. It hissed again and it snapped at Tanner, who swung his axe at the base of the branch. The creature's bite missed his head by a hair's breadth, and he hit the branch a second time, chopping it off, and consigning the monster to the embrace of the fires beneath.

Striving not to look down, Tanner ran in that direction. The rest of the band was lost in the mayhem, and he wished them luck as the first Locust came for him, brandishing a short spear.

The first thing Grim thought when he saw the flames eating at the city of the elves was that all of his stuff was in his room. Spell components and spices for cooking, all that was left of his shop, of his quiet life, a million years before. For that reason, while the others ran looking for a way out, he ran back in and quickly collected his satchel and, on the way out, Doctor Emery's leather bag.

Outside the door, the hot air hit him like a hammer. The others were gone, and everything was burning. The wide ramp they had followed coming in from the council crashed with a thunderous sound. This changed the balance of the whole structure, and it was like the world had tilted to one side. Grim stumbled and rolled down the balcony, hitting the balustrade hard.

The impact knocked his breath out. He tried to grab a hold, his fingers ice cold despite the heat. Nothing was scarier to him than death by fire, the pain and the horror of the flames. He managed to move to a safer position, but the bags dragged him down and hindered his movements. He cursed himself for a fool. To die for a handful of spices and an old man's collection of curios.

Beneath him the flames rose to grab him.

"Not today," he whispered. He pulled at the straps of the two bags crossed over his chest, and on all fours, slowly, went looking for a way out.

More Uthuk warriors came for them, crawling like ants along the suspended bridges and the hanging walkways. Brix pushed Emery back, and stood side by side with Kestrel, one shield and two blades trying to keep the incoming adversaries at bay while they retreated.

One of the brutes threw himself at them. He slammed into the shield and pushed, growling. His hand grabbed the upper rim of the shield. Brix cut at the fingers just as Kestrel pushed back and stabbed the Uthuk in his side. The narrow gangway forced their adversaries to come at them one at a time, and the poorly disciplined Uthuk hindered each other as they tried to rush forward. Gadan was holding their rearguard, milling his spear at the incoming assailants. Emery was pinched between them, trying to keep low, and mumbling an uninterrupted litany of grief.

The heat and the smoke made everything more difficult. The two women fell into a simple rhythm: stab, push back, retreat, stab again, push back. This way, they held the gangway, and slowly moved towards one of the hanging platforms. Limping and short of breath, Doctor Emery got there first, and waited, holding on to one of the three cables that kept it hanging over the inferno. He scanned the surrounding treetops, and gasped as he saw more Uthuk swinging from one branch to the next, approaching fast.

"Go on," Kestrel said to Brix as soon as they walked onto the platform.

"What–?"

But then Gadan was there, using his lance to push them both forward.

"Run!" the elf commanded, shoving both women towards Emery.

Brix collided with the old man. By her side, Kestrel slipped and fell. She grasped her by an arm and helped her up. She turned in time to see Gadan gut the first of the incoming Uthuk with his lance. The dead warrior rolled away, and the lance snapped. More warriors were coming, and the elf lifted his arms, defying them.

"No!"

"Get out of here!" he shouted again, without turning.

Emery pulled Brix back. Together with Kestrel, they ran to the closest ramp, which wound in a spiral around the colossal trunk of an ancient tree.

As Kestrel helped Emery negotiate the descent, Brix turned one last time, to see a dozen Uthuk surrounding Gadan, screaming in rage and triumph as he twirled his sword, cutting at them without pause. A monster with knife-like teeth and a spiky back circled him slowly, its razor-like tail swinging. But still Gadan kept them at a distance. This only increased the murderous fury of the raiders. More came, the platform swaying under their weight. A beast like a rusty snake accompanied them, sharp teeth and a flaring spiky cowl.

Brix took one step towards Gadan, brandishing her sword. He looked in her eyes, and what she saw there stopped her in her tracks. The blade of the elven sword flashed in a tight arc, and the closest support cable snapped like a whip.

Brix cried out in horror as the platform tilted, and all the occupants were delivered to the white-hot maw of the roaring flames.

For a heartbeat, Brix leant over the abyss, her arm uselessly stretched. Nobody was there anymore for her to help.

A hand pulled at her shoulder.

"Come," Kestrel said.

Brix followed her and Emery down the spiraling ramp like a sleepwalker.

She lost all sense of time. They were walking past a swaying rope bridge, and they heard children screaming. The sound brought Brix back to the present. She stopped.

"You go on," Kestrel said.

There were children, running from a collapsing residential structure. Menacing shapes moved behind them. "No," Brix said.

The elf shook her head. "You'd slow me down," she said, and Brix remembered Laurel's same words, a lifetime before. "Go, and I'll see to the children."

They nodded once, silently wishing each other good luck, and went their separate ways. Brix turned once, as she was about to take a spiraling ramp downwards. She saw Kestrel lead the children along a thin branch. The elf was carrying a very small one in her arms, and dragged another along by the hand. Three more, a little older, followed.

"They'll be safe," Emery said.

Brix wished he was right, and led the old man down the ramp.

•••

Creaking and groaning, a flaming tree crashed on the ground, cutting off Tanner's trail. Protecting his face and his eyes with an arm, he backed onto a damaged stepladder and against his best counsel climbed to a rickety platform, halfway up a giant birch tree. From his vintage position, he scanned the nightmare of flames and smoke, trying to find a clear way out.

He felt the shuddering of the platform under his feet before the Uthuk raiders started screaming. He turned in time to intercept the first with his axe. Tanner pushed him back, into the two others that followed. The two warriors pushed their companion forward, and Tanner's weapon bit into the Uthuk's shoulder, cleaving him down to the sternum. The orc kicked the dying Uthuk back, and twirled his axe, his eyes trailed on the two survivors. He could take them both. He knew he could. He shouted out in defiance.

The first one lunged at him just as the platform's stilts snapped, and they fell.

Grim was lost.

He had followed a narrow walkway up close to the leafy cover, trying to stay as far as possible from the flames below. The narrow path of planks snaked through branches and vines and finally came to a stepladder going further up.

Breathing heavily, Grim climbed the ladder, and found himself in a small garret-like structure. He spent a minute on all fours on the floor, coughing and shuddering. Finally, on trembling legs, he stood and grasped the edge of the parapet with his hands.

He was in a small circular tower that rose above the top of the Bloodwood trees. In every direction, a sea of reds and crimsons rippled under the stars, catching the rays of an almost full moon. The fires on the floor of the forest casting a sinister, spectral light through the branches. Huge billows of dark smoke, scattered through with firefly-like embers, clouded the stars and the moon, marking the spots where the major fires were eating at the city of Methras. The crackling of the fires and the screams of the people on the run, the din of the fights – all sounds were distant and muffled, like an afterthought.

"Fortuna's eyes," he whispered in awe.

From his bag, Grim took his small metal flask, and washed his mouth of the taste of smoke with a gulp of brandy. He watched in horrified fascination for long minutes, a sense of emptiness creeping over him. He wondered what had happened to his friends.

Old Doctor Emery would have a hard time running from the fire and the Uthuk. And there was not much that Tanner could do but run with his long legs. But Tanner was not the kind that ran from a fight. The same was true of Laurel, and this was her home burning, after all.

He saw a column of embers rise in the sky where a tree had collapsed in a fiery crash.

And Brix…

He chuckled. The cat-woman would probably try and swashbuckle her way through the Uthuk. He sighed, and shook his head. Those fools would be lost without him.

Slowly, carefully, he started down the stepladder. The last thing he wanted was a twisted ankle. Methras was lost, the forest was turning into a fiery trap, and he needed to find the others.

•••

Tanner shook his head, trying to get his bearings. He was still holding his axe, and he used it for support as he pushed himself back to his feet. The heat was like a hot slap in the face, and he raised an arm to protect his eyes. The movement sent a stab of pain through his shoulder. There was burning wreckage all around him and his ears were still ringing from the impact with the ground. He took a few steps away from the flames, limping. As he turned, he spotted one of the Uthuk, impaled on a length of broken plank.

The crack of longbows led him to a ledge on the forest floor. Beneath him, a band of elven hunters was engaging a bunch of rabid Uthuks. A first line of spearmen kept the incoming raiders at bay, while the archers on the second line aimed their arrows.

Tanner looked around, searching for a way to climb down his vintage point and join the elven fighters. A tree leaning over the edge of the scarp gave him an idea.

As he negotiated the roots of the large oak, slowly climbing down, there was a sudden lull in the fight. The Uthuk had retreated and the elves, emboldened, took three steps forward, their formation loosening. Tanner stopped, surprised at the sudden stillness. The elves regrouped, and one of the archers spotted him. The elf pointed at Tanner, and he waved a hand, trying to signal he was a friend.

Then, with a mighty roar, the Uthuk surged forward. It was a mindless rush, fearful in its recklessness. Tanner cursed under his breath and watched as the barbarians crashed into the level spears of the elves. They ignored the rain of arrows and kept pushing. They fell by the dozen, brought down by arrows or cut down by spears, and still they kept coming. It was, Tanner thought, like there was something far scarier than death on the elven spears urging them on.

Then he saw what was behind the Uthuk.

Cillian had three lines of archers holding the access to Ledish Schall. They stood on the thick branches of the oldest tree in the city, raining death on the Uthuk Y'llan. Wave after wave of warriors had come at them, and forfeited their lives. Not a man accustomed to speculation, Cillian could not help but wonder what would become of his people. He had sworn to protect them, and he had failed.

"You take Dareine to safety," he had said to Travaran. He could no longer say if it had been minutes or hours before. In the fiery twilight, time had lost its meaning.

The wizard had grasped his arm in a brotherly farewell. "Do not waste your lives."

Another band of Locusts came for them. The archers took their time and selected their targets. More bodies piled at the foot of the great tree.

"They seem to have lost their boldness," Cillian said to Delsanra. The woman stood by his side, apparently untouched by the mayhem that surrounded them. Cillian had been surprised when she'd remained behind with his forces.

The sorceress' face was impassive. "Someone's coming," she said.

"Get ready," Cillian said to his hunters. They had been counting how many arrows they had left in their quivers. They were burned and wounded, their armor dented and broken. Tired and scared, they looked like survivors of a year-long war. Yet they waited for the newcomer side by side, in silence.

He came for them with long strides on his strangely jointed legs, his bone whips cracking. Just like the human Grimald had said, he was tall and almost emaciated, his pale skin scarred and stretched over sinewy limbs. Behind him, a tangle of crimson horrors, like a gaggle of massive, scaled millipedes, screamed murder, sharp teeth shining. The largest towered above the rest, leathery cowl flaring menacingly.

A crackling ball of lightning grew between the hands of Delsanra, and then hurtled towards the Uthuk champion. The blue light engulfed him, and he screamed in fury. The fire spread to his crawling train. The smaller snakelike beasts screeched and yelped, curling and twisting in pain.

With a sound like a thunderclap the blue light died, its power exhausted, leaving behind a strong smell of stormy weather and burned flesh. Unscathed, the Uthuk champion roared his anger and snapped his whips. The segmented bones intercepted the incoming arrows, casting them aside.

Delsanra shuddered, despite the heat from the rising flames.

"Take your men to safety, Cillian," she said, coldly, her fingers weaving another blue ball of electricity. "There is nothing you can do with this one."

He looked at her. The finality in the woman's voice extinguished the last spark of hope he had clung to.

The whip cracked again, and two of the archers were caught and dragged from their perch and into the flames. He had to take his hunters to safety, Cillian thought. Standing here they were doing nothing good.

"Go," Delsanra repeated, echoing his thoughts. "And warn the scions."

Grim fell through the hot air, the fiery embers smacking his face, stinging him like burning mosquitoes, the blazing wreckage of the walkway streaking in the darkness around him. He'd been running along a flying bridge, looking for a way down, when the struts had snapped and the whole thing had collapsed with a thundering crash.

He felt fear, and surprise, and a strange sense of vertigo, and then he hit the surface of the pond head on, and the warm, sulfurous water closed around him, breath escaping in a burst of bubbles through his mouth and his nose. His hands touched the gravel at the bottom and he pushed himself up, breaking the surface and gasping a large lungful of hot air.

A tract of burning walkway had crashed in the pond with him and now rested, half-submerged and scorched, a black trellis wrapped in flames, reflected in the water. And above, the sky was hidden by black clouds of smoke and yellow tongues of fire.

Finding the bottom of the pond with his feet, Grim pushed toward the shore, and once there he rested on all fours, coughing and spitting and thanking his good luck.

A hand grabbed him by the hair, and painfully forced his head up.

A grinning Uthuk lifted his twisted iron hatchet.

Grimald of Guyot felt extremely stupid as his eye caught the mark on the warrior's chest, the rough circle crossed by three oblique scars.

The iron blade hissed as it swung down. Grim closed his eyes.

The maws of the leonx snapped on the Uthuk's arm, crushing the bones with an unpleasant sound. The warrior shouted and let go of Grim's hair. The man fell to his knees and scrambled as far as possible from where Hewma was making short shrift of the Uthuk.

It was fast and brutal, and Grim turned away, nausea boiling up in his throat.

With a grimace of distaste, Grim picked up the fallen blade

of the dead assailant. The leonx stretched, moved closer, and prodded him with her head.

"Yes, girl," he said, his voice shaking, "I am happy to see you too."

Somewhere behind them, a tree crashed in a cloud of embers, and a breath of warm air buffeted them.

"Let's get out of here," he said.

Tanner was bleeding through a dozen cuts, and his sight was swimming. His head throbbed. He had been running through the burning floor of the forest, blindly. The line of archers and spearmen had been broken by the charging monsters, it had been every man for himself. Running away from the enemy, he did not know if the Uthuk Y'llan had found him, or he had stumbled on them. They faced off on a small platform, suspended fifteen feet over the burning forest floor. Tanner had no idea of how he'd got there, his brain dulled by exhaustion.

Now he lunged, wielding his axe, his arms aching. He dragged his left foot, and stumbled on the body of the third Uthuk he had killed. He staggered, and the bone spurs on his adversary's left wrist caught him under the ribs, on the right side. Tanner snapped his arm close, to try and limit the damage, which further compromised his stance. The Uthuk gave him a grin filled with sharp teeth, and lifted his right to strike. He was holding a misshapen black iron blade, the edge glinting malignantly. An arrow went through his arm, and another caught him in the hollow at the base of his neck. The warrior gurgled, black blood pouring out of his mouth, and fell backwards, and off the platform, into the fires below.

Tanner turned, panting.

Laurel nodded at him, and helped him up. He whispered a thank you, his voice broken. He coughed, and held on to her with all his remaining strength.

Delsanra had never contemplated the perspective of her own death.

She had been too busy exploring her life, to make it into a work of art. It was one of the reasons that had brought her to the Bloodwood, her desire to be free, to enjoy life to the fullest according to her own rules, and not those of Caelcira. As she went through time, commanded only by her whims, existential philosophizing had been something for which she had had no interest. Hers was to be a long, wonder-filled existence, and she did not care for its extremities.

And now that she was about to die, she no longer had time to consider the ramifications. That this was the end, she had no doubt. Ledish Schall was coming down in flames around her, and her future would be measured in heartbeats. Therefore what she would do with those final heartbeats was all that counted.

With a flick of her fingers she extinguished another life by summoning a searing bolt of pale lightning. The Uthuk Y'llan warrior in front of her froze as the energy coursed through his limbs and then he collapsed, steam rising from his remains. It gave her a brief moment of respite. The Locust Swarm was holding back, the heat from the flames was pressing on her.

A shambling shape stepped forth, and shouted his challenge.

Delsanra looked at the Uthuk Y'llan champion. He was much like the human spirit-talker had described. She struggled to remember his name: Grimald of Guyot.

It was important, in this moment, to remember as much as

she could. Memory, after all, would be all that was left of her in a moment.

A nightmare creature all angles and spines, built around a poisonous core of pure hatred, the champion towered above her by a full head and shoulders. She wondered briefly what circumstances had shaped him, what Ynfernael patron had fed his growth.

The champion grinned, showing teeth like a shark. His long arms snaked at his sides, and two long whips unfurled. The backbones of some animal of the wild, turned into a weapon. He was good at turning living things into weapons, this monster out of the Ru wastelands. Something that transcended evil burned in his eyes.

He cracked his whips.

Delsanra took a long breath, and pulled the last but one ampule from her harness. She could not allow herself the luxury of fear, and she was glad, in a way, that she was given this last opportunity.

She cast the glass bottle. The champion intercepted it with his whip, shattering it in midair, a cloud of glass shards and black powder, spreading a strong smell of aniseed. Then he laughed at her.

Delsanra retreated. The wall of fire behind her scorched her back, steam rising from her dress. Nowhere to run. This was it.

"You should not be afraid of dying," the champion said. His voice was rough, his accent rougher. She could barely understand his words, but the look on his face was unquestionable. For the first time in centuries, Delsanra felt a spike of fear go through her heart.

"I don't plan to kill you," the champion said. He was slowly circling her, his eyes boring into hers. Delsanra held his gaze, and moved slowly, like in a dance. She put her thumb and forefinger together, and then opened them, a long spark of blue energy crackling. He looked at her hand, and then back at her face. "I will let you live," he said. His gravelly voice was horribly persuasive. "I will take you as my pet. My servant. My bloodhound. There is so much I can teach you. You will love every moment."

Delsanra hurled a bolt at him. The lightning discharged at his feet, and he laughed. Defiantly, he stepped over the black scar her bolt had burned in the floor of the pavilion.

"You'll be beautiful when I'm done with you," he said.

He was close now, very close. His grin widened.

"Look down, champion," she said, irony coloring her ice-cold voice.

He hesitated for a moment, suspecting a trick. Then he screamed, more in surprise probably than pain, and pulled back. He stumbled, holding his wrist.

A flaming tree crashed at the edge of the floor, exploding in a cloud of flying embers. But the champion had other things to worry about.

There was a certain black moss that grew in the caves and shady recesses in the damp, benighted tangle of the Greywood. It looked like soft black velvet, and it carried a faint scent of aniseed. It was also aggressively acid. It would eat through flesh and metal, cloth and bone. Scouts and hunters, the few who braved the Greywood, knew it and gave it a wide berth, but Delsanra had once taken an interest in these things, and the freedom of the Bloodwood had allowed her to conduct some experiments that would have been frowned upon in more civilized society.

She had kept a small sample of the rotmoss among her things.

In the few moments after the vial's breach, the spores had found purchase, and the mold had eaten through the bone whip in the champion's right hand, and was now burning the flesh of his fingers. He tossed the melting remains of his weapon away, and turned a look of pure hatred on Delsanra. His right hand was black, erupting in horrid purple pustules, the sickness quickly spreading towards the elbow.

Cracking his remaining whip to keep her at a distance, the champion retreated, his teeth set. "Get her!" he screamed. "Kill the elf!"

A colossal shape burst through the wall of flame.

The larger caecilian, Delsanra observed dispassionately, the smaller ones of the brood coming after it. The monster opened its maw and screamed, the sound like a hundred trumpets.

Delsanra pulled the last of her ampules free, and wondered briefly what waited for her beyond the Veil.

CHAPTER SIXTEEN

There was more violence, a mind-numbing feast of death and destruction, more than any individual would care to contemplate, or remember.

Doctor Emery held back while Brix flailed her sword around, hissing and cursing, her tail snapping behind her. They ran through the burning trees and smoke, sometimes joining small bands of fleeing elves, sometimes alone in the madness and the noise.

He felt like a fever was going through him, shivers shaking his limbs, and a dull ache numbing his mind. The hanging city of the elves had been a thing of beauty, the perfect merger of nature and nurture, of ingenuity and patience, an achievement that spoke of history, passion, and civilization. Now it was all wreckage and horror, blackened remains and fire. As he hastened to keep pace with the rabid bundle of fury that had once been Brixida Lovell, Arnost Emery was surprised at the sense of pain the loss of Methras was causing him. A deep sense of prostration he had not even felt at the loss of the Great Cathedral of Kellos.

He looked up ahead and saw two twined trees, standing like

a portal at the head of a living bridge. Both trees were burning, two columns of flame marking the passage.

"Beyond the river we'll be safe," he said.

Brix looked at him, without seeing him.

"Safer," he corrected himself. And grasping the cat-woman by the wrist, pulled her in the direction of the gorge and the burning gate. Brix resisted for a moment, and then let him pull her along.

"Doctor!" Tanner appeared at his side, limping. Laurel was with him, and was helping him stand.

"Across the river–" Emery said, and coughed. He squeezed the hand of the boy, glad he was alive. Tanner placed a hand on his shoulder, and together they hastened to the river.

They slowed as they approached the two burning trees, the heat biting at them like a watchdog. They moved in single file, keeping their distance from the flames.

Laurel gasped and faltered. A rough barbed shaft had gone through her right thigh. She stumbled and fell to her knees. More arrows fell around them.

"Hurry!" Emery shouted and pushed Brix across the river.

At his side, Tanner handed him his axe. It weighed like a mountain, but Emery held on to it. He started on as Tanner, with a mighty groan, lifted the elf and threw her across his back. "Let's go!"

A band of Uthuk was behind them. Emery reached the other side of the gorge as the first of them passed through the burning trees. Tanner stumbled and fell by his side, breathless.

Emery watched in horrid fascination as the Uthuk ran towards him, like a single horror with a score of legs and as many arms, ten heads screaming all together.

He tightened his grip on the axe and shifted his weight. This would not be like chopping wood for his mother, a lifetime ago. He barely could lift the weapon, but he took what he hoped was a martial stance, his old bones crackling like twigs. He could smell the rank odor of the Uthuk, so close now. The intertwined roots that made the bridge erupted in flame and warped, creaking and groaning. With a long, painful cracking sound, the two trees collapsed one into the other, and then the whole wonderful structure folded and dropped into the river down below, taking the screaming Locusts along with it.

Emery dropped his arms, the blade of the axe scraping the ground. He realized he had been holding his breath.

"We need to keep moving," Tanner said. He stood and picked Laurel up in his arms, and pushed into the undergrowth.

Emery went to where Brix had collapsed, and helped her up. The cat-woman was crying. The old man put an arm around her shoulders and led her on, following in the steps of the orc. The realization that Grim was not with them made him stumble. He looked around, squinting at the dancing light of the fires, and wondered what had become of the man. He felt too crushed to feel any real worry. He pulled Brix closer, and together they followed Tanner, too exhausted to speak.

There were other survivors, marching alone or in small bands away from the flames. They did not draw near, nor try to speak, and Emery was happy to ignore them.

Deep into the night, the flames consuming Methras shone like a distant sunset. They battled the silver light of the moon, casting deceptive shadows that made the going trickier than it would normally be. The fires were like the roar of a storm at sea.

Tanner did not know how far from the river they managed

to go before the last of his strength waned, and he was forced to stop. He found a shady nook between two thick roots at the foot of a big tree, and laid Laurel on the ground. Emery and Brix joined them. They were ragged and covered in soot and ash. Tanner could not even imagine what he looked like. But he could not crash yet. He pushed the pain and dizziness back, blind determination fueling him.

In the false dusk of the fire, he examined the wound in the elf's leg. The jagged stone head of the arrow had pierced through her leg, and jutted out at the back of her thigh. Tanner touched the skin with the tip of his thumb, and Laurel groaned.

"The shaft's gone through the muscle," he said. "It doesn't seem to have touched the bone. Doesn't seem to be poisoned either. It's a clean wound."

Laurel was sweating profusely. She shuddered. "Take it out," she said.

She tried to grasp the tail of the arrow, but Tanner slapped her hand away. He turned to Brix. "Can I have your dagger?"

The cat-woman looked at him like she'd never seen him before. Her voice was low, wary. "What do you want to do?"

"I can cut the shaft," he said, "and then pull it through."

She stared at him, wide-eyed. Laurel groaned, but nodded.

"I've done it once before," he said, trying to sound reassuring. "My brother got an arrow through his arm when we were kids. It hurts, but it's a clean thing. It will just leave a scar."

Laurel nodded. "Do it."

"It's her dagger, after all," Brix hissed as she pulled out the weapon and handed it to him. "Do you need any help?"

He shook his head and clicked his tongue. "You can come here and hold the arrow as still as you can."

Laurel turned onto her side, carefully, to give him better

access to the injury. Her skin was damp with sweat. Blood dripped along her thigh.

Brix eyed Emery. "You keep an eye out," she said. The old man nodded.

Tanner knelt by Laurel, and took hold of the arrow. "Here we go."

He held the gaze of Laurel for a moment, and she gave him a nod to go ahead.

He used the dagger to cut off the feathered tail of the arrow. He held the dagger against his thumb, like he was pruning a sapling, and cut through the wood. Then he threw the feathered end away.

The elf did not make a sound, but Brix hissed as more blood poured through the wound.

"Now we pull it through," he said.

"This is going to hurt, but I'll make it fast," he said.

She nodded. "Go on. It's not my first wound."

He heard the sound of cloth tearing. Emery was cutting strips off his silk tunic. "You'll need bandages," he said.

Tanner nodded. Then he wrapped his fingers around the blood-slick arrow, just above the arrowhead. Brix let go, and he pulled it through.

Laurel hissed and cursed, but did not scream. Tanner was not really surprised. His brother had screamed, all those years ago, but Laurel was different.

They applied the bandages, stopping the gushing blood.

"It would be nice to have some clean water and some chamomile ointment," Tanner said. "Or something alcoholic."

"You could use slippery elm bark as an ointment."

They all turned, and Brix let out a loud gasp. Grim was leaning against the tree. He was disheveled and dirty, his face and hands smeared with ashes. The leonx Hewma was sitting by his side, her large eyes glowing in the shadow. "Or marshmallow. I used to sell the stuff. Both work a marvel. But this," he added, handing them his flask, "might work just as well."

There were a lot of questions whirling in his head, but Tanner was just too tired now. Relief felt like a gulp of cold water. They were all safe. He sniffed at the contents, and arched his eyebrows.

"Special supplies," Grim said.

Tanner took a gulp, and then poured the liquor on the bandage. Laurel gasped and gritted her teeth. Then she took the flask from Tanner's hand and drank a mouthful. She coughed and handed the flask to Brix, who sniffed at it, cleaned the neck with her hand, and drank. Then she handed the flask to Emery.

The doctor glanced at Grim, who shrugged. "Be my guest, doctor."

Brix's eyes were bright from the liquor. She rubbed her hands together. "Where have you been?"

"How did you find us?" Tanner asked.

The short man sat down by Brix's side and let out a long sigh. "My friend here followed your trail like it was glowing in the dark," he said. The leonx growled and purred. "You guys are fine?"

The others mumbled an answer. Tanner slapped him on the back.

"I missed you, my friend," he said, and handed back the flask. Grim upturned it, and not a drop fell. "I am glad we all made it."

They sat in silence for a moment. Brix rubbed her eye with her wrist, and mumbled something about the ashes.

"We need to keep going," Grim said, pocketing the flask.

"Where?" Emery asked, and coughed again. In the uncertain

light of the raging fires, his face was streaked with tears that had cut through the soot.

Grim ran a hand through his hair. He patted his tunic, nodded, and pulled his hat out of it. He shook it and put it on. "To the Well," he said.

Tanner had never seen him so determined. Something had changed in the man. He wondered what he had seen in the burning ruins of Methras.

"Are you crazy?"

"Do you have a better idea, old man?"

Emery pointed a shaky finger at the rippling red to the west. He opened and closed his mouth twice, and then shook his head. "This is madness. Putting ourselves in the very eye of the storm is not what we wanted."

"The eye of the storm is usually a pretty peaceful place," Grim said.

"But never for very long," Emery snapped back.

"The doctor is right," Brix said, in a level voice. Tanner looked at her, frowning. He had not expected her to side with the doctor. She had helped Laurel sit up against the tree, and now was sitting by her side. "This is not what we wanted. What we wanted was peace, and safety. It was what we were seeking on the Old Road. We would have happily settled in Mayvale, and stayed out of the chaos and the fighting through the winter. But that was an illusion. And safety and peace was what we were looking for in Methras. But even Methras was no sanctuary."

She took a deep breath, and looked at Doctor Emery.

"It is not our fault," she said. "It simply is, I believe, that the Uthuk Y'llan will not allow us peace and safety. That we want them is of no consequence. And therefore it does not matter where we go, we will always be on the run, and scared." She shrugged, and Tanner saw what she had been driving at. "So I say we go to the Well of Tears, and there we take our stand."

Grim was right, Tanner thought. She was the brains of their small band.

Doctor Emery shook his head.

"Dareine sent for help," Laurel said. She was clearly in pain, but her voice was clear. "To the other enclaves in the Bloodwood. To the Aymhelin. They also called on some other allies we have in these woods. They will come to the Well, and show the Locust what the rage of peaceful people feels like. I will go to the Well of Tears. Whether you come with me or not, that is your choice."

"You can't walk with that leg," Emery said, but his voice was uncertain.

"She can ride Hewma," Grim said. Then he turned to Tanner, with a questioning look.

Tanner looked down at his hands. There was still blood on his fingers. The blood of the elves was the same color as his.

"To the Well," he said. "I am tired of running."

"I seriously doubt the wisdom of seeking safety in the middle of a battlefield," Emery said, tiredly. "But I see we are not seeking safety anymore, so I ask, what are we seeking now?"

They were silent for a long moment, the surf-like sound of the burning forest all around them. All eyes turned to Brix.

"Closure," she said.

Doctor Emery nodded. "It being so," he said, "we go to the Well of Tears."

PART THREE

IN THE EYE OF THE STORM

CHAPTER SEVENTEEN

Where the trees stopped, ten standing stones surrounded a little knoll, dotted with the remains of what looked like a maze garden. And at the top of the knoll, a low circular enclosure sat surrounded by thick thorny bushes, blooming with roses. The flowers were fist-sized, with velvet-like, dark red petals. Like crawlers they hugged the stones, a black web of thick branches dotted with deep crimson. Cruel, sharp thorns extended like arrowheads pointed at any intruder. The wall was little over twenty feet tall, and from a distance the ancient redoubt looked squat, utilitarian, and long abandoned. Two tall, iron doors, black and forbidding, gave access to whatever was within the walls. Or would have, had they been open.

"Looks like rust has sealed them closed," Grim said, making a face. The leonx by his side growled, and made a show of sniffing the air. The others wandered closer to the enclosure, warily.

"And yet this is the place," Brix mumbled.

"Not very impressive, truth be told," Doctor Emery observed.

Tanner gave a call, "Hoy, of the castle!", but when the echo of his voice faded, there was no response. Only the rustling of the red leaves of the trees, and the stillness of the ancient redoubt.

They advanced through the bushes, staying clear of the sharp spikes. The gravel creaked under their feet.

"This is not what I expected," Brix said.

Grim turned to her. "What did you expect?"

She shrugged. "Something more – heroic, maybe? More mystical." She remembered the paintings and the illuminated manuscripts, with their portrayals of magical wells by which long-haired elven princesses pined for their long-lost love.

Grim laughed. "Well, it's a round stone wall, I guess it does look like a large well."

"I guess the well itself is inside these walls," said Tanner.

"It figures."

"This was a bad idea," Emery mumbled.

Tanner hit the iron doors with the pommel of his axe. The sound echoed like a mighty bell, but once again there was no response. Birds flew from the nearby trees, a cloud of fluttering wings that spun twice over their heads before it settled back.

"It looks like the messenger from Ledish Schall never made it to the guardian," Tanner said. They had crossed the forest, making haste and taking no pause. For three days and three nights they had traveled, Laurel finding the way for them as she rode Hewma. Seldom stopping for rest, they had followed a track marked by secret signs, carved stones hidden under bushes and the course of small brooks. The elves of the Bloodwood, Laurel had explained, did not know where the Well was, but could find their way there. And yet, it was clear they were the first in this place in many years.

"Looks like the guardian is long gone," Grim said.

"If there ever was one in the first place," Brix said. She cast a glance at Laurel, who shook her head.

Doctor Emery lifted a hand to shield his eyes from the low sun. "Certainly, nobody has taken care of the garden for a long time."

Brix followed his gaze, taking in the rose bushes and the thorny vines wrapped around the bastion wall. Doubts were creeping at the back of her mind. Had the Fae tricked them into wasting their time? She glanced at Grim. Had he gotten the Fae's message wrong?

"The place is abandoned," Tanner said.

"Any ideas?" Brix asked Laurel. She was at the end of her wits.

The elf was pale, and having dismounted from Hewma's back, now leaned on Tanner's arm. She shook her head. "My people know to stay away from this place."

Brix frowned. "Why? This is your forest."

"But this is the Well's domain."

"I am beginning to wonder," Tanner said, "if it was a good idea after all. Coming here, I mean."

"Well," Grim sighed, "it's a bit late now."

He took off his hat, and used it as a fan. "Now wouldn't it be a hoot," he said, "if all the armies of the elves and the Locust Swarm were to come here, to fight over an overgrown garden and an old ruin?"

Brix scanned the woodland behind them, and then looked up at the stone tower. "What now?"

She caught a blinding light burning at the top of the wall, like sunlight on a warm summer afternoon. She squinted, and lifted her hand to shield her eyes.

•••

The polished planks of the floor creaked under Brixida's weight as she walked into the gymnasium. The sound was familiar and reassuring. Like her father, after long years of training, Brixida was able to spot the exact place where a foot was being placed based only on the sound.

In a fight, her father had taught her, it is one's duty to use everything to one's own advantage.

"Trust your eyes, but do not forget your other senses."

But her father was not here now.

She looked at the slender silhouette standing in front of her, framed in the glare of the southern arch. She squinted, and raised her left arm halfway, to shield her eyes. She was holding a wooden training sword in her right.

"Is this what I raised my daughter for?"

Her mother's voice was reproachful and more, disappointed.

Brixida tightened her grip on the wooden sword and took a step forward. The floor greeted her weight with a weak groan.

Dositea Lovell placed her hands on her hips, a dramatic gesture accompanied by the jangling of the bracelets on her thin wrists. She tossed her head, and her braid fell on her shoulder. A fine copper fur covered her body, and she had large emerald eyes, the slit pupils unblinking as she stared at her daughter.

"I'm doing nothing wrong," Brixida said, weakly. How many times had they had this conversation? Yet her mother still failed to see her point.

Her mother hissed. "But you're doing nothing right, either."

To buy time, Brixida walked to the wall where the weapons panoply was, and slipped her wooden sword in the basket with the other practice weapons. Turning her back on that piercing stare caused her heart to slow down.

"Is this the future you want for yourself?"

"I am just–"

"You fancy you will go to sea, and be a buccaneer princess, like you read in your silly stories?"

"This is not about the stories," Brixida said, defensively.

It was like a swordfight, she realized, this discussion with her mother. Dositea was pressing her, with her presence as much as with her words, forcing her back, pushing her in a defensive pattern that would be her undoing.

"Would you rather me be a dancer?" she replied. "The top of a table in a tavern would be better than the deck of a buccaneer ship?"

Dositea's eyes flared, and her golden earrings clicked as she instinctively flattened her ears. "I was never a tavern dancer," she said, proudly.

She was dressed in fine amaranth velvet, with a tight-laced bodice and a high neckline, her legs hidden by a bell-shaped skirt, but Brixida could still see the dancer in her mother's moves, in the ease with which she glided over the polished floor. The creaky planks were silent where she passed. She was a governess now, in the house of a wealthy guildmaster, and she had frost in her hair, but she still moved with the feline grace of her youth.

A grace Brixida had inherited, together with her mother's keen senses and fiery spirit. She was just putting those gifts to a different use.

"The sword is not a young woman's accessory," Dositea said. "And a padded doublet does not compliment your figure."

Brixida could hear a faint music, drifting in from somewhere outside.

She wondered passingly if this was festival day.

She wondered what day this was.

"Come dance with me," her mother said, spreading her arms in a welcoming gesture.

"Stand straight, and be silent."

Tharadax stumbled on the carpeted floor, blinded by the bright light coming from the window, and his brother's hand steadied him. Behind them, the man that had brought them here closed the door, and stood with his back against it, his arms crossed. He was big and rough featured, and somewhat orc-ish in stance, if not in ancestry. Maybe he thought they would try and run.

Tharadax turned again to the bright window, and the polished desk that sat in front of it. There was a high-backed chair behind the desk, and a dwarf sat there, smoking a long-stemmed pipe. He had a shock of pale yellow hair, and a thick beard. The honorable Crothair Ludger, one-time master of the Artificers' Guild, and steward of the stretch of woods where Tharadax, his brother Ricomer and their mates had been caught as they hunted for pheasant eggs, mushrooms and blackberries.

He had never been to such a grand house, and he was too busy looking around with wide-eyed wonder to feel really scared of what would come. Yet his heart was thumping in his chest.

"So these are the famous poachers," the dwarf said, exhaling a thin cone of blue smoke. He eyed the two orcs. "What happened to you?"

Tharadax looked down at his shirt, a large purple stain spreading over his chest and his belly.

The man at the door slapped him on the head. "Answer Lord Crothair!"

"Leave him alone!" Ricomer snapped. He was the oldest, and was always looking out for Tanner.

The man shook his fist. "You shut up, or–!"

"Order!" Lord Crothair barked, slapping his hands together. "Well, answer my question. Why are you bleeding blue on my carpet?"

"Black–" Tharadax stuttered. "Blackberries, sir."

The dwarf arched his eyebrows. "That looks more like blackberry jam."

"I put them inside my shirt for carrying, sir, and when I fell..."

Clumsy, his brother always said. Tanner was tall, even for an orc, and he was often limping home with scraped knees.

The dwarf sucked on his pipe. "I see."

He turned his eyes to his groundskeeper. "And so these are the criminals damaging my fields and stealing my game. The foxes in my chicken coop, so to speak."

"Two of them, sir," the man replied. "There were three more, but they ran."

"Indeed."

"But these two know their names, sir. We can make them tell."

"How lucky we are that you caught them, huh?" the dwarf said. He gave Tharadax a humorous glance. He was a cheerful old man, Tanner thought fleetingly. But any sense of safety was soon dispelled. The groundskeeper slapped Ricomer on the head.

"This one stopped to help his friend up. That's how I caught them."

Ricomer massaged his head, and directed a poisonous look at the man.

"That was not very smart of you," Lord Crothair said. "When push comes to shove, it's every man for himself. Were you never told that there is no loyalty among thieves?"

"He ain't no thief." Ricomer stood straight, defiant. "He's my brother."

The dwarf looked down into the embers in his pipe, and nodded. "I see."

He stood, and walked around his desk. He was very short, reaching only to Tharadax's chin, but he was a striking figure, with his gold buttons and his square-finished beard. There were fine brass buckles on his shoes. There was a humorous light in his eyes, hidden underneath bushy brows. Tharadax's heartbeat slowed to normal.

"And what should I do with you two now? There are laws against poaching, you know?"

"By your leave, sir, I think we should make an example of them."

"I was not asking you, Bruno."

"Sorry, sir."

Lord Crothair looked into Tharadax's eyes. "What do you suggest, young man? What should be the sentence?"

"I think…" He stopped, his cheeks burning. He was afraid the man Bruno would hit him again. Crothair gestured for him to go on. "I think you should be merciful, sir. Especially with my brother, sir, because he should not be punished for helping me."

Lord Crothair suppressed a smile. "Looks like we have a young man of principles here, what? And what of my blackberries, then?"

"Those, sir, I think they are gone." The dwarf's level voice and kindly humorous manner were making him bold. He pulled at his shirt, where it was sticking to his skin. "But your brambles will grow more. And it's not like you were needing them for eating, I think."

The dwarf turned to Ricomer. "And you, don't you have anything to say?"

"He's the one that usually does the talking. Sir."

"I see."

The garret window projected a square of bright light on the worn carpet, and its glare made the small room look even emptier than it was.

Grimald sat on the bare mattress of his bed, his hands on his knees, and took a deep breath. So this was it. He had sold most of his stuff, and placed what remained in a wooden box that now sat by the door. A few books, a leather tube with some scrolls, a leather pouch with his geomantic compass. The money he had made from his books and his tools had paid the overdue rent for these quarters, and he still had enough for a coach ride to Guyot, provided he traveled cheap, sitting on top of the coach, with the other passengers' luggage and servants.

But he could walk and save the money. It was not like he was in any hurry, and the weather was good.

There was a knock on the door.

Before he could answer, the door opened, and in walked his fellow student Ramir Pecanin, his brocade riding coat swishing, his knee-high boots polished. He was carrying a silver-pommeled walking stick as an affectation. He stood in the middle of the sunlit floor, and the bare room felt suddenly crowded.

He did not offer a greeting or a salutation. "I hoped to find you here still," he said. He had a high-pitched, nasal voice, and the insufferable habit of sucking in his cheeks, which gave him the look of someone about to spit.

"I won't be here for long," Grimald said. He opened his hands wide, and looked in the other man's face. "And as you see, I'm busy going through my correspondence, so if you don't mind–"

"Ha ha," said Ramir. Not a laugh, but a pretense of laughter. "That's the right attitude, old man. Humor is important in moments like this. I just dropped by because I wanted to offer, you know, my sympathy and stuff."

"Much appreciated," Grimald replied. "The stuff especially. Now if you don't mind…"

Ramir gave him a vacuous look. "Yes, fine," he said then. "The fact is, something came to me as I was walking here, you know?"

"Really."

"Sure. You know how sometimes an inspiration can hit you–"

"I'm afraid I'm not familiar with that."

"Yes. Well, I mean, the long and short of it, you know, is I have kept an eye on you these last two years, and I must admit I was impressed. And no matter what the old fools say, I think it would be wrong to waste your skills and expertise, for us to show you the door just like this–"

Ramir loved the sound of his own voice, and had this habit of acting like he was one of the teaching staff and not just another student, albeit well lined with his father's money.

"A pity the old fools don't share your view."

"But as you know," Ramir went on, ignoring him, "I have a certain allowance, granted to me by my father–"

As long as you stay out of his way, Grimald thought.

"–and I was thinking I might offer you a position, as part of my retinue."

Grimald gave him a look. "Your… retinue?"

"Yes, you know, acting as a secretary of mine. We will make up a convenient title and position to justify your permanence here in Greyhaven. This way you could keep attending classes. You are quite good at taking notes, aren't you? I am sure you are. And there was that bit of research you did about spell weaving and musical composition. I took a look at it a while back. Brilliant, believe me. It would be a crime to let it go to waste, and I could expand on it and see that it is given its due."

The sheer unashamed dishonesty made Grim speechless for a moment. "But wouldn't passing my work off as yours," he finally said, "be a rather grave breach of the academy's rules?"

Ramir sucked his cheeks in, and shook his head. "Well," he said peevishly, "rules are made to be broken, you know–"

"At least until they catch you."

"Exactly! And what do you have to lose, after all? It's not like you can be kicked out of Greyhaven twice, right?"

Grimald looked at the vapid young man standing in front of him. A crow come to feed on the carcass of his academic career. No, he corrected himself, a crow was too noble a creature.

"I'm afraid I cannot accept your kind offer," he said.

"Are you sure? I could make it worth your while. Money is not an issue. Within reason."

Grimald sighed. "I'm pretty sure, yes."

Ramir did that thing with his cheeks again, and looked around the empty garret room. "In that case, are you doing anything with your alchemy notes? I mean, you won't have any use for them as you serve mead behind the counter of your father's tavern, right? And I guess you might find a couple of crowns useful on your way home."

Grimald felt terribly tired. He nodded at the fireplace. "I burned them," he said. "As a farewell to my career."

"Oh, that's a pity."

"Is it now."

Ramir pulled up his collar and sucked his cheeks in for one last time. "Well, then, I better be going. You know, classes tomorrow morning–"

His hand on the door knob, he stopped and looked into the wooden box in which Grimald's few belongings waited. "Is this Gurloes' *Collectanea*?" He picked up the volume and turned it in his hands. "This is pretty rare, isn't it? Where did you get it?"

"Somewhere."

"How much do you want for it?"

"It's not for sale."

"Ten crowns?"

There was a predatory eagerness in Ramir, such a hungry need to buy a piece of him, that caused Grimald to shudder. "Twenty," he said.

There was a boar in the bushes.

Laurel could hear it move. She closed her eyes, cutting out the distracting glare of the spring sun through the branches, and concentrated on the sound. She turned slowly, the fingers of her right hand holding gently onto the arrow end.

A big one, by the way it disturbed the undergrowth. Twigs rustled as it passed through, slowly. A fine catch, and a lot of food.

Laurel pictured the animal in her mind's eye. It was curious, likely baffled by the intruders in its kingdom. Cautious, it kept moving, and watched. It wondered what the two-legged strangers were doing in this sector of the Bloodwood. It tried to understand if they could be a menace.

It tried to decide whether to fight or flee.

The rustling came closer, and Laurel's hold on her bow tightened.

Not too much, though. Too much strength holding the bow might cause the arrow to go astray. A beginner's mistake. She relaxed the muscles in her forearm, felt the muscular mound at the base of her thumb soften.

"Here it comes," Redstar whispered.

The rich tone of her voice rippled through the trees. The animal was no longer curious. It was scared. A scared boar was dangerous.

With a ferocious squeal, it charged through the tall grass and the undergrowth.

Laurel opened her eyes, and caught Redstar pulling her bow, in the corner of her eye, just as she saw the path of the incoming boar, branches snapping, soft leaves flying. It erupted through the wall of greenery, a brown and black bolt of muscle and fury, more felt than seen. The elven bow creaked as Laurel pulled back the string, the tip of her thumb caressing her jaw.

With both eyes, like she had been instructed to do, she sighted.

Down the shaft, past the arrowhead, through the rapidly decreasing distance and into the shortened muzzle, the sharp tusks, the fear-fueled fury of the beast.

She inhaled slowly. Holding her breath would be another beginner's mistake. Pulling the bow and releasing her arrow was to be part of the natural cycle of her breathing.

She caught the movement of the boarlets just as air started

flowing out of her lungs. They were following the large one. They cried out, excited.

A mother. Defending her little ones from the intruders.

In the space of a heartbeat, she flicked the bow upwards, and the arrow shot through the blood-red leaves of the nearest tree, just as the raging boar drew closer.

Redstar cursed. Her arrow caught the charging boar between the neck and the shoulder, piercing its side and finding its heart. By the time it crashed and rolled at Laurel's feet it was dead already.

Laurel whispered a few words to the wood, for their taking of the boar.

The boarlets trotted closer, crying. One of them prodded the dead boar with its snout. Then they ran as Redstar broke cover and walked closer. She also was carrying a longbow.

"That was stupid," she said. "What were you thinking?"

"What of the little ones?" Laurel asked.

The tree boarlets huddled under a bush, too scared to wander far from their dead mother.

"What of you, had I not been here?" Redstar asked.

"It's a laurel bush," Laurel replied, caressing the long leaves. "Isn't that strange?"

Sunlight filtered through the tall windows, painting colorful mosaics on the marble floor of the second floor reading room. The place smelled of old paper and dust. Pages rustled like the leaves in an autumn woodland, but the air was warm on a late spring day.

Arnost Emery stopped, one hand leaning on the closest table, and looked around, trying to get his bearings. He squinted in the glare of the tinted windows. His mouth felt dry and he coughed, a bad taste on his tongue. He pushed back a strand of blond hair. He'd need a barber soon. An old man in a skullcap looked up from the musty old parchment he was reading, and arched his eyebrows. Emery pulled back his hand, whispering an excuse. Then he saw Eyleen, sitting alone at a reading table. She waved at him, a bright smile illuminating her features. She was wearing her novice tunic, her honey blond hair covered by a thin veil. Her violet eyes sparkled mischievously as he took her hands in his.

"Emery!"

They all called him that, the teachers and the lecturers, and even Eyleen. It was like his given name, Arnost, was too angular and unwieldy for them. It sounded like a twig snapping, he thought.

"How did it go?" she asked, leaning close.

Somebody shushed them, and she turned that way and stuck out her tongue. He chuckled. That was his Eyleen.

Then she looked at him as he sat in front of her. "Well?" she asked in a whisper. "How did it go?"

Emery frowned. "How did it go what?"

She rolled her eyes. "Don't be a tease!" she hissed. "Master Kinloch! You passed, didn't you? How did it go?"

Master Paterson Kinloch, of course. The old man had questioned him for over one hour on the third and fourth stanzas of the Second Chronicle of Beier the Meek. He had had to stand in the darkened studio of the old bore, and recite verse upon verse, stopping and starting again as Master Kinloch asked questions about each of the characters from history and legend mentioned in the verses, and to whom Beier the Meek had petitioned for help against the incoming horror of the First Darkness. The old poem read like a long list of names, titles and fiefdoms, and it was a legend among history students for the dry boredom of it.

"You promised!" Eyleen snapped at his hesitation.

Emery opened his mouth and then closed it again. He looked away from her, and caught the disapproving stare of the old man in a skullcap.

"My parents are waiting for us!" she insisted. "The dales are wonderful at this time of the year. As soon as your literature examination was done, you promised we would go. So, did you pass it or not?"

"Of course I passed it," he said, his cheeks warming. She had helped him learn it by heart. "The old man was quite impressed when he found out I knew who Lavas Laersk was."

Somebody again hissed at them to be quiet. The invigilator, a tall, gaunt woman with haunted eyes, perched like a vulture at the lectern, gave them an admonishing look. Eyleen did not care, nor did Emery.

"I knew it!" she said. She stood, and smoothed the folds of her tunic. She took him by the hand. "Come, let's take a walk."

"Wait," he said.

She looked at him, a frown creasing her high forehead. She tossed her head, and pulled her veil back. "It's a beautiful day," she said.

He glanced at the tinted windows, squinting at the bright light. "Yes, I know, but–"

Something like a discordant note was ringing in his ears. He felt a fluttering in his chest. Again he drew back his hair, which had fallen across his eyes.

She pulled at his hands and forced him to stand. "We can go to Market Square," she whispered in his ear. "If you are really nice, I will allow you to buy me some candied ginger."

Her lips were so close, he could smell violets on her breath. Emery remembered that perfume so well. He remembered how much she loved candied ginger, and long walks in the marketplace, talking up a storm about the fabrics and ribbons and the garish songbirds in their cages.

He remembered all that, from long, long ago.

"Who are you?" he asked.

Eyleen's frown deepened, and she released him, her arms falling at her sides. "Arnost Emery!" There was a hint of mocking reproach in her voice. "What are you talking about?"

With a little effort, he looked down at his hands. He could see the liver spots, the lines, the thin scars and, on the right hand, the thick writer's callus on his middle finger. He looked up at her, trying not to be blinded by her beauty. "Please," he said. "I went through all of this once before, and it hurts. I would rather see things for what they are."

Her features softened. "That is interesting," she whispered. She took a step back. The air had suddenly lost its warmth, and her colors were fading. The library rippled like a reflection in a pool of dark water, and Eyleen crossed her arms, regarding him like a cat would look at a sparrow.

Doctor Emery pulled his cloak closer. He was standing among the rose bushes that surrounded the Well. In the waning light of the autumn afternoon, for the first time he saw rusted pieces of armor in the bushes. A long thorny tendril was wrapped around a sword, the blade brown with age. An elongated elven skull grinned at him from the ground. He shuddered, and turned his eyes from that morbid display.

Where Eyleen had been, in front of him was a tall elven woman, her skin the color of terracotta, her hair black like a raven's wing and soft as mist. A single white streak ran through her tresses, starting in her widow's peak. She wore a many-layered dress in shades of ivory and mauve, its design unfamiliar to the old man. Her eyes were the same violet as Eyleen's, but there any resemblance ended. There was something in her stance and expression that reminded him of the elf Delsanra. But there was a different warmth to her, and there were fine lines in the corner of her eyes and her mouth, the sign of wit and an easy smile. Emery had an impression of great age, and of even greater power.

Slowly, she paced around him in a circle, thumb and forefinger caressing her sharp chin. There were silver bracelets on her arms, and a lone amethyst hung in the hollow at the base of her neck.

"Who are you, my lady? And what does all of this mean?" His head hurt, but he had too many questions to heed the pain.

"What an unusual find," she said, pensively. She had a pleasant contralto voice, with a faint lilting tone he could not place. She sounded nothing like Eyleen. "A man who wants to see things for what they are."

Somewhat stiffly, Emery bowed to her. "Your illusion was very good, my lady."

She scoffed. "Not my illusion, but the Well's."

"Is there any difference, my lady? Are you not the Guardian of the Well of Tears?"

Dareine had mentioned a guardian. It felt like a thousand years had passed. And yet, that was the reason why they were here.

"A world of difference, Arnost Emery. I am not the guardian. You speak of things you do not know."

It was like treading on thin ice. "I beg your pardon, my lady, if I was out of line. But I wish to learn, and I carry a message to the Guardian of the Well."

"You will find it hard to deliver, Arnost Emery."

Again, he bowed. He spread his hands, showing her the palms. "Please, my lady–"

"Enough of this pleading," she said. "You have no reason be afraid of me, but there is not much I can do for you."

He bowed a third time, his bones creaking. "It is not fright, my lady, but awe."

Her lips twitched. "Such gallantry."

"Not gallantry, my lady, but fact. An old man can afford to be sincere."

Her fine eyebrow arched, an ironic smile brightening her features. "You keep contradicting me, but you do it with a tongue of silver."

"There is no cheaper silver to be had, my lady."

She laughed, a short sincere burst of mirth. "Fates ward me from a man of wit," she said.

"And from a woman of beauty," he replied, completing the old adage. He felt a pang of guilt for finding this exchange so enjoyable. He should keep his guard up, but what could he do, really, against such a powerful creature?

The black-haired woman crossed her arms on her chest, and regarded him dispassionately. "You are far away from the halls of your library, Arnost Emery," she said, suddenly serious. "What leads you at this time, in such a strange company, to the Bloodwood, and to the Well of Tears?"

"By my lady's leave, and as I mentioned, it is the Guardian of the Well we seek–"

"There is no guardian, I told you." Her frown deepened.

"The Well needs no guardian. Just as you witnessed, it is quite excellent at guarding itself."

"Through cruel illusions."

"It weaves together memories, wishes and dreams, in which the unwary are caught. It is like a spider's web. Few escape it."

"And yet, my lady, you were there, speaking the words of someone that's long gone. Are you the spider, then, in this strange web, or are you also trapped in its weave?"

"I am no spider, Arnost Emery." Her left shoulder rose and dropped, a half-shrug that ill-matched her majesty. "I but inhabit these illusions, from time to time and on sufferance, being as I'm a long-time guest of these places. I walk through these dreams, and meet the men and women the Well ensnares. Thus I find distraction, and brief company. A small concession the Well makes for an old associate, if you will."

"A cruel concession, my lady, if you don't mind me saying so."

"To those like me," she said, "cruelty can become a habit."

She ran her fingers through her hair, pulling the strands away from her cheek, and for a moment she was Eyleen again. A cold hand squeezed Emery's heart.

"No, please," he whispered.

"She was beautiful," the elven woman said, and she rippled back to being herself, a strange, sad smile on her lips.

"She was young, my lady," Emery conceded, composing himself. He did not like talking about his private life. Never had. "Youth is always beautiful."

"And what of old age? Is it not beautiful, Arnost Emery?"

Emery sighed. "Comfortable, like a well-worn boot, maybe. Familiar, and undemanding. But beautiful? I do not think so, my lady. Not often, at least, and not for long."

"What happened to her?"

He gave her a stern look. "Don't you know?"

Was she toying with him? And yet she did not seem as cruel as she claimed to be.

"I only know what the Well weaves and allows me to visit. Everything else comes from your mind, and there it remains. I cannot read your thoughts any more than you can read mine."

Emery felt a pressure on his chest like he had not felt for many years. "She is gone."

"Gone? Just like that?"

His voice was hollow. "Is there any other way?"

She lowered her gaze. "I'm sorry."

He could not say whether she was sorry for asking those questions, or for what had gone before, or for Eyleen. But he could see sorry was not a word she spoke often, and was grateful for her simple gentleness.

"No day goes by without a memory," he said, quietly. "And sometimes I wish she was by my side, to share what I see, and find, and learn. But that is how it has to stay. She's but a memory, and memories are not real."

"Some would contend our memories are the only reality, as we live trapped in a fleeting present we cannot grasp."

"That may be, my lady. But I am an old man. And with old age comes a wariness for memories, they can become a labyrinth, not different from the spiderweb you mentioned but even trickier. A maze in which many lose themselves, and realize too late."

"But not Arnost Emery." Her lips curled into a smile, and again a shade of sadness colored her eyes. "You are a wise man. How old are you, Arnost Emery?"

He pushed on his staff and straightened his back, ignoring

the crackling of his bones. "Seventy-three springs, my lady, and counting, as long as I will be able to count."

"You are but a child in elven years."

"But alas, my lady, I am no elf."

"Your people put great stock in a long life, more than they should. A life's worth is not measured in its length, like cloth in a tailor's shop."

"Much depends, I guess, on what we make of the years that are allotted to us by fate. Just like a tailor can make a good warm cloak or a jester's motley with the same length of cloth. But in both cases, having enough cloth is as important as the skill of the tailor."

"A wise man," she repeated, and nodded. "Or a witty one. Walk with me, Arnost Emery. Let's seek your friends."

With a sigh, and leaning on his staff, Emery moved to her side. She strolled away from the tower's shadow, and into the rose bushes. It seemed to Emery a long time since he had walked into the garden with his companions. But the shadows had not lengthened much, and the woodland was still bathed in the late afternoon sunlight. The birds were singing in the trees, and the whole scene had an air of simple rural charm.

And yet, there were remains trapped in the thorny bushes, skeletal shapes of men enmeshed in the roses, pressed against the wall of the redoubt, their clothes faded, their armor spotted with rust. Emery shuddered, and looked away.

"You have strange companions, Arnost Emery," she said.

Scattered among the flowerbeds, Emery saw his friends standing, their eyes lost in the distance. In the lane leading to the bastion gates, Tanner had dropped his axe, and Brixida was swaying gently, like on the drift of some unheard music.

Her long tail moved left and right, following a silent rhythm. Further back, Laurel's lips were moving, like she was talking to someone. She had forgotten her bow that rested idly in her limp fingers. She was sitting on a stone plinth, her hurt leg stretched in front of her. Emery scanned the overgrown garden, and finally saw where, at the edge of the trees by an old sundial, Grim was sitting on the ground, his chin on his chest. The great cat Hewma was by his side, purring like a beehive and trying to rouse him, prodding him with her muzzle, without effect. Each one trapped in a dream, he imagined, in their own personal labyrinth. He dared not imagine what memories were entangling them. It was not for him to pry. But he had to do something.

"A man, an elf, an orc and a cat-folk," the elven woman said. "A mageling, a hunter, a warrior and a skirmisher. We have never seen a company such as yours this deep into the Bloodwood. It is like something out of some legend of old."

"Maybe we should all play an instrument," Emery chuckled, "and become strolling minstrels."

Her laugh surprised him. "I remember that old ballad," she said, and for a moment she sounded like a young girl.

"My lady, could you by any chance unravel the web in which my friends are trapped?" he asked. "Please?"

"The web, I told you, is not of my making. And you endow me with more power than I ever had. But I do not think they will be entangled for much longer now that you have torn through the illusion. Be patient."

He cleared his voice. "My lady–"

"Stop calling me that," she said with a sigh, and she turned to him. "My name is Suhlwen Calhurnar. I am of the Well. The Witch of the Well, some used to call me, long before you were born. I am not the Well's guardian, but its servant. And servants are not ladies."

"With all due respect, in the Barons' court or in the wilds of the Bloodwood, a lady remains a lady. It is a consequence of demeanor, not of birth or circumstances."

Her smile was warm. "You are good with words, Arnost Emery."

"I am an old man, my lady. Words and memories are all I have."

She took a deep breath, but before she could say anything more, a string of curses echoed from where Grim had opened his eyes, and found himself staring in the jaws of Hewma. The big cat growled and lashed at her sides with her tail, happier to see her friend awake than he was.

"See?" Suhlwen said. "I told you it would not be long."

Tanner gasped and looked around, lost. By his side, Brix faltered, pirouetted twice on her feet, and fell on her back with a loud oath. Laurel batted her lashes as if waking from a dream, and turned her gaze on where Emery and Suhlwen were standing. Her eyes widened as she saw the doctor's new companion. She pulled herself slowly to her feet.

Talking all together, shaking their heads and dusting their clothes, they walked closer. Hewma growled and hissed, and pressed against Grim, and he seemed happy for once to have her close. Only Laurel was silent, her eyes glued to the woman by Emery's side.

"What sorcery was that?" Brix was the first to ask. She gave a sideways look at Suhlwen, and then stared at Emery. Her hand went to her sword.

"I was with my brother," Tanner said. "It's been years since we..." He shook his head, and then he saw Emery. "Are you all right, doctor?"

"Sorcery," Laurel said.

Grim shuddered, and Brix nudged him on. He shook his head, and she snorted and took a step forward.

"We seek the Guardian of the Well," she said, in what to Emery sounded like a rather belligerent tone.

"Alas, Mistress Brixida," Suhlwen replied, "as I have explained at length to Arnost Emery, here you will find no guardians. I am all you will find, in fact. I hope I'll be enough."

"And who are you, if I may ask?"

"My name is Suhlwen Calhurnar," she replied, with a hint of haughtiness. "I am of the Well."

"She's a friend," Doctor Emery said. "And allow me to introduce–"

"I know their names," Suhlwen said. "Just like I knew yours, and for the same reason. It is not often I receive guests, but you are quite welcome, and I will be happy to share what little comforts I have with all of you." She turned to Emery. "Do you play chess, Arnost Emery?"

"I do, my lady. And nobody calls me Arnost. I am just Emery to everyone."

"But I am not just everyone," she replied, piqued. "We shall play, then, and you will tell me what you want with the Well, and what the Well wants with you. Come, I have quarters inside."

And before Emery could say another word, she locked his arm in hers, and they walked towards the gate in the Well tower wall, which now gaped open.

CHAPTER EIGHTEEN

"Once, the place was covered," Suhlwen said, as she led Emery out of the tunnel-like entryway. The others followed, talking among themselves, and came into the enclosure. "In the summer, a great tarpaulin, like an ocean ship's sail, was stretched over the courtyard, providing shade around the well but letting the cool breeze in. That was when people still used to come here often, before the compact between the Fae and the Dimora was broken. Before the wars, before the Shadow Tear."

She turned towards them and smiled. "I am not that old, of course," she said, her tone ironic. "But memory is what the Well pours forth, and I have sat by its wall for a long time."

The circular courtyard was large but not as great as the doctor had thought, and in the midst of it, a simple stone well, with three buckets of different sizes resting on its lip. Steps led to the top of the enclosure, and doors opened in the inner wall. The bastion was riddled with large rooms at the ground level. Only one of the access doors was closed by a thick curtain, while the others gaped like empty eye-sockets in the bone-white stone of the wall.

Along the inner walls, between one door and the next, plants grew in bunkers. A vegetable garden, somewhat ill-kept and wild, with peas and lentils, peppers, onions and parsnips. An edge of herbs and officinal plants grew by the curtained door, hyssop and jasmine, rhubarb, sage and rosemary. After so much time spent under the blood-hued canopy of the Bloodwood, so many shades of green looked novel and fantastic.

"It's like a fable of old," Brix whispered.

Grim by her side groaned. "The one about the old hag feeding on children?"

She prodded him in the side with her elbow. Emery turned to Suhlwen, but if she had heard, as he believed, she did not seem to care.

"Doesn't look like a hag to me," Tanner said. But he was keeping his axe ready.

Between the well and the plant bunkers, the courtyard was a circular ring of cobblestones. The travelers looked around warily. Grim leaned on the edge of the well and looked down.

Emery was by his side, and did the same. He saw a crescent of sky reflected in the still water, maybe ten feet below.

"What were you doing out there?" Grim asked in a low voice. The well gave it a faint echo.

Emery arched his eyebrows. "Philosophizing. Mostly."

Grim gave him a look, and then shook his head.

"You are wounded," Suhlwen said to Laurel. The elven huntress retreated when the other woman approached her. Suhlwen smiled. "The water from the Well will heal your wound." She turned her gaze on the others, pointed at the bandages on Tanner's arms and side. "All of your wounds and sores, of course."

"At what price?" Tanner asked, guarded.

The elf arched her fine eyebrows. "Price?"

"One hears stories..." The orc shrugged.

"Never partake of the food of the Fae," Brix said, "or you'll be trapped in their realm for a hundred years and a day."

Suhlwen chuckled. "You give too much credit to the old ballads. And do I look like one of the Fae?" She fixed her violet gaze on Grim. "Fetch a bucket of water, will you?" Then she gestured towards the curtained door. "Come inside."

Grim and Emery traded a glance, and then the short man picked a mid-sized bucket and dropped it in the Well. It hit with a cheerful splash.

Inside, a large room on the ground floor was furnished like a simple apartment, with shelves of scrolls and books, a desk and two chairs, and, in a curtained alcove, a bed with a pile of cushions and a fur cover. In a large circular fireplace, a bed of embers still radiated a pleasant warmth.

"Sit and show me your leg," Suhlwen said to Laurel. The huntress gave a look at Brix, who hurried over and helped her as she limped to a chair. Grim came in holding a bucket, Hewma by his side. Emery followed him. He gave a questioning look at Tanner, who kept back, and didn't come through the door.

"Set the chessboard," their host said to Emery, gesturing to the side of the door. "This will not take long. And you, bring that bucket here."

Emery found a square table by the side of the door, holding an ancient-looking set of chess pieces. "We might not have time for games, my lady," he said.

Suhlwen ignored him. She lit a floating lamp, of the kind the elves were clearly fond of. Dragging the light along, she knelt by Laurel. "What was it?"

"An arrow," Laurel said.

Suhlwen looked at her. "Is there war in the Bloodwood?" she asked.

Laurel nodded. "The Locust Swarm has come."

The other woman looked long into her eyes, and then turned and looked at the others standing around. "This explains your strange band of wanderers." She looked at Emery. "We will need to talk."

"Yes, of course–" he said, urgently.

"But not now." Suhlwen dipped her fingers into the bucket and took some water in her cupped hands. She poured it on the dirty bandages on Laurel's thigh, soaking the fabric. This she did three times, until the water dripped on the floor.

Laurel frowned, and then undid the ties of the bandage. She pulled the rags away to reveal her leg healed, a faint scar, a pale circle marking the point where the Uthuk arrow had run through the muscle.

Suhlwen stood and looked down at her hands, then turned to Emery. "So what is this thing that brought you here?"

The travelers looked at each other, and then all started talking.

"Please!" Suhlwen said, with a grimace, clapping her hands. "Take no offense, but I've been alone too long to be able to stand you all talking at the same time." She pointed. "On the other side of the court you will find rooms where you can settle. Empty, mostly, and somewhat stale, but reasonably clean, I am sure. You go and rest yourself. Arnost Emery will stay here and explain to me what this is all about."

Nobody seemed willing to leave. Suhlwen waited for a moment, and then waved her hands at the door. "Go. Find a place to stay. Clean yourself up." She looked at Laurel. "You too, dear."

Tanner and Brix silently questioned Doctor Emery.

"You go," he said with a sigh and what he hoped was a reassuring smile. "I will explain."

They shuffled out of the room, again talking among themselves.

Suhlwen nodded at the chessboard. "Come," she said. "You can tell me everything while we play."

"What do you make of her?" Grim asked as they crossed the courtyard.

"She's strange." Brix shrugged. "She doesn't look like the other elves we've met."

"Because she is not like us," Laurel said. They stopped and looked at her.

"She's high-born Darnati," Laurel said. Brix frowned, and Grim and Tanner looked at each other. The orc shrugged, and the short man shook his head.

"From one of the high-born clans of the Darnati Highlands," Laurel explained.

"I'm afraid this is beyond our knowledge of elven geography," Grim said.

"And politics," Brix added.

"They're a proud people," Laurel said. "They're famous weapon makers, and sacred fighters."

"Sacred fighters?" Tanner asked.

"They make a vow of silence," Laurel said.

"Clearly not the case here," Grim scoffed.

"They hail from the southwest, where the Aymhelin thins out." She had been there, years before, during her travels. She remembered the people. "The land makes them hard-edged."

"Not as fun and easygoing as you of the Bloodwood, huh?"

It was Laurel's turn to stare at him. He used words to keep fear away, but sometimes it became distracting.

"Sorry," Grim said with a sigh. "I was being silly. Please go on."

She shrugged. "There is not much else I can say. She is a sorceress of some kind. She is also very old."

Grim cast a glance at Tanner. "She looks fine to me."

The orc nodded, and Brix rolled her eyes. "You mean old for an elf?"

Laurel nodded. "She is older than Dareine. I'm not sure she is telling the truth when she says she does not remember the Second Darkness."

"How can you tell that?" Brix asked.

The question reminded Laurel how different they were. "Just like you can tell Doctor Emery is older than Grim," she said. "It is something I see."

"And who is she?" Tanner asked. "I mean, what is she doing here?"

"She claims she is not the guardian," Brix said. "Then what is she?"

"Can we trust her?" Tanner asked.

Laurel shrugged again. She wished she had all those answers. "Maybe."

"Well, she seems to have taken a shine to Emery," Grim said. "So she can't be completely bad, right?"

Tanner made a face, puffing his cheeks like he was about to whistle. "Maybe they have something in common. If she's as old as Laurel says – like seeks like, as the saying goes."

Grim sighed. Then he rolled his head, cracking the kinks in his neck. "Well, let's see what she has to offer in terms of accommodations."

They picked one of the gaping doors, and beyond they found a large room with wall-niches for bedding, and a circular fireplace in the center. Laurel hung back with Brix, and they let the men go forth.

"Cozy," Grim said. He stepped into the center of the hearth and looked up. "Something made a nest in the chimney. No fires in here."

"But it's dry," Tanner said.

"And it's not like we'll have to spend much time here," Brix added. Her words hung in the air.

"Well," Grim said, "we can spend the little time we have in good comfort."

"And a good rest is important before a fight," Tanner added.

Laurel sat in one of the niches and listened to them bickering. They were like birds chirping, using their song to reinforce their bonds.

She thought she liked it.

Suhlwen was an aggressive player, ruthless in her handling of her own pieces. Doctor Emery strove to bring his king to the safety of the board's edge, while at the same time telling his story.

He told of the Uthuk Y'llan pouring in from the Ru Darklands and spreading like a plague through Terrinoth, as Suhlwen cut his tower's retreat.

He spoke of the flames and destruction of Vynelvale, and the desperate scramble on the Old Road afterwards, just as she pushed his king back towards the center of the board.

He saw an opening, and bagged one of her knights, but too late he saw this was a trap, and his sage went down. He told her of their coming to Mayvale, and the long walk through the woodlands and into the Bloodwood.

"You were very bold," she said, removing another piece from the chessboard, "or very stupid, to seek the help of the Bloodwood elves. In my time, there was no love lost between the Latari and your people."

Emery placed his fingertip on his king, but did not move it. "Are we not all at the mercy of the Uthuk Y'llan?"

She looked at him. "The Uthuk Y'llan know no mercy."

"Exactly," he said, and he captured her courier.

She smiled. "Smart."

And so he came to the meeting with the Fae, and the game suddenly stopped.

"You should not mock me," she said, staring hard at him.

"I mock you not, my lady. This is no lark I am telling you, and it is not on a whim we came here. There is war in the Bloodwood, and Methras is burning."

"Wait," Brix said, and climbed nimbly up the steps to the top of the bastion. "Let's see what's up here."

The two men followed her. They had left Laurel in their new quarters, resting. Hewma was guarding her. Grim took a quick look at the Well, and was the last in the line reaching the top.

The redoubt was built like a circular building with a thicker outer wall and chambers opening on the inner courtyard, and the rooftop was a wide terrace running over the circular bastion, with six evenly-spaced staircases leading up. A low battlement, little more than a parapet and without any merlons, ran along the perimeter. Grasses grew in the cracks between the stones, and the rose bush hanging on the wall extended its tendrils over the parapet.

"It's beautiful, don't you think?" Tanner said.

The redoubt sat on top of a low hillock, and from up there

they could see red treetops stretching in every direction like a blood-colored sea. Brix took a deep breath, grateful for the clear air and the light. Beneath them, the overgrown garden was already in shadow, a dark tangle of thorny bushes and narrow passages up to where it met the Bloodwood. On the border, the standing stones were like fingers pointing at the sky, or sentinels guarding the Well.

In the distance, towards the north, the black columns of smoke marked the spots where the Uthuk Y'llan had set fire to the Bloodwood. They looked terribly close.

Their enemies were probably closer, Brix thought. A sudden flight of birds caught her eye, and she squinted at the trees.

"Look at that!" Brix pointed.

Something was moving at the edge of the wood. Something huge. Whatever it was, Brix didn't see it, but she saw the trees shaking as if from a great wind, and more birds take flight, screeching. The blood-red canopy shook at the mysterious thing's passage, like a lake disturbed by some large fish swimming close to the surface. Stepping closer to the wall, they followed its course as it moved swiftly from east to south, circling the Well. Then it retreated deeper into the Bloodwood, and they lost it.

"What was that?" Brix asked.

Grim shook his head.

"Whatever it was," Tanner said, "I hope it's on our side."

In Suhlwen's quarters, Emery was still sitting at the chessboard, while the elven woman paced the room.

As the others entered, she stopped and looked at them.

"Is this the one?" she asked, pointing her finger at Grim.

Emery nodded. "Master Grimald used to be at Greyhaven."

Suhlwen snorted. "But not for long."

"Long enough, my lady," Grim replied, piqued. Emery answered his reproachful glance with a gesture of denial. The man believed he had revealed more than he should, but he was sure this was the Well's doing.

"What of this Uthuk champion who's marching on the Well?" she asked. "What of the Fae's interference in the affairs of elves and mortals?"

"I tried to explain–" Emery said, but she lifted a hand, shutting him off.

"Let the man speak for himself," she commanded.

Grim huffed. "There is not much I can say about the champion, but it rages with hatred for the Latari–"

"Which is to be expected," she said.

"– and even the Fae fear him."

"Which is both unlikely and disquieting," she said.

"I saw him."

They all turned to Tanner, who was lingering by the door. The orc nodded, sighed, and came forward, his shoulders drooping. "While I was making my way out of burning Methras," he said. His voice was quivering with emotion. "I saw him. As tall as I am, but wiry, like an insect more than a man. Taking long strides on legs like a bird, or a lizard. A head crowned with spines."

Brix started articulating a question, but Suhlwen quieted her too, with a gesture and a hard stare.

"He was driving his warriors forward, whipping them. He screamed, and they ran forth, disregarding the flames and the arrows of the elves. With them were animals, some like the monsters we met on the road, but also animals of the wild, spurred on by his whipping. They looked crazy with bloodlust.

It was like a nightmare. And behind him was a beast like a colossal maggot, the color of dead flesh, and bigger than an ox."

The face of the orc was streaked with tears. "I watched as the monster grabbed an elven hunter, and devoured him. I watched, and I did nothing."

He sat heavily on one of the chairs, and put his face in his hands. "I did nothing," he repeated.

Again Emery made to speak, and again the elven woman stopped him. Suhlwen walked to where the orc sat, and placed a hand on his shoulder. "The thing you describe looks like one of the abominations of the Ru steppes. It has a name that I forget right now. The man you saw had no hope the moment the creature grabbed him."

"I should have helped him."

"And forfeit your life for nothing?"

Tanner gave her a hurt look. "For nothing? Maybe he would have had a hope. Maybe he had family, children–"

"You could not have saved him, like you could not save Methras," she said, and Emery caught a kind note in her level voice. "But you live, and as anyone alive, you can still make a difference. Your potential is not spent yet."

"I was a coward."

Grim snorted. "Nonsense."

"What of your friends?" Suhlwen asked.

"What of them?"

"Would have they made it to this place, without your help?"

Tanner shook his head. "Who knows?"

"Right," she said. "Then let's not talk of what we cannot know. We have no time now for what-might-have-beens."

He looked up at her, and nodded.

"Do they call you Wen?" Grim asked, out of nowhere. She

turned to him, arching her eyebrows. "Your friends. Do they call you Wen? Or Cal?"

"Neither, most certainly," she replied, dryly, and Emery was reminded of a similar dialogue, many days before, and many miles away.

"Not many friends?" Grim grinned.

She closed her eyes. "Not many, no."

"I was asking because Suhlwen Calhurnar's a bit of a mouthful, you see–"

She sighed. "Please say what you mean, Master Grimald."

"It's Grim. That's what my friends call me. That's what I meant."

She looked at him, and then at the others. "It must be wonderful to have friends."

CHAPTER NINETEEN

"I came to the Bloodwood a long time ago," Suhlwen said. "Back when there wasn't even any Ledish Schall, and Methras was an idea more than a city. A lot of us felt the Bloodwood would allow us the freedom that we did not have in the Aymhelin. Freedom to decide our course, and build something different. I guess what we did was deemed scandalous by the Latari in the halls of Caelcira. We did not care. We only saw potential and opportunity. But even the idea that was Methras was not what I was looking for. There were still too many rules, too many constraints. Our potential was still being stifled by convention. And of course I had heard the stories about the Well of Tears ..." She made a dismissive gesture. "We'd all heard those. And so I set out to find the Well. It was the isolated, lonely place I was seeking."

"Why did you want to be alone?" Emery asked.

She tossed her head and looked at him, and he was suddenly aware of how her humanity was something she was striving to wear like a mask. "For the usual reasons," she said.

The silence hung heavy around the table. Grim had arranged

a simple dinner, much to Suhlwen's amused surprise, and now they were all sitting together, listening to her story.

"I'm not a spirit talker," she went on. "I don't know how the Well operates. I know that it managed to ensnare me, like it seems to do with anyone that enters the rose garden."

"But not the animals, and the birds," Grim said.

"Birds are animals," Tanner pointed out.

Grim gave him a look and rolled his eyes.

"Whatever it is that triggers the Well's response," Suhlwen went on, "seems to have to do with intelligence."

"And mind you," Grim said, "I've met people that were a lot less intelligent than your average bird."

They laughed.

"It is probably memories," Emery said. "After all, that is what the Well uses against the interlopers."

"Animals do have memories," Tanner said. "Ravens can hold a grudge for years."

"Most creatures live in the here and now," Laurel said. "They do not imagine a future, built on their memories of the past. The animal mind is like a child's, simple and focused. We are the ones that remember, and growing up build stories in our heads. About the past, and the future. Only we do." She turned to Tanner. "And maybe ravens."

"It may be," Suhlwen said, pensively.

"How did you escape the web of the Well?" Emery asked.

"Who said I escaped it?"

There was an uneasy silence around the table, but then the elven woman laughed out loud. "I came to the Well at the peak of winter. It was a new moon, in the coldest days of the year. The sky was so clear it felt like you could stretch a hand and grab a handful of stars, and there was a thick layer of snow on the ground, so white it seemed to glow. It was so cold, so bitter: a biting cold." Her eyes unfocused for a moment. "It was the cold that broke the illusion. It pierced through the memories the Well was feeding me, and there I was, curled up in the snow."

She lifted a hand, the fingers spread. "My fingers were blue, and I couldn't stop shaking."

She drank a bit of Grim's soup. "My thoughts were slow, confused. It was very hard to focus. For some reason I had discarded my cloak. Something in me realized I was going to die out there. Unless I did something. So I gathered myself and I pushed the cold back–"

Laurel's eyes widened, and she said a single word in her language, something that sounded to Tanner's ears like "Dawn tyme".

Tanner looked at her. "What's that?"

"Storm sorceress," Grim said.

All eyes were on him and then on the elven sorceress.

Suhlwen nodded.

"A storm sorceress?" Brix said, slowly. "Like in the legends?"

"I am not familiar with the legends," the sorceress said.

Brix blushed violently.

"Powerful, capricious and lethal," Grim said.

Suhlwen arched her eyebrows. "Powerful, capricious and lethal," she repeated, slowly. She picked up her cup and drank a sip of wine. "Harsh, but generally correct, yes. And not prickly?"

Grim grinned. "Hopefully not."

"We met one of yours," Laurel said. "She calls herself Delsanra. She is of Ledish Schall."

Suhlwen shook her head. "Delsanra is a name of the

Bloodwood. I do not know who she might have been in my time." She arched an eyebrow. "Although I have some suspicions."

"You never told us Delsanra was a storm sorceress," Tanner said. He turned to Grim.

Laurel shrugged. Grim shrugged too.

Suhlwen put down her cup. "Anyway," she went on. "I climbed the wall because the doors were locked. My hands were so cold I did not feel the thorns as they ripped through my flesh. I did not care. I reached the battlements, and found quarter in this room. That's how I escaped the Well's web of illusion."

"And why are you still here?" Tanner asked. Then he looked down in his bowl. "If you don't mind me asking, my lady."

Suhlwen took a deep breath. "For the usual reasons," she said.

"You described yourself as a servant of the Well," Grim said. "How are you in its service?"

She shrugged. "I keep the redoubt in order, and take care of the garden. I do sometimes help the stragglers that get caught in the web. Or did you never wonder how news of the Well of Tears spread through the world? In exchange, the Well provides me with food. There is a pleasant view from the terraces. And this place provides me with the solitude that I cherish."

"A solitude we have invaded, I am afraid," Emery said.

Suhlwen bowed her head in his direction. "Sometimes–"

"Silence!" Brix snapped. Emery froze, a spoonful of soup halfway to his mouth, and looked at her. Grim frowned, and Tanner put down his bowl.

The storm sorceress arched an eyebrow. "I beg your pardon?"

Brix pointed at the cup in front of her. The surface of the

wine was rippling. In a moment, all the crockery on the table was trembling and ringing.

Hewma ran out of the apartment, roaring.

"Earthquake," Emery whispered.

"Someone's coming," Grim said. The sound of his voice caused everybody to look at him, momentarily forgetting their meal. The short man was pale as a ghost, his eyes unfocused. He dropped his wooden spoon.

"Thirty-eight, coming from the northwest," he said, like he was talking in a dream.

Brix called his name out loud, and jumped to her feet. She moved as to grab his shoulders, but then she stopped and pulled back. Outside, Hewma roared, her voice echoing in the night.

"He's right," Suhlwen said, standing in turn. "We have visitors." She made for the door and they left their food behind, running outside. Tanner grabbed his axe from where it rested by the door. Emery leaned on his arm as they stood in the courtyard. A pale blue light was burning beyond the walls, and it had made the stars disappear.

They climbed the nearby steps to the top of the wall, and froze.

"Whoa," Tanner exclaimed, stopping so suddenly Brix bumped into him.

The standing stones along the perimeter were burning with blue fire, casting an eerie glow on the overgrown garden and turning the shadows of the woodland into black, hungry pools. The light rose and ebbed with a rhythm, like a deep, slow heartbeat.

"What does this mean?" Emery asked.

Fine blue lines twisted and turned on the dark surface of the stone pillars, tracing complex, maze-like designs. As they watched, the blue light intensified, and crackling bursts of lightning started arching between the stones. There was a vibration in the air, like the tuning of a colossal lute, that seemed to seep into the ground, and tickle the very soles of their feet as they stood on top of the battlements.

"I have no idea," Suhlwen whispered in a breath.

Her eyes on the forest, Hewma roared again, and another leonx answered her call, and then another.

And then, in a ragged column, a band of elven warriors marched out of the wood. In the blue glow of the stones, their armor was dirty and dented, and they advanced with guarded wariness, archers with arrows ready and spearmen guarding the sides. Two large leonx traveled with them, and upon coming into the overgrown garden, they roared and arched their backs, and Hewma did the same, greeting them.

"The Well will ensnare them," Emery said. He looked at the advancing warriors, his heart sinking at the thought this would be all the help they would get.

Suhlwen shook her head. "I don't think so."

The elves were approaching the iron gates unhindered. Behind them, lightning exploded with a resounding crackle. In the blue light, it was like the forest was afire, bathed in underwater flames. Emery felt the hair on his neck rise, like in a thunderstorm.

"Let's go and greet them," the elven sorceress said.

Brix was the first to turn around. "Where is Grim?" she asked.

For miles and miles around, the world was music. It rose and ebbed like a tide, like the pounding of a mighty heart, and there was nothing else.

Grim could perceive the rolling land like a steady, simple rhythm. The trees were short bursts of notes, tangles and copses playing variations on a lilting melody that was the Bloodwood. A mosaic of chords braided in a complex fugue, the oaks marking the beats like clear tenors, with the beeches, the birches and the larches adding to the chorus, sopranos and baritones and contraltos. Each tree in the Bloodwood a single, individual, distinctive voice. The running water of the streams and the creeks was a flowing cadenza, like trumpets and flutes, at the core of which a dark, sensual knot of notes repeated insistently, like a melody within the melody. Close, urgent, and mournful.

The Well of Tears.

As his fear retreated and his breathing steadied, Grim's perception of the landscape grew, and he picked up details in the melody that had escaped him at first. The flurry of little animals and the hanging mist, like bursts of music and light. The distinctive trill of the elven enclaves, each a variation on a theme, like a reprise of some strand already played in the background.

Underneath it all, the constant pull of the sun and the moon was a note too deep to be heard, but still strong and steady, and felt through the bones. And as the landscape widened, the music changed, twisted and turned and expanded, until he felt a change in rhythm, a new drive to the chorus. More voices, more sounds.

The Aymhelin, as full and complex as an ancient symphony, and yet not as quirky and unique as the Bloodwood. Clearer, and with a simpler structure in its movements. Like a song with a simpler chorus. Dark deep forests rumbling with basses fading into clear, high-pitched coasts, the sea cutting into white rocks like reedy voices.

And burning bright at the core of this new symphony,

another tangle of notes, luminous and joyful where the Well of Tears was mournful and ominous. The Fountain of Purity.

Something suddenly distracted him, and Grim felt like he was falling back, the music shifting again to the chiming voices of the Bloodwood.

Pain.

He was feeling pain.

The close, intimate individuality of what his body was feeling pulled him out of the sea of sound. But the music was still enveloping him, lush and soothing, but he was falling away from it, faster and faster.

A single discordant note rose in the north, with the pounding aggression of a war drum.

The Uthuk Y'llan were coming.

The pain grew and pushed the music back, and he fell through the blackness and silence.

The elves walked through the iron doors and were a poor sight indeed. Their armor was dented and stained, their weapons caked with the grim remains of battle. They were tired and fatigued, covered in dust and ash. Some leaned on their companions for support. They dragged their feet, and looked around the courtyard with haunted eyes.

At their head, a single warrior limped into the Well courtyard, a bent shield on her arm.

"Kestrel," Laurel said. She had been watching them as they entered, hoping to see a familiar face.

The leader of the column left her followers behind and came forward to embrace Laurel, who stood by Suhlwen to greet them. She removed her helmet, revealing her drawn features and her pale face.

"They are a day behind us," Kestrel said, and collapsed.

"You have oatmeal in your hair," Brix said, pointing.

Grim nodded and ran a hand through it. He was terribly pale, his lips an unpleasant livid color, and his breath came in short rattling bursts, but he claimed not to be in pain. She did not believe him, but this was not the time to debate that.

"Just imagine," he said, his voice broken, "coming all this way to drown in a bowl of gruel."

He stood, and then bent in a crouch.

Brix gasped, but he lifted a hand and smiled. "I am fine. I'm just short of breath."

She had found him still at the table, face down in his bowl of oatmeal, left behind as they rushed outside. She had screamed and slapped him awake, and could still see the red marks on his cheek where her extended claws had ripped his waxy flesh. She felt sorry for that, but for a moment she'd been sure he was dead.

He finally straightened his back, and took a few tentative steps. Then he went to one of the alcoves in the walls, pushed a pillow aside, and sat down. He nodded again at her, smiling what he probably thought was a reassuring smile.

"What happened to you?"

He made a vague gesture with a hand. She poured a cup of water, and went and sat by his side. He took a sip.

"Spirit talkers – proper spirit talkers, that is, have to learn discipline, and ways to guard themselves. The spirit world might otherwise take advantage of them. Which is what happened, back in the woods, and now, too."

"The Fae again?" she asked, shuddering at the memory of their previous meeting.

"The Well," he said. He swallowed some more water. "Its voice, or its will." He chuckled. "The will of the Well."

She frowned. "The Well spoke to you?"

He shook his head. "Not speaking. It was more like pouring all of it inside of me." He gave her a lopsided grin. "It did not show the same restraint as the Fae, and the experience was somewhat overwhelming."

He checked his own pulse, and shook his head. "I never trained properly, of course. The Greyhaven curriculum does not cover that. And I'm not very good at keeping the spirits out of my head, apparently."

She was curious now. "What did you see?"

Grim shrugged, and stretched his back. "Everything, as far as the farthest reaches of the Aymhelin, and beyond. Everything at the same time."

"How is that possible?"

"Just like when you listen to some music, and you perceive each instrument or voice simultaneously, and they form a song. You enjoy the song because you get every. thread that's intertwined in it, even if you do not realize it." He grinned. "Only the Well played it very loudly to me."

"Why did the Well do this to you?" While wary of it, she was fascinated by the Well.

Grim shook his head. He took another sip of water.

"I think it was trying to show me the elves as they approached the redoubt. But either it was not able to restrain itself, or I was not skilled enough to filter the flood of things it showed. It was going to show me the whole of Mennara, and only the pain pulled me out before it poured the whole world inside my mind."

He placed his open hand on his chest, and for a moment listened to his own heart.

"How are you?"

He nodded. "I'll live."

They sat together and listened to the sounds from outside, where Tanner and Laurel were trying to find quarters for the newcomers. From a distance, they had seemed a poor lot, and they had clearly gone through a great deal.

"The Uthuk are coming," she said.

He nodded, a hard light in his eyes. "I know."

As the sun rose over the redoubt, Tanner walked up the steps to the battlements. He looked into the courtyard, where the elves had settled and made camp the previous evening, preferring the night sky to a roof over their heads. Thirty-eight warriors and two leonx, bringing the total forces holding the Well to forty elves, two humans, a cat-woman, an orc and three leonx.

The stuff of ballads, he thought, as he climbed the stairs.

On the terrace, Brix was training, dancing and sliding on the stone floor, a sword and a dagger in her hands, twirling like silver blurs as she parried and struck imaginary opponents. He watched as her moves became faster and faster, her long tail streaking behind her as she twisted, flexed her legs and leaped forward, landed in a crouch and rolled to the side. He could see the fighter and the dancer in her, and wondered what it must have been like for the children of the rich merchant to be in her charge. Then she sprung up, both blades crossed to parry a heavier weapon.

She saw him, and nodded as she disengaged her invisible adversary, turned on her heels, and did a second parry, this time intercepting an upward stab.

She spread her arms, crossed them over her chest and bowed, then it was over.

"You are very good," he said.

She grimaced and huffed. She was not even short of breath. "I had a good teacher."

They leant on the battlement, and looked at the savage garden and the trees beyond. In the morning light, the blue fires of the standing stones were barely visible, and the buzzing sound they made was as an afterthought.

"I wish they were here already," Brix said.

Tanner glanced at her. He recognized her impatience, but did not share it. "They will be, soon."

"The wait is the worst part," she said.

He shrugged. "It's like when you are out hunting," he said. "You need to learn patience."

She chuckled.

"What?"

A shrug. "I used to say to my wards they needed to learn patience. Sit at their desk and learn their lines, because Doctor Emery would test them in three days, and they were to be ready. But now I'm here burning, and I have no patience."

"It's not a history test we are about to face."

"In a way it is. What we are doing here–"

"The stuff of ballads."

She nodded. "That's what they say, isn't it?"

Tanner snorted. "Ballads are a lot more fun when you're not inside one."

One of the chambers in the redoubt was filled with a collection of old weapons and assorted equipment. Kestrel and two of her hunters searched through the piles of jumble. They were looking for arrows, mostly, but any piece of armor and any weapon in good condition would be a boon.

Perched on a low stool, Grim was not interested in implements of warfare as he dug into a large chest, delicately picking up bottles and setting them aside. He had piled a few old books on his left. Mages were in the unnerving habit of using codes and private languages to obfuscate their work, and he intended to use the books to decode some of the more cryptic labels. The fact that most of the material was of elvish origin and in elvish script did not help, but it would have been quite unpleasant should anyone mistake a fire accelerant fluid for an anti-inflammatory salve.

And then there were the things other adventurers had carried, rough cheap runestones and dubiously spelled blades, sluggish concoctions that were supposed to heal wounds and rat-eaten scrolls with illegible spells. Grim half expected to find some of the things he used to sell to questing parties and mercenaries.

He shook his head. The things some people entrusted their lives to.

"Anything you can use?" He turned. Suhlwen was standing behind him, her arms crossed.

"This is a veritable magic shop," he said, "if somewhat debatable. I'm inventorying what we've got, and then we'll be able to concoct something, I'm sure. Nothing earth-shaking, but still effective."

She nodded. "Fine."

She picked up one of the books and browsed it. She arched an eyebrow.

"Where does all this stuff come from?" he asked.

She gave him a bored look. "You mean you don't imagine?"

Grim could easily imagine. The people outside, the ones whose remains were entangled in the rose bushes, the ones that had succumbed to the illusions of the Well. All this had been scavenged from their bodies by Suhlwen.

How long had she been here?

He watched Suhlwen go through the door and into the brightness of the courtyard, and shuddered. Kestrel gave him a questioning look, but he just shook his head. They were all in awe of their hostess. If awe was the right word, and not just plain fear.

The elf woman came closer. She nodded at the departing sorceress.

"Do you think we can trust her?" she asked.

That seemed to be the question in everybody's mind. One they had all been asking each other in the last few hours.

Most of the time, especially when Arnost Emery was there, Suhlwen acted like a reasonably friendly person, for an elf. And yet there was something about her, a sense of strangeness that still gave them all pause.

She was, in certain moments, the most inhuman elf Grim had ever seen so far. He had come to the conclusion she had to be somewhat eccentric. By her own admission, she had chosen solitude to living in Methras. Right now, she seemed to tolerate their company. Even enjoy it, in Emery's case. But Grim wondered how long her friendly attitude would last.

"She has spent a lot of time alone," he said. Kestrel did not look convinced. "She says she serves the Well," he went on. "That at least means she's on our side."

Kestrel looked at the collection of objects surrounding them.

"I hope you're right," she said. She collected three quivers of blue-feathered arrows, and went out. Grim went back to the contents of the chest.

•••

"I still feel uneasy," Brix said. She was walking the boundary between the overgrown garden and the Bloodwood, going from one standing stone to the next. In the early morning light, Laurel walked by her side.

"Uneasy?"

They looked at each other. Brix sighed. "Scared," she admitted. She did not like to put it in words, but even that was better than silence.

Ever since the coming of the elves, the stones had been alive with blue lights, strange patterns etched in glowing lines over their surface, and the occasional lightning discharge. But it was not that what scared Brix.

"I'd hate to get lost in a daydream again," she said. She cast a glance at one of the bushes that punctuated the slope to the iron gates. Pale bones intermingled with the rose stalks, and rusty pieces of armor.

"What did you see?" Laurel asked.

Brix stopped, and took a deep breath. "I was in my father's gymnasium. My mother was dancing with me. I was, I don't know, maybe fourteen or fifteen."

The elf gave her a sympathetic look.

"What did you see, instead?" Brix countered.

"I was in the Bloodwood, with my cousin Redstar. We were hunting boars."

"As one does," Brix chuckled.

"We can't all be dancers," Laurel replied, and walked on, towards the next stone.

Brix snapped her tail and followed.

"Have you wondered why the Well chose those moments and not others?" Brix asked. "I did."

"Did you find an answer?"

"No, not really."

"We should place sentries along the path of the stones," Laurel said. She pointed. "They'd be in sight of each other, and in sight of the Well."

Obviously Laurel did not like to talk about whatever the Well had shown her. "You think the Uthuk will try and take us by stealth?"

Right now, they had soldiers in the trees, one hundred yards from the stones, on the lookout. The elf shrugged. "It's what I would do. And they used stealth in Methras. Caught us off guard."

Brix looked into the wood. The undergrowth was thick here, close to the Well. She had left a piece of her coat and a strand of her hair in the brambles. "It's not what you'd expect from the Locust Swarm, is it?" she said. "Stealth, I mean. The Uthuk are brash and brutal. What they did in Methras required planning."

"The champion that leads them is different."

Brix nodded, and frowned. "We saw a thing in the wood, two days ago," she said suddenly. She turned to look at Laurel. "It was here, at the edge. Something big enough to shake the branches of the trees. Any idea what that might be?"

Laurel in turn eyed the deep shadows under the red foliage. She nodded, and started to speak.

A long buzzing sound rose through the trees, like the call of a wild deer buck, raging. It rose and fell with an increasing rhythm.

An elven bullroarer.

The two women looked at each other. Brix's breath caught in her throat, and she gasped. The shadows among the trees turned threatening as she looked around. Both of them remembered the Old Road, what felt like a whole lifetime before.

"They are coming," Laurel said.

Brix was already running up the hill. Laurel followed her.

Halfway up, they were joined by the elven warriors that had been stationed in the trees. They came out of the undergrowth and raced up to the iron gates.

The deep shadow of the access gallery welcomed them, and the doors slammed behind them.

The siege of the Well of Tears had begun.

CHAPTER TWENTY

The Uthuk Y'llan came two days after the elves, later than expected but still too soon. They came walking slowly, carefully, and not in a bloodthirsty rush. The bulk of their army remained in the trees, and a small vanguard was sent forward to scout the terrain.

Tanner squinted in the early morning light as a dozen warriors walked past the standing stones and into the savage garden. They made sure to stay clear of the stones. Tanner wondered if it was just superstitious fear, or if they knew something the defenders didn't. They were carrying bone axes and rough blades of scavenged metal. Their red loincloths and scarves were in stark contrast to their gray skin.

A bow creaked to Tanner's left. "Steady," he heard Kestrel say.

They were all standing on the battlements, a thin line of archers and spearmen covering the whole perimeter. They had patched up their armor with the bits and pieces found in the stores of the redoubt. They looked like a strange band of scarecrows, Tanner thought.

When the first gray-skinned warriors had made their

appearance at the northern edge of the garden, Laurel and Brix had moved to the south, expecting the newcomers to be a decoy. But it did not look so.

In the eerie silence of the autumnal late morning, the Uthuk Y'llan scouts walked slowly uphill, fanning out in a very loose formation.

"They show more restraint than their kin," Emery observed.

Grim leaned on the battlement wall. "The Well is getting them."

The Uthuk Y'llan scouts were slowing as they climbed. First one, then two others stopped altogether. One of them sat down by a rose bush, and his weapon slipped from his fingers. Another warrior stopped and then started again, wandering aimlessly between the rose bushes.

Grim's shoulders relaxed and he straightened up. "Looks like the Well is taking care of itself, after all."

Tanner turned, too wary to feel relieved yet. On the other side of the battlement, Brix lifted a hand, signaling that there were no incoming attackers there. The elves relaxed their grip on the bows.

A second group of Uthuk Y'llan came past the standing stones about ten minutes later. One of the archers spotted them and gave the signal. There were five of them, moving swiftly uphill from the west side, trying to make it to the wall. Tanner went there, and was joined by Brix and Laurel.

"They are testing our perimeter," Tanner said. The elf nodded.

These five lost themselves too, enraptured by whatever illusion the powers of the Well wove around them. Their momentum spent, the raiders slowed down and stopped. One of them walked around in small circles, his arms hanging limp at his side. The others just stood on the spot, swaying a little, as if moved by a light breeze.

"It looks like it won't be much of a battle," Tanner said.

"We could just go down there and slit their throats," Brix replied. She crossed paths with Kestrel as they traded places.

In that same moment, an arrow flew from the shadows in the trees. It struck one of the standing Uthuk Y'llan between the shoulder and the neck. The raider went down without a sound.

Brix gasped.

"Steady!" Kestrel shouted from the other side of the redoubt.

More arrows were raining on the dazed raiders. Some barely scratched their bone plates, others stuck in their limbs and their chests. But they kept falling, flying in a tall arch from the shadows of the wood. In a few moments, all the Uthuk Y'llan in the overgrown garden were dead or dying, struck by the arrows of their own people.

"This is madness," Brix said.

And the drums started.

A hollow, rhythmic beat, primitive and brutal, that thundered in the trees and rolled like a tide against the walls of the redoubt.

A thing came hurtling from the trees. It had been hours, and the hollow drone of the drums had never stopped, grating on their nerves. Tanner welcomed the diversion, and watched as the creature came forth.

It was as large as a black bear, short-legged but with overlong, muscular arms that ended in colossal black talons. Surprisingly fast for its massive bulk and short legs, it crashed through the undergrowth, and made a beeline for the closest standing stone. As it approached the rock column, the animal increased the speed of its charge, and then slammed with its whole body against the stone.

Tanner had never seen such a creature, nor such a display of raw aggression. He kept staring, his mouth hanging open.

The blue energy crackled and discharged into the ground in bright arches. Sparks burned into its black tufts of fur as it touched the stone. Blue lines flared on the gray rock, blue fire pouring along deep-etched grooves. The gray skin of the thing burned as it roared, and pushed against the rock.

The faint buzzing of the blue energy grew in intensity as the brightness of the light increased. The creature clawed at the rock. The ground shook as the vibration of the standing stone dropped to an impossibly low note. It rose on its hind legs and once more attacked the stone, with no effect.

The creature paused, as if to regain its breath. It let out a mournful groan, and it took a few tentative steps, slowly. It tried to get away from the standing stone, but it was too late. It staggered and fell, and it was still.

"Now we know how the stones work," Grim said.

Tanner glanced at him, and then at Suhlwen, standing still by one of the merlons. "Do we?"

"Sort of like a soulstone rune," the short man said.

Tanner shook his head. Mages had their ways, and he would rather stay clear of them.

"A soulstone rune drains life and transfers it to the user," Grim said.

"This is how the rose garden feeds the Well of Tears," Suhlwen said. Then she turned and walked off the battlement. Tanner shuddered, and felt a pang of guilt about it. She was one of their own, after all.

•••

It was late in the afternoon when the Uthuk came again.

The drums had not stopped beating for a moment since the morning, a monotonous, overwhelming reminder of the presence of the Uthuk in the trees. The warriors on the battlements had tried to ignore the sound, to not let it grate on their already strained nerves.

Kestrel had kept walking up and down their line, making sure the defenders kept their focus. She had spoken to the ones she had seen were more nervous, and traded a few words with Laurel, where she stood scanning the wood.

Now, a band of warriors emerged from the trees, charging up the hillside, screaming and waving their weapons. Like the ones before they wore red rags and carried strange, misshapen weapons. Instead of cautiously walking, they pushed up the slope without slowing, and the Well did not seem able to interfere with their charge.

On the battlement, Kestrel tightened her helmet's strap, and took her position at the head of the line of archers. All the warriors fell into place, grateful in a way for some action after the long wait. Kestrel barked an order, and a volley of arrows hit the incoming force, felling a handful of raiders. But the others kept coming. The elves let their arrows fly three more times before the survivors of the charge slammed into the redoubt wall and started climbing the vine-covered stone. They grabbed the network of thorny vines, ignoring the damage. Some climbed over their own companions. They were like desperate men trying to get out of a pit, but driven forward by bloodlust and anger, and the sheer terror of their own leader.

Archers and spearmen pushed them back. They aimed for the eyes and for other weak spots. They stabbed downwards, and retreated to avoid being grabbed and dragged away. Kestrel felt sick. It was a dirty, messy affair, a fight without honor.

Then the Uthuk Y'llan reached the battlement, and the true fight began.

Joining the defenders, Tanner chopped at the legs of the first warrior standing on top of the parapet. His axe bit into the muscle and the bone, and the Uthuk lost his balance and toppled back.

Two more warriors rolled onto the terrace, wielding their jagged weapons. Brix intercepted the first, was pushed back, and managed to dodge the second. When a high whistle warned her, she dropped on the floor. The archers on the other side of the redoubt had turned inward, and their arrows found the two invaders, killing them both.

A broad-shouldered brute vaulted over the parapet and landed on his feet in front of Grim. The short man screamed and fell on his back. The Uthuk hefted a pickaxe fashioned out of an animal's jaw. Kestrel cursed under her breath and hastened there, sword drawn.

With a roar, Hewma slammed into the Uthuk and dragged it down into the courtyard. The raider landed on his back, and the giant cat crushed him under its weight. Kestrel helped Grim up and went back to the fight.

Along the parapet, spearmen pushed the incoming Uthuk back, while the archers shot down the length of the wall, picking their targets with care. Kestrel kept her voice level, commanding them to bide their time. The elven archers were mortally efficient. The dead piled at the foot of the wall, and served as a platform to those that kept coming, screaming and waving their weapons. There seemed to be no end to them, and for each one that was killed, two more came to the wall.

Then they were gone, and only the drum remained, insistent and menacing.

The survivors retreated, leaving behind their dead. The men and women on the battlements cheered, but each one of them felt the Locust Swarm was only testing their strength.

“So, if they run fast enough, the Well cannot trick them,” Tanner said.

“I do not think it’s the running,” Grim said, handing back the water-skin.

“What then?”

“They are giving nothing to the Well,” Laurel said. “No thoughts, no memories.” She gestured towards the darkening woods. “It’s to do with the drums.”

“It’s an old trick,” the orc said. “They are meant to unnerve the defenders. Us, that is. Like with most endless, repetitive loud sounds, in the long run either you don’t hear it anymore, or it drives you to distraction.”

“It is not just that,” she replied. “The sounds are used to fill the heads of the warriors. Their continued repetition smothers the mind. Nothing remains but their bloodlust, their frenzy and the pounding of the drums driving them on. A void remains between their will and their actions. No thought, no imagination. They become like animals, like rocks rolling down a hill. They no longer have a mind the Well can trap. They just run, and scream, and kill.”

Tanner cursed under his breath.

They had made great drums out of hollowed tree trunks, and now they were pounding on them. Two dozen muscular, determined warriors, raising a thunder like the mother of all storms, a sound that caused the very earth to shake.

Th'Uk Tar walked along the line of drummers.

He still carried, as a necklace, the skull of the elven sorceress that had fought him in Methras. Gorgemaw had been badly wounded, before managing to crush and devour her. Now the beastmaster pensively caressed the arc of her eye socket. It had been a pity, he thought, being forced to kill her. It would have been good to trap her and educate her, twist her to make her one of his servants. It would have been such a pleasure, to break and remake such a proud creature. A welcome diversion in the long nights in the Bloodwood, marching through the damp, the mud and the shrubs. But elves were not that pliable, and he now could feel the ones in the tower on the top of the hill. He could feel their evil eyes staring out of their den, could hear their malignant whispers.

He would drown those whispers with the sound of his drums, and then he would crush the elves under the sheer weight of his army. Smother their defiance, humiliate their pride.

And then, he would take the Well.

Th'Uk Tar could feel its power, calling to him. Like a beacon.

To the south, the Fountain of Purity was like a sun, a painful spike of light burning through his mind's defenses. So much power that the brain refused to encompass it. The Well of Tears was more manageable. Less blinding in its light, but in a way fiercer.

And it was close. So close.

Little more than an arrow's flight from him.

He looked down at the blistering, burned hand he had dipped into the fire to clear the curse of the elven sorceress. He flexed his fingers, and pain stabbed through his burned skin. The scabs broke and crumbled, and yellow ichor dripped through the cracks.

Th'Uk Tar screamed for the drummers to play louder. Behind the drummers stood a line of others, ready to relieve them. The drums would not stop. They would silence the snickering voices of the elves on the hill. Silence the pain coursing through his hand.

He would take the Well.

The Well would heal his hand.

And through the Well, he would take the Fountain of Purity.

Poison its waters, corrupt its power.

The Aymhelin would become his playground, for him to do what he wanted. He would remake the Latari, he would weave a whole new landscape. He would command the fabled Scions, and bend them to his own will.

All he had to do was take the Well.

Wipe away the puny elves that clung to it.

He would smoke them out of their anthill.

He would turn their Bloodwood to ashes.

Th'Uk Tar cracked his bone whips, and ordered the fires lit.

Trembling red dots appeared beyond the blue glow of the standing stones.

"They are setting fire to the Bloodwood," Laurel said.

"No, they're not." Laurel and Brix turned. Suhlwen was coming up the staircase. She had replaced her old-fashioned gown with a leather vest and a flaring silk skirt, the color of dry leaves. She had braided her hair, and bound it with a red ribbon. She was wearing a belt with pouches and bottles on her waist, and she carried a long staff, topped by a rough-cut crystal, pale yellow with speckles of gold in its depth.

She stood at the edge of the terrace, and squinted at the torches dancing in the shadows of the forest. "Not while I am here," she said, and smiled a cruel smile.

She slipped a glass vial from her belt, and unstopped it with a flick of her thumb. An ominous purple vapor rose from the mouth of the small bottle, rising in a slow spiral.

"I think we better step back," Grim said. Brix heard the serious tone in his voice, and moved aside.

As the purple smoke rose, Suhlwen lifted her staff, and started chanting a repetitive sequence of syllables.

The torches were moving in the distance. In Methras, they had piled dry leaves and branches to start the fires. Brix guessed they had done the same here.

Suhlwen's words rose in volume as the rough crystal atop her staff started sparkling, the gold specks inside of it dancing. The glass vial kept belching purple smoke, thicker now, brighter.

Soon it was as if all the birds in the Bloodwood had taken flight, screeching in panic. They flew over the top of the trees, in ample circles.

"We're still too close," Grim said, and slowly retreated by the staircase. He placed a hand on Brix's arm, and gently pulled her along.

The wind rose.

A soft breeze first, cool and caressing. Then its intensity grew, just as the sorceress' words became louder, and faster. And yet the vapor from the vial rose in a straight column connecting the earth and the sky, undisturbed by the growing wind.

Clouds were gathering above the Well, turning and churning with increasing violence as the wind rose further. The column of purple vapor was like the axis around which the clouds were twisting and dancing in tighter circles, and where the vapor reached them, darkness spread, like a bruise.

The ominous murmur of distant thunder echoed in the sky. Brix's hair stood on end and her ears flattened. She saw Laurel grow pale, her eyes widening in fear.

Soon, a low overhang of black thunderclouds was spinning over the Well of Tears, and a single bright light shone under it, the crystal on Suhlwen's staff burning like a miniature sun. The wind howled as Suhlwen screamed her incantation, her face drawn, her arms stretched. Her braid undone, her hair was like a black storm cloud around her face, and the white strand rippled through it like a lightning bolt.

Thunder roared closer in the black sky.

The trees of the Bloodwood shook and bowed under the force of the growing storm.

Brix grabbed Laurel's arm. Grim cursed.

Suhlwen was suddenly silent, and the silence was like a second thunderclap. All sound was gone, and Brix felt dizzy. The howling of the wind, the thrashing of the tree branches, the frightened calls of the birds and the animals in the wood. Everything seemed to be perfectly still for two full heartbeats.

Then, with the roar of a colossal beast raging, a column of purple lightning connected the battlements and the clouds. Immersed in the fluid purple fire, Suhlwen threw back her head and laughed, her arms outstretched, her hair a wild black cloud. A single word erupted through her lips, and rang like a mighty bell.

Lightning bolts crashed in the overgrown garden and in the nearby forest, as the full fury of the storm was released, and rain poured down from the sky in a thundering cascade to which there seemed to be no end.

The overgrown garden was turned into a swamp, the battlement was washed in rainwater that poured down the steps of the staircases like a waterfall. Barely visible through the wall of icy-cold rain, the fires in the trees sizzled and died out.

Alone at the edge of the battlement, Suhlwen's shoulders dropped, and she leaned on her staff. Her hair was sticking to her face, wet, and ragged breath escaped her lips in soft clouds of steam. For the first time Brix truly realized how ancient the elven sorceress was, and how powerful.

"There will be no fires in my woods," Suhlwen whispered.

CHAPTER TWENTY-ONE

Beastmaster Th'Uk Tar screamed his rage at the pouring sky.

Rain dripped down the red leaves of the Bloodwood, soaking his warriors and his beasts, turning the undergrowth into a swamp. The fires sizzled and died, and the drums slowed and lost their tempo. He cracked his whip, and the head of the closest drummer rolled in the mud. The drums resumed their steady beat.

Th'Uk Tar stalked through his camp. It was little more than dying fires and squats where his warriors had waited for the moment to strike. Now everything was drowning in the rain, and he could feel the laughter and scorn of the hateful Latari, hiding in their stone fortress, mocking him.

So they had sorcery at their command.

It would not make any difference.

The crack of his whips echoed the sound of the thunder.

"Rise and be ready!" he commanded.

The warriors rose in irregular lines, waiting for orders. The flesh rippers roared, the surviving caecilians hissed and bawled. All craved the fight. And he would give it to them.

He would wipe the laughter off the faces of the Latari.

He would take the Well, and he would take it now.

He gave the word, and his army responded with a chorus of bloodthirsty delight. Black iron weapons glinted in the haze of the lightnings, and the Uthuk Y'llan marched on the Well of Tears.

"Arnost Emery–"

By the lip of the Well, the doctor had donned a rusty, reinforced leather overcoat, and was leaning on a spear. He looked up at Suhlwen as she walked to him.

"My lady–"

"I told you already," she said, softly, "that I am no lady."

She was wearing her leather jacket and her belt with the pockets and vials. Now she propped her staff against the lip of the Well, and put her hands behind her neck to undo the clasp of a thin silver chain.

"I want you to have this," she said. A dark blue stone, the size of a thumbnail. "It is not very powerful, but it might help you in what's to come."

"I don't…"

What was to come was weighing on his soul. He felt his age dragging him down, and now this unexpected gesture had all the markings of a farewell. He lifted a hand to stop her.

She ignored him, and hung the stone around his neck. Then she leaned close and whispered a single word in his ear. It had the fluid sound of the elven language, and it eluded the grasp of his mind. It slipped into his ear and was gone.

He looked into Suhlwen's eyes.

"Stay safe in the middle of the battle," she said then, as she retrieved her staff. "I want to play you again."

•••

"Here they come," Tanner said.

There was no time for rousing speeches, no final words of courage and sacrifice. No contests of song, no gallant challenges of champions. Kestrel was too busy running around the rampart, giving the last orders, and as for Tanner's companions…

Tanner had heard a lot of stories and ballads, about brave warriors and champions. This was nothing like that. He thought Doctor Emery could have said some good words, but he was by the Well, ready to bring water to the wounded.

He glanced at Brix. The end of the wait did not seem to make her any happier. Together with Laurel, the cat-woman moved on the other side of the redoubt.

The elves had spread along the battlement, bows ready, lances waiting nearby. They were a very thin line. Tanner thought about the help they had been wishing for, Dareine and the armies of the Aymhelin. They would not be here in time, if they were coming at all.

They were alone.

"Just like in the ballads, huh?" Grim had donned an ill-fitting leather jacket, and had draped across it a bandoleer of pouches and pockets. Tanner slapped him on the shoulder.

"On my order!" Kestrel shouted.

The creaking of the bows overcame the pouring of the rain.

Behind them, Suhlwen climbed the staircase, the gemstone on her staff burning sinisterly.

The Uthuk Y'llan came running from the forest, warriors and war beasts together, without any order or strategy. They ran past the standing stones, and many of them drifted too close and lost their momentum, their energies sapped. They were overcome, pushed down and trampled by those that came after them. The war cries of the warriors mingled with the incessant drumming from the forest in a cacophony that overwhelmed any other sound.

Tanner stared as, crazed in their bloodlust, some of them cut themselves with their own weapons, black blood pouring, and shouted challenges at the as yet unseen elves.

Uphill they ran, their feet churning the mud of the hillside, entangled in the thorny branches of the rose bushes. Tearing away the overgrown vines and the grass, turning the slope into a crawling mass of mud-splattered bodies, a shapeless horde of beasts that hungered for destruction.

Their rage was like a wave that washed over the battlements, and Tanner felt it like a punch in his chest. The long-fanged hunter beasts were the first on the battlements, coming in leaps and bounds across the mire. The archers took out two of them, lucky shots that caught the animal's eyes or open maws.

"Don't waste your arrows!" Kestrel shouted.

Half the archers on the bastion shouldered their bows and picked up their lances, and when the beasts clawed their way up the wall, stabbed with all their strength, pushing the animals back, and looking for weak spots in their bony armor. Their companions on the other side of the redoubt turned, and used their arrows to cover the spearmen.

Tanner flexed his muscles and cut with his axe. The head of a clawed horror fell on the stone floor of the rampart, eyes still rolling, jaws snapping on empty air. A few feet away, an elf caught a leaping beast in the gut, but the animal's momentum carried it forward and it clawed its killer as it pushed him off the bastion and into the courtyard.

Then the horde of berserkers slammed into the walls of the

Well, and the redoubt shuddered under their weight like a lighthouse in a sea storm.

"Snakes!" Laurel shouted.

They looked like snakes and like snakes they crawled, but their hide was covered in rusty bone plates, and they had square-jawed heads, bristling with sharp teeth. The animals came from the southern edge of the Bloodwood, and after them a horde of Uthuk, running across the murky length of the overgrown garden.

The archers had been shooting at the growling beasts on the other side of the battlements, but now turned and aimed their arrows at the incoming enemies. Many had dropped their empty quivers, and were going for the old arrows they had recovered from the stores. Brix knew they could not keep shooting much longer.

Then swords and spears would decide the battle.

The slitherers gathered at the foot of the wall, and then pushed themselves up, coil after coil, finding purchase in the web of vines and branches that covered the stones. From above, Brix looked into their fevered eyes, and into their slavering maws, and gasped. The animals hissed and barked like dogs, and their tongues lashed the air. She pulled back and left her place to Laurel and the archers. The bows creaked and snapped as the arrows flew. The first volley bounced off the creatures' armor.

"Aim for the eyes!" Laurel shouted. "Save your shot!"

Then the world turned upside down, and Brix was on the floor, her neck and shoulder hurting, and a mud-splattered Uthuk was standing over her, a scythe-like blade in his hand. Brix screamed and stabbed him in the foot with her dagger.

The warrior bellowed in pain, and as she rose to her feet she found his heart with her sword, the blade slipping between two bone plates in his armor.

She let him fall and pulled another dagger from her belt.

"Is this what I raised a daughter for?" her mother's voice asked. Brix ignored her, and ran to cover Laurel's side.

Time ceased to exist for Tharadax Tanner. Blood and mangled limbs, the snarl of the Uthuk Y'llan as they clawed their way up the wall, the incessant drumming, was all there was. No camaraderie and no jokes among the defenders, no keeping count of the dead: friend or foe.

The ballads had made war sound heroic, but this was simple brutality. There was only the rhythmic swinging of his axe, his arms heavier with each hit, and the distorted faces of the Uthuk Y'llan as they came for him, and he chopped at them like a lumberjack, cutting them down as they climbed on the wall. It was not a fight, it was a massacre.

The Uthuk Y'llan were endowed with supernatural vitality, but as they reached for the top of the wall and started climbing towards it, they were defenseless. Arrows, spears, axes. It was enough to wound the incoming berserkers and push them back, and they would be trampled and killed by their own as they pushed on.

A few managed to reach the terrace.

Glimpses of the fight flashed in front of Tanner's eyes as he moved rhythmically, cutting at the incoming attackers. An elven archer was lifted bodily and crushed by a brute the size of a pony. He threw the broken body into the courtyard, Kestrel stabbed it in a leg with her lance. The monster roared and swung at her with a bone billhook. She parried, and behind her Grim pulled a vial from his bandoleer and threw it at the Uthuk. A bright flash of green fire enveloped the creature. Still it came for Grim and Kestrel, arms flailing, shrouded in green flames, screaming. The elf tripped him with the shaft of her lance, and as it tottered, she pushed him off the wall. Tanner felt a spark of relief. Then a tall warrior wielding two black iron swords came for him, and there was only the fight. He cut sideways, knocked the enemy down, and finished him.

And still the Uthuk kept coming.

The drums thrumming in his ears, Tanner lost all sense of time. The attackers retreated, regrouped, and came forward again. The archers were dropping their bows, their arrows spent. During a lull in the fight, Tanner saw Grim again. Sitting at the top of the staircase, the man poured brandy on his hand, hissing an oath, and wrapped it in a strip of rag.

"That was stupid," Tanner said. The short man had raised a hand to defend himself from the slash of an Uthuk iron hook.

"Go and see Emery," the orc said.

"I'll survive," Grim replied. He grimaced as he tightened the bandage. "I only wish those drums would let up."

"Fat chance."

Brix watched in horror as a bloated shape trampled through the mud on stumpy legs, pushing aside his companions. Its gray skin was slick from the rain, and he towered above them, and swung what looked like a tree trunk with iron spikes at its end. She remembered the colossus they had met on the Grey Steps.

Without stopping, the creature reached out with its free hand and grabbed one of the Uthuk Y'llan warriors by the head. He lifted him up and then, opening a mouth like a black pit, bit him in half. The other warriors cleared a path for him, and the creature marched on, chewing happily on its snack. A volley of arrows stuck to his blob-like body, and he ignored them.

Brix wondered if he would be able to climb the wall of the redoubt. More importantly, she wondered if she'd be able to take him. Then a cat-like monster, all fangs and sharp talons clawed its way through two merlons, growling, and she stabbed at its open maw. She did not have the luxury to think too far ahead.

Lightning bolts fell from the sky, exploding into the crawling horde. The archers and the spearmen welcomed the moment of respite as Suhlwen held her staff high, calling upon the elements.

One of them limped down the stair to the Well, one arm hanging limply at her side, her chainmail hauberk ripped in the shoulder and the chest. Emery handed her a cup of water and a few words of comfort. The water healed her wound, just washing it away. She hastened up the steps as the lightning stopped, and only the rain and the distant drums remained. Emery watched her go, his heart heavy. Her next wound could be too much for the water to heal. There was only so much the ancient magic could do, and he was feeling powerless, and frustrated, as the wounded came and went.

He closed his hand around Suhlwen's gemstone. Magic should make life better, he thought, not death easier. He helped one of the wounded as the elf tried to pull up a bucket from the well. The elf thanked him, and Emery wondered fleetingly if he was really as young as he looked. But did it make any difference?

Someone shouted for more arrows. He saw the archers on top of the wall pass along the last of their quivers. Many had dropped their bows and picked up spears and swords.

Emery looked at the length of the rampart at the thinning line of defenders and wondered if there would ever be an end to this.

The fight was like a dream, and at the same time, her wits had rarely felt this sharp and awake. For this reason Laurel kept fighting, dodging axes and billhooks, cutting and slashing at the Uthuk Y'llan as they crawled up the wall of the Well of Tears. Their trance-like fury made them blind like sleepwalkers, blunting their attacks. Her own trance-like state made her fully aware, and deadly.

As she turned on herself, two short swords twirling, she saw one of the archers fall, a black iron dagger in his eye. She slashed at the wrist of the killer, the elven blade biting deep into the gray flesh. As the Uthuk pulled back and topped off the battlement, in a single movement she dropped her blades, picked up the fallen archer's bow, and released three arrows in quick sequence, killing another marauder.

She felt the bone pickaxe before she saw it. She turned, avoiding the hit, just as Brix slid by her side, sword and dagger crossed, and intercepted the blow. The strength ofher opponent pushed her down on a knee. Behind her, Laurel shot an arrow into the eye of the Uthuk, and then pulled the cat-woman away before the dead body could crush her. She moved on, seeking another target, before Brix could whisper a thank you.

Standing at the edge of the forest, drums pounding in his ears, Beastmaster Th'Uk Tar whipped his beasts and his warriors forward until his arms ached, and watched in growing frustration as the cowardly elves rained thunderbolts on them, and fought them back on the ramparts of their stone tower.

The flames of his fury surged as he saw the last of his flesh rippers torn to pieces by the defenders of the Well.

They thought they were safe.

They thought their spells and their longbows and their wall put them beyond his reach.

A terrible grimace crossed the lean features of Th'Uk Tar as he watched the dead pile against the gray wall of the Well of Tears.

So much death was what he needed.

There was still a favor he could invoke. One last surprise for the hated Latari.

It was time to put an end to this game.

The earth shook and a colossus emerged from the forest, in a storm of wrecked trees and torn lumps of dirt. It threw back its head and roared to the sky, climbing in long strides up the hill to the Well. It disregarded the warriors and the beasts, trampling them mercilessly as it went.

The archers on the rampart were frozen in terror, as Kestrel shouted to resume shooting. By her side, Tanner stood and struggled to believe what he was seeing.

A body that was neither animal nor insect, it stomped on four massive legs, its rust-colored armor creaking. Muscular arms flailed in the air, with sharp-toothed mouths at their end that snapped like snares and bit into the living and the dead. A crest of hooked spines ran down its back, and a bony tail whipped the air, again armed with a gaping mouth. The Uthuk Y'llan screamed in terror and pushed even stronger against the walls of the redoubt, like they wanted to get in themselves, not as conquerors, but to escape this new nightmare.

Reaching to the closest standing stone, the creature grabbed it with its vise-like hands, and a low growl resounded as it ripped it from the earth and, ignoring the bolts of energy scorching its rust-colored hide, it lifted it high and threw it at the walls of the Well.

Still trailing blue sparks, the stone flew through the rain, and then it crashed into the wall. The redoubt shuddered under the impact. The stone rolled down, its energy vanished, and it steamrolled the besiegers that were not fast enough out of its way. Then the thing with many mouths finally reached the Well, its head taller than the merlons of the battlements.

Tanner pushed an Uthuk warrior off the wall and looked up, open mouthed. His mind was blank as he stared the monster in the eye.

Pure horror seemed to radiate from the creature like stench from a dead carcass. The line of elves wavered. Some of the spearmen dropped their lances, and one of them crouched on the floor, covering his head with his hands.

Ashen-faced, Kestrel ran up and down the battlements, inciting her warriors to hold their position.

Grim stood paralyzed. "What in the name of Kellos is that?"

Suhlwen stood by him and pushed him gently aside. "It's mine."

She raised her staff, and a column of electric fire poured from the sky and slammed into the monster. The creature roared and grasped the top of the wall with its right forepaw, the mouth open wide, its thin tongue flapping obscenely. Tanner intercepted the jaws, pushing with his armored shoulder against the sharp teeth, while battering the arm with his axe. The teeth punctured his shoulder pad, his breastplate creaked, and he kept hitting blindly, screaming an unending string of curses. There was pain, ringing at the back of his perception, but it was nothing compared to the horror. Tanner kept swinging his axe as everything else faded away.

A second blast of raw lightning crashed down on the monster, and spread to the unwary that had remained closer to it on the ground. The creature spasmed and let go of Tanner. The orc collapsed on the floor. The demon-beast reared back on its hind legs and roared, thin tendrils of smoke rising from the cracks in its armor.

Tanner crawled away as the creature punched the wall with its clawed-mouth fists, and the rock crumbled. Two elves were crushed and swallowed by the gaping maws of the monster.

New roars echoed in the courtyard, and through the pouring rain, three leonx climbed up the battlements and jumped at the demon-creature. One of the leonx hung by its teeth to one of the creature arm's, the second circled it and attacked the flailing, biting tail, and Hewma clawed her way up the back of the monster, and sunk her teeth at the base of its neck. The monster screeched in rage. It twisted and turned, trying to dislodge the leonx. With blind fury, it slammed its arm against the stone wall of the rampart, once, twice, until the leonx let go of its hold and fell at the foot of the wall, and was still. Clinging to the shoulder of the creature with her claws sunk between two of its plates, Hewma bit again and again in the neck. The monster bucked and jumped, shaking the earth and trampling the Uthuk Y'llan that had not yet fled the slope. Its tail smacked the second leonx in the muzzle, and it landed back on all fours by Tanner's side.

Grim was suddenly there, grabbing the orc by the shoulders. "Get up, mate."

Confusedly, Tanner wondered why the archers had stopped shooting. Then he realized they were trying to find more arrows. He didn't know if there were any.

For a third time Suhlwen lifted her staff, and its gemstone flared, summoning the power of the storm. Somehow, Hewma sensed the coming attack, and finally let go and jumped back by Grim just as a third pillar of raw energy crashed down from the sky.

As the elemental fire engulfed the monster for a third time, one of its snapping maws came in a swift sweep, pushing Tanner to the side. It closed on the midriff of the sorceress. The snakelike tail of the creature lifted Suhlwen from the battlement and tossed her to the other side of the rampart. She slammed into the battlement and went down on all fours, coughing and bleeding.

The demon creature burned. It rammed the wall, causing a new fall of debris. Cracks opened in the walls of the redoubt, and part of the battlements collapsed, carrying some of the defenders with them. Black smoke was pouring through the monster's mouths and nostrils, and the plates of its armor were growing black at their edges. A plume of oily smoke rose from the base of the neck, where Hewma had wounded it. On the opposite rampart, Suhlwen tried to pull herself to her feet. Laurel and Kestrel were by her side, helping her stand. She swayed, blood pouring from her side, and she crumpled and was still.

Unable to quench the fire, the monster clawed at the iron doors of the redoubt, and the metal hinges creaked and cracked. One of the two doors twisted and hung sideways.

Tanner hit the biting arm of the monster once more, and again was pushed back against the parapet. There were black spots blinking in front of his eyes, and the pain in his side and his back was like fire. He sensed more than saw Grim as he lunged forward.

Suhlwen was standing, leaning on Laurel. She shouted a warning as Grim picked up the broken staff where she had dropped it, and hefted it like a mace. The burning monster lowered its head to look at the small man with the sparkling gemstone. Tanner called out but Grim ignored him. He tried to move, to go cover his friend, but his legs failed him. Exhausted, the orc knelt down, leaning on his axe, each ragged breath burning in his chest.

Grim covered his face with his arm against the heat, and smashed the storm crystal on the edge of the battlement. The stone shattered into a thousand shards that twinkled in the air like frozen fireflies. The monster tried to pull back but it was too late. A miniature maelstrom blossomed in the midst of the shards, a black whirlwind bubbling with translucent foam that expanded and stretched as it sucked the fire from the monster's body, and the monster with it.

A long tongue of flame spiraled into the black pit, and the creature followed. Stretching, twisting out of shape, screaming in agony as an unseen wind pulled the plates off its armor and broke its frame. Fire, smoke, misshapen limbs, everything turned and plummeted into the frozen constellation of burning shards, as a resounding bellow, like a giant's bronze trumpet, rose in volume and pitch until it drowned the drumming of the Uthuk Y'llan, the thunder of the storm, and the sounds of battle.

The final blast swept the ramparts and echoed into the courtyard of the Well, as the remaining standing stones burned with wraithlike fire.

Tanner crawled to where Grim was crouching against the parapet, his clothes smoking, his face burned.

CHAPTER TWENTY-TWO

The Uthuk Y'llan warriors fleeing from the wrath of the Gw'reth Chuik were met by their master with the burning caress of his bone whips. The first did not survive, while the others stopped, caught between the horror of the Ynfernael creature ravaging the walls of the Well and the prospect of the beastmaster's wrath.

As Th'Uk Tar strode towards them, Gorgemaw slithering behind him, they turned, and like a wave washing back on the shore, started running again up the hill, stumbling on the corpses of their companions, seeking a kill or, missing that, a swift death.

The drums guiding their steps, the last of the Uthuk Y'llan charged the Well of Tears. In front of them, the colossal shape of the many-mouthed beast burst into flames, casting a dancing red light over the nightmare landscape.

Those that hesitated at the sight were killed. His gnarled hand hurt as he gripped his new whip, freshly fashioned from the spine of one of his beasts. He spun it in the air, cracking it repeatedly. Th'Uk Tar had no time for the craven and the weak.

Fire erupted on top of the Well.

Th'Uk Tar watched as the Gw'reth Chuik fell foul of one last wizardry, and vanished with a sound like the scream of all the voices of the Ynfernael. It was a sight undreamed of. But where a lesser warrior would have reacted with fear, an anger like never he had felt before erupted through the champion's chest and he screamed in fury, his voice lost in the din. Once again, the Latari were mocking him, with their magic tricks and their craven tactics. A steely determination moved him. He would need to put an end to this battle himself.

When the sound died down, everything was still for a moment. Only the drums kept drumming, and Th'Uk Tar marched forward, followed by his most trusted warriors.

No more thunderbolts were raining on them, the storm was subsiding, and Th'Uk Tar knew that triumph was his. He did not care for the end of the Gw'reth Chuik. The creature had fulfilled its purpose, putting a stop to the storm sorceress' interference and damaging the Well's protective circle.

No more cowardly elvish trickery.

No more hiding behind walls and invoking ancient magic.

Now strength would decide the fight.

He grabbed one of the spines in Gorgemaw's cowl and swung on the back of the creature, riding it in triumph. The doors of the Well were broken, the defenders in disarray.

Beastmaster Th'Uk Tar entered the Well of Tears riding over the corpses of his enemies and his own warriors. He ignored the cries of the wounded and the panicked shouts of the survivors. He did not care for the thin, needle-like rain that washed over him as he emerged through the entrance tunnel. The only thing that mattered was the Well.

•••

"The gate!" Kestrel shouted. "Cover the gate!"

A handful of archers moved above the black iron doors. The champion was riding his snakelike monster to the gates of the Well. The defenders' last few arrows rebounded on the spines covering his shoulders.

"The eyes! Aim for the eyes!"

Roaring in frustration, Tanner slammed his axe into the ruined battlement, and as the rocks of the parapet loosened and moved, he threw down his weapon and pressed with all his might against the damaged wall. They had lost their magic, but they could still use brute force.

With a mighty crash, one of the doors broke its last hinge and fell to the ground. Tanner doubled his efforts, and now Kestrel and two elves were by his side. They braced their backs against the wall and pushed with the last remains of their strength and the full power of their desperation. The wall rocked, dust snowed down.

The champion's ride pushed the remaining door aside with its massive head, and started slithering into the access passage.

With a final desperate heave, the battlement crumbled and fell, a landslide of rocks and mortar that buried the gate, trapping the tail of the red snake creature. The Uthuk started climbing over the pile of rubble. On top of the wall, the elves put hand to their swords, and prepared to meet them. Grim limped to their side, rummaging in the pockets of his pouch belt.

Tanner picked up his axe and looked into the courtyard, where the champion was dismounting, Arnost Emery alone between him and the Well. Tanner took a deep breath, cast a glance at Brix and Laurel where they stood on the opposite battlement, and jumped.

•••

Doctor Emery closed his hand around Suhlwen's gemstone. His own spear was propped against the Well, out of reach and useless. He looked into the face of the creature riding the red snake into the courtyard, and saw nothing human. The emotions that animated the ash-gray features of the champion were too extreme and twisted to have a human counterpart. He watched him whip the side of his mount, horrid glee in his eyes.

The serpent came to an abrupt stop, and the champion swung one of his misshapen legs over its back.

Brixida was screaming somewhere behind him, but Emery would not take his eyes off the creature in front of him. He was determined to not look away as death came for him. He squared his shoulders, a defiant look on his face.

And something snaked at the back of his mind. Something that had the fluid musicality of the elven speech, and a will of its own. Doctor Emery took a deep breath and saw young Tanner dive into the void. The stone was burning the palm of his hand. Time crawled, and a single word pushed to the fore in his mind. He thought he was no mage, and this was foolishness. Then Arnost Emery spoke that single word the sorceress had given him.

Tanner landed on the back of the snake, his axe biting into the thick scale of its hide, just as a screaming ball of blinding blue lightning engulfed the creature, its rider, and half the courtyard, and a thunder shook the very walls of the redoubt.

The orc had to hold on for dear life as a mighty wind swept the enclosed space, and more detritus fell from the ramparts, further burying the body of the snake.

A fat chunk of rock hit Tanner over the head, and a black

veil fell over his eyes for the time of a heartbeat. The courtyard cobblestones hit him in the face, and when he shook his head he was on the ground, dizzy, his axe still stuck to the serpent's back, ten feet away. He must have broken his nose. His temple throbbed, half-formed thoughts milling in his head. He wiped blood out of his eyes.

The still form of Doctor Emery was propped against the Well, sparks still crackling in his hair, steam rising from his coat.

Gorgemaw only knew hunger and bloodlust, and the need to be close to Th'Uk Tar. Its sides brushing the walls of the corridor, it tried to crawl on, screeching. The weight of the fallen wall pressed on its tail, trapping it half in, half out of the tunnel.

Gorgemaw tried to twist and buck free. Each movement caused a stab of pain where the blade of the orc had stuck. This new thought reminded the animal of its assailant, and it looked around and saw the orc where he was trying to push himself back to his feet. Gorgemaw smelled blood. Flaring its cowl, it opened its mouth to roar defiance at the orc that had dared to challenge it.

The orc did not wait for the beast to move. He scrambled on all fours and he reached out to where the old man's spear had fallen. He picked it up just as Gorgemaw's teeth closed on his left leg, crushing muscle and bone.

The orc bellowed as pain added to pain, and stabbed with the spear into Gorgemaw's muzzle, trying to free himself. Gorgemaw shook its head, further tearing into the orc's leg and causing him to scream again.

His knuckles pale with the effort, the orc pushed the spear

between Gorgemaw's teeth and worked them open by sheer force of desperation. The shaft of the spear snapped, but the jaws of the creature opened long enough. His mangled leg free, he rolled onto the ground, one hand reaching for Gorgemaw's side.

Staggering from the blast of blue energy, Th'Uk Tar left Gorgemaw behind and strode to the center of the courtyard. His feet splashed over the slippery cobblestones. He ignored the dying old man on the ground, crushed a bucket under his heel. He lifted his pain-seared right hand. Now this too would be healed.

An arrow hit him between the neck and the shoulder and bounced off his bone plates, little more than a pinprick. Th'Uk Tar stopped and looked up. A second arrow hit him in the chest, a brief, negligible stab of pain. He distractedly snapped the shaft off.

For some the fight was not over yet. There were two women standing on the battlements. A strange half-human in a stained white shirt and blue britches was climbing down the staircase. She had cat-like ears and a long tail. Her eyes were large and yellow. She twirled a sword and a long dirk as she came towards him. Above her, and covering her friend, an elf woman in ragged chain mail was pulling on her bow for a third time, sighting down the shaft. Her face was a mask of red warpaint.

The cat-woman stopped on the bottom step of the staircase and silently pointed her sword at him with a flourish. Black homicidal mirth bubbled to Th'Uk Tar's lips. She was defying him. He would grant her her wish.

Slowly, a grin spreading over his face, Beastmaster Th'Uk Tar unfurled his twin bone whips. While his right whip drew a large curve in front of him, the other shot towards the ramparts and caught one of the elven lancers that had strayed too close to the inner parapet. With a flick of his wrist, Th'Uk Tar pulled the weapon back, and the two halves of the dead body slammed on the ground either side of him.

The hybrid woman and the elf did not flinch.

Th'Uk Tar decided he would cherish this last diversion.

Brix waited for one moment on the bottom step of the staircase. She remembered what her mother would say to her every morning as a child when she got out of bed. "Get up and step into the world."

She had used the same phrase with Lysette and Remin, back in the Petremol house. She wondered passingly what had become of the two, of their parents, of Léa. Of all the scared people on the road, and the tired captain of the militia, and all the people she had met and left behind, to come here, now, to this place.

The sword was like an extension of her arm.

She pushed back the memories, just as she pushed back the din of the fighting still raging on the wall. She studied her adversary as he unfurled his jagged bone whips. The Uthuk champion was tall. He had good reach, augmented by his unusual weapons. His limbs folded in a strange way. There were bone plates over his shoulders and around his neck, a natural armor like a sea urchin. But she could see his ribs when he breathed.

His weapons, she realized as he snapped them viciously, were the bones and tails of two of the beasts that usually accompanied the Uthuk Y'llan. The realization caused an unexpected shift in her, as the last nugget of fear in her chest dissolved, and all she felt for this creature was disdain. She bent her wrist, pulled her arm up, and twirled her sword in a swift salute, like her father had taught his students. Then she extended her arm, pointing the tip of the sword at the champion's heart.

Claiming him as her own.

She tightened the grip on the dagger in her left hand. Then she took a deep breath, and stepped into the world.

The two bone whips snapped.

The champion swung them in a crossed pattern, left and right, left and right, one striking at his foe while the other curled in front of him in a defensive arch, stopping the adversary from coming close enough to use her thin blade.

Brix stepped carefully on the wet stones, her blade swinging gently, studying his moves. He seemed to be favoring his right hand. The skin was cracked, the fingers gnarled. When he came forward, she retreated, biding her time. The champion of the Locust Swarm stared at her, as if fascinated by the blade she was pointing at him.

The bone whip creaked, hissed and cracked, about one foot in front of the cat-woman's eyes. He pulled his arm back, twisting his left wrist to retrieve the whip and reload, just as he started the upstroke with his right whip. His right hand was betraying him. The whip distended with a snap and with a flick of her blade, Brix pushed aside its forked end. There was a weakness there, and she could use it.

She arched an eyebrow, and smirked. The anger over his inhuman features was unmistakable.

"Some fighters are their own worst enemy," her father said in her ear. "They pay too much attention to their feelings."

The champion maneuvered nimbly his left-hand whip,

twisting it and sending a loop to curl around the cat-woman's leg. By instinct alone she jumped out of the way. She twirled and danced away, and parried the backstroke of his right whip. She had to dive on the ground and do a cartwheel to again evade the backward sweep of the second.

Th'Uk Tar laughed.

Both of his whips slammed on the ground, as Brix rolled away, pushed against the wall and flipped back on her feet. It was obvious to her that the champion was toying with her, but in so doing he was revealing the rhythm of his own dance.

"It is just like a dance," her father said in her head. Her mother agreed.

A silent music playing in her mind, Brix lunged, driving her sword past the loop of bone and sinew encircling the champion.

She almost got him.

Th'Uk Tar laughed as he twisted a loop through his right whip and entangled the sword of the cat-woman. The bone disks of the weapon wrapped around the blade and caressed the hand that held it. One more turn of his wrist and he could rip her arm off.

She let go of the hilt, pulling her hand back. She saved her limb and lost her weapon.

She hissed, just like a cat, and the sword rattled on the ground behind Th'Uk Tar and she stood in front of him, switching her dirk from the left to the right. Her long tail snapped.

She moved nimbly on her feet, avoiding a spiraling coil that almost entangled her, and then ducked under the other whip. An elegant creature, but as frail as men and elves.

The sound of the drums and the screams of elves and Uthuk

locked in the melee on the battlements were the music of carnage to which his whips and the cat-woman were dancing.

He had enjoyed the dance more than she had, but it would soon be over, Th'Uk Tar thought. She could not keep evading him forever.

He snapped his left whip back. The bones scraped the ground and then rose in an ample loop, keeping the woman at a safe distance. There was not much she could do with her dagger. His right hand sent barbs of icy pain up his arm as he repeated the movement with his other whip. But he did not care. It was time to finish this.

Then the world went black and pain burned half his face.

Brix dared to glance sideways and saw Laurel standing on top of the ruined bastion. With her last arrow stuck in the left eye of the Uthuk champion, the elf had no more use for her bow. She used it to parry a vicious swing from the champion's whip, and let it go.

Brix tried to reach for her sword, but narrowly avoided a blind whiplash. Any other opponent would not have survived her arrow, but the champion was still standing and fighting, his teeth gritted in anger, or from the pain. He twisted his other whip in an overhead swoop, trying to hit Laurel, and in that moment Brix lunged again.

Half blind and consumed with anger, the champion was standing with his left arm raised, and the right-hand whip snaking close to the ground, still entangled in the longbow. Brix sidestepped the slower right-hand whip, entered the guard of the Uthuk Y'llan, and drew a long cut on the champion's left side with her dagger. Black blood oozed, and she danced away, but not fast enough. The monster hissed, and hit her with a kick, sending her reeling against the steps of the battlement. The left whip cracked and swooped down to her. She rolled off the steps. A sharp pain made her cry as the tail end of the weapon missed her head but clipped the tip of her right ear.

In that exact moment, the drums fell silent, and it was as if time had stopped.

CHAPTER TWENTY-THREE

"There's no end to them!"

Grim dropped his last incendiary bottle and stepped back from the rampart. Kestrel and a handful of her elves were all that remained of the redoubt's defenses, and still the Uthuk Y'llan pressed against the walls, scrambling over the heaped bodies and the piled rubble.

Looking for a weapon of some kind, Grim turned around in time to watch Brix stab the gangly Uthuk champion in the side. Tanner, a limping mess of blood, gore and ripped chainmail, was holding on to the back of the thrashing red serpent with all his might, and reaching for the axe stuck in the beast's armor.

"Father of Nordros," he whispered.

The drums stopped. The silence was so sudden it echoed like thunder, and for a moment Grim felt lost, like something had taken away the very air he was breathing.

Then the elves started shouting.

"Scions!" they said. "Scions!"

All around the Well of Tears, the forest moved.

The Uthuk Y'llan raiders closest to the trees did not see

it. The Bloodwood simply reached out with long arms and grabbed them, pulling them into the darkness. Many did not even make a sound. Other cried, in surprise, and in pain. The drummers were the first to go, grabbed and silenced forever, one by one.

This alerted their companions under the walls. The charge forward lost momentum as the Uthuk Y'llan stared in horror at the Bloodwood as it shifted and advanced on them. Walking on long legs like hooked roots, running on all fours like a bloodhound or striding like a human being. Stretching arms that had branches for bones and vines for sinews.

The rain had died down and there was no wind, but blood-red leaves rustled and twigs snapped as the monstrous shapes advanced.

The charge of the Uthuk Y'llan came to a halt. The eerie glow of the standing stones painted the scene in a ghostly light.

Another line of raiders disappeared, grabbed and dragged away screaming, before their companions shook themselves out of their surprise. Axes were lifted, weapons readied. A lone ripper beast sprung and snapped with its long fangs at the closest of the advancing shapes. It was intercepted in midair by a large, gnarly hand, three long fingers closing on the slick body. The beast's talons scratched the bark of the arm holding it. A rope-like vine was severed. The tree-thing roared to the sky, a twisted crack opening in its elongated, gourd-like head. A second hand grasped the back legs of the ripper beast. Screeching in fury, the tree monster pulled its prey apart and tossed the remains at the warriors.

Then it came forward, defiantly, its strange legs treading the soft water-soaked dirt. Many others came after it, a seething, boiling mass of limbs, branches, leaves and roots, radiating fury and malevolence. An Uthuk stood in the way of the creatures, arms outstretched, hooked blades raised high. He screamed his defiance. The closest tree-thing slapped him out of the way with a casual gesture. His broken body landed ten yards away, and was trampled by more of the advancing horrors.

Wailing in panic, the Uthuk moved again, pushing towards the redoubt, slipping and sliding in the mud. Uncaring for the thorny bushes, they scrambled uphill, without a strategy or a plan. The largest of them pushed through the crowd, trampling their weaker companions into the ground, wild with unthinking fear.

In the sudden silence, Th'Uk Tar's hiss of pain sounded like a bugle call to his monstrous ride. The beastmaster was in danger. The beastmaster needed help. Ignoring the annoying orc clinging to its side, the beast turned towards its master and companion, eager to bring him succor. Still trapped under the wreckage of the wall, it pulled with renewed strength, and finally freed its tail from the rubble. It sprang forward with a satisfied roar.

Holding on to the side of the beast with one arm, Tanner was no longer thinking. All he knew was he had to stop the creature. Blinded by pain, his strength almost spent, Tanner swung his axe one last time at the base of the monster's leathery cowl. Irritated by the distracting sting of the blade, the caecilian swung and coiled and shook the wounded orc off its back. Tanner fell back, groaning. Drunk on pain, he tried to crawl away, clawing at the flagstones of the courtyard. The monster deigned the fallen warrior little more than a sniff, its long tongue snaking through its teeth, and then turned again to find its master.

What it found was instead was Doctor Arnost Emery, dirty and disheveled, armed with a broken spear. His body shaking, his sight veiled with blood, Tanner watched in awe as the old scholar grunted and huffed and plunged the blade in the monster's eye. The caecilian shuddered and thrashed. In its dying convulsions, its head slammed into the old man, sending him rolling on the ground. Tanner tried to call out the old man's name, but nothing but a rattling breath escaped his lips. A black pit swallowed up the orc as the caecilian moved forward a few feet, confusion addling its simple brain, and then it crashed on the cobblestones and was still.

Grim watched in horrified fascination as the tree-creatures that the elves called scions advanced on the terrified horde of the Locust Swarm. There was something uncanny and subtly mechanical in the way the scions moved, scuttling on the muddy ground seeking prey. Because there was no doubt, in the weak gray light of the coming dawn, that these newcomers would not rest until the Uthuk Y'llan were vanquished. And their absolute silence only added to the horror.

Whatever they are, he thought, at least they are on our side.

Trampled and beaten, the Uthuk Y'llan tried to counter the onslaught of the scions. Their black iron blades cut the bark of their enemies, and they broke branches and cut limbs. It availed nothing. The scions were unstoppable, and where a band of warriors managed to gang together and beat one of the creatures, three more came forward and took the place of their fallen comrade. It was like the Bloodwood itself, Grim imagined, had come to avenge the injuries the swarm had caused it.

An obscenely bloated abomination, taller than two Uthuk

raiders, managed to grab one of the scions. As the tree-thing scratched its gray skin, the Uthuk lifted it bodily, and opening its mouth, tried to swallow it whole. Into the gaping mouth of the Uthuk went the red leaves and the top branches of the scion, its roots scissoring in the sky. Then the Uthuk froze, and emitted a terrified gurgle. Its body stretched and twisted, and then the scion ripped its captor from the inside. Then the scion slowly walked back into the Bloodwood, ignoring the carnage his kin were wreaking on the Locust Swarm.

On top of the wall, the elves around Grim were no longer cheering. They all watched the massacre as it played out on the slope, in awestruck silence.

Beastmaster Th'Uk Tar did not see his faithful caecilian fall, nor care for the desperate shouts of his warriors beyond the wall. Nothing mattered to him but his rage. He turned on his feet, his left whip snaking defensively, as he tried to keep the two cursed women in his sights. They were mocking him, slowly turning around him on his wounded eye's side.

Roaring with frustration, he snapped the shaft of the arrow still stuck in his eye. The shock sent a stab of pain into his head. His vision blurred, and he took a step back. He cracked his whip at the elf and caught a glimpse of the cat-woman as she tiptoed past him, and the glint of triumph in her eyes as she retrieved her blade. He whipped at her, and she parried with her dagger before retreating and switching the blades in her hand.

Pain searing through his head, in his right hand and along his left side, Beastmaster Th'Uk Tar perceived for the first time in his brutal existence the faint possibility of defeat. It was a strange, hollow sensation in the pit of his stomach, something he could not kill or cow in submission. It was fear.

He looped his whips in a defensive swoop, marking a perimeter into which the Latari and her cat companion would not dare to enter. Turning slowly, trying to keep the two in sight, he started looking for a way out, until he finally saw the still coils of Gorgemaw.

Surprise and the pain in the rotting flesh of his arm betrayed him, and his right whip missed a beat. It dragged on the ground, raising a fan of thin water droplets. Th'Uk Tar realized his error in the same instant the elf saw an opening and struck. Pushing aside the failing bone whip with her blade, she charged him. He tried to stop her by looping his left whip on the downswing, but he could not see on that side. The murderous coils of the whip missed the elf as she came close enough to Th'Uk Tar to plunge her blade into his gut. The sword slid over a bony spur, and missed the Uthuk's vital organs, but his black blood poured copiously from the gash. Th'Uk Tar screeched in pain and anger.

Cursing her, he kicked her back, and cracked his whip at the cat-woman who was coming at him on his blind side. The decapitating blow missed her neck but slapped in her face, lacking the strength to kill. The cat-woman staggered back, her face a mask of blood.

An eye for an eye, thought Th'Uk Tar with cruel glee.

Hissing with killer fury, the woman twirled her dagger in her left, and threw it.

Her opponent parried it easily, and again his left arm was raised as the whip looped for a high swooping hit. But his flank was open. Shaking the blood off from her eye, the cat-woman danced on tiptoes into his guard. With a scream like nothing Th'Uk Tar had ever heard, she pushed her sword blade between his ribs.

Th'Uk Tar staggered, black blood pouring from his mouth.

He choked and coughed as the blade snapped close to the hilt, and he crashed on the ground. He arched his back, kicked with his feet, and was still.

Panting, Brix offered her hand to Laurel and helped her up.

"Your eye–"

The cat-woman shook her head. "I'm fine." She could feel her heart pulse in her cheek, but after what she'd been through, the pain was an afterthought. She used her cuff to clean her face of the blood.

She squinted, her face hurting more. She still had use of both eyes, and she turned towards the staircase, which Grim was hurrying down. It took her a moment to realize what was distracting her. "This silence–"

Her words were echoed by the savage roar of the caecilian, as the snake thing came back to life, opened its remaining eye and charged towards her and Laurel. The elf pulled a short dagger from her belt, and both she and Brix braced for the assault of the monster.

But the creature was not interested in them. Coiling itself around the remains of Th'Uk Tar, it picked up its master between knife-like teeth and then, carrying it in its mouth, sped up a nearby staircase, over the battlements, and outside, to the Bloodwood, in the mournful light of the early dawn.

EPILOGUE

It was noon the next day when the Latari arrived, Dareine and Cillian, and Travaran the war mage, and a thousand silver-clad elven warriors from the Aymhelin, like a tide of quicksilver pouring forth from the Bloodwood. They carried spears and standards, and there was a troop of leonx riders warding their flank. They had a full troop of archers, their armor as clean and shiny as spun silver. They marched through the wreck of the standing stone ring in silence, and then stood at the edge of the chaos of blood and dead bodies that had been the overgrown rose garden.

In silence they rode up to the redoubt, fearing what they would find.

Carrion crows saluted their coming, and the Well of Tears did not entrap them in its weave of illusion.

A single scion stood guard by the shattered gate, its root-like feet grasping the pile of rocks and rubble that half-blocked the access, like an old tree clinging to a ruin, and whether it was asleep, or just at rest, it was impossible to say.

Everything was still as in death, and shrouded in mist.

•••

"How's the eye?"

Brix squinted at Grim as he sat down on the last step at the top of the battlement staircase, Hewma curled by his side, sleeping. His face was shiny from slippery elm bark ointment for the burns, and he had somehow lost his black hat. Brix's face was bandaged, and she had not changed her blood-splattered shirt yet.

"Shall we get you an eye patch? Together with the clipped ear it would make you look quite piratical."

"It is fine," she said. She self-consciously touched the end of her ear. "No eye patch, this time. But there will be a scar," she added, almost proud. She had refused the water from the Well, claiming the wound was merely a scratch. "Your hand?"

He looked down at his bandages. "I'll live. There will be a scar."

Brix leaned against the parapet and arched her back. "Where's everybody?"

Grim shrugged. "Emery and Tanner are over at the Latari camp with Laurel and Kestrel." He chuckled. "Dareine and their bunch are so shocked at what happened here, they are probably going to make us honorary elves. Mark my words, I half suspect Dareine might do just that, if only to shock the Aymhelin crowd."

Brix laughed.

The Latari had set camp by the edge of the Bloodwood, a small city of many-colored silken pavilions and fluttering silver banners. The Aymhelin elves had showed a cold courtesy to Brix and the others, but they had taken Tanner in, and their healers were working on his leg. For some reason, the water from the Well of Tears seemed to have lost some of its powers. Something to do with the damage to the stone ring, Grim had suggested. The elves were busy recovering the broken stone, with the intent of putting it back in its place.

Hewma shifted position, opened her eyes, looked at Brix, and then pushed with her head against Grim's shoulder, purring.

"Looks like Doctor Emery is not the only one who found a paramour," Brix grinned.

"An elusive one like all elves are said to be," Grim smirked. "Suhlwen made herself scarce when the Latari arrived, and while Emery and I looked up and down for her this morning, she was nowhere to be found."

"Whatever her reasons, something tells me she's not very far," Brix smiled. "And I wonder if we'll ever learn the truth about her story."

"I guess one of us will," he said. Brix shook her head reproachfully, but chuckled at the same time.

They were silent for a long moment.

"And you?" she asked. "How are you?"

Grim shrugged again. "I am terribly tired, and I only want some quiet. It would be nice to sleep for a week. Get some peace."

"Can we get any, with the Locust Swarms rampaging through Terrinoth?"

He leaned back and made a face. "Once I would have asked you what difference we could make," he said. "But I've got this feeling right now that's a loaded question."

"We really did make a difference, didn't we?"

"Like a pinch of common sand in a fine piece of clockwork," he said.

She laughed. "But they are still out there," she said then.

"And we are still here. And…"

Hewma looked up as Laurel came up the stairs, holding a scroll. She was out of armor and unarmed, a rare occurrence. Grim gave her a look and stood. "I'll leave you ladies alone," he said. "I'll go and find something to eat." He patted the leonx on the side. "You coming with me, girl?"

The elf gave him a nod, and he slowly descended into the courtyard, the big cat trailing behind him.

Brix looked at the papers in Laurel's hand, and up into her eyes. "Redstar?"

Laurel nodded. "Her letter came with Dareine. She is... there is a great danger, and she is hunting it down. Up north, into the Blind Muir Forest."

Blind Muir was but a name to Brix. Something out of the adventure stories whose heroes she no longer envied. She smiled. "And you are going to her."

It was not a question. The elf nodded, the joy of the hunt sparkling in her eyes.

"When are you leaving?"

"Now."

Brix was not surprised. The elf knew no separation between thought and action. But she did surprise herself. "I'm coming with you," she said.

"No."

She did not look away. A human would, Brix thought, but not Laurel. "Afraid I'd slow you down?"

Laurel turned away now, and looked at the distant tops of the Bloodwood forest. "No, but this I must do alone. And our friends will need you here."

Brix chuckled. "Can't let the men go it alone, right?"

"You are the brains of the band," Laurel said, and smiled.

•••

"An elf artificer was here a moment ago," Tanner said, "to share a design for a new leg. It will be spell-sung from living wood into a thing of real beauty. The healers agree I will walk much like before, with a little exercise."

Laurel had left, and now the survivors of the battle of the Well were sitting at dinner as the sun set over the Bloodwood. A table had been set in the pavilion in which Tanner was staying, and a selection of foods and beverages had been laid out for them by servants as silent and discreet as old ghosts. Grim failed to recognize half of the dishes, but he did not care. He would learn as he went.

Suhlwen was still nowhere to be found, much to Emery's chagrin, but Kestrel joined them, a strange creature out of her chainmail and tunic, that Grim almost failed to recognize. She had pulled up her hair, and was wearing a dress as red as the leaves of the wood and silver jewels on her ears and fingers. There was a lingering perfume of cinnamon about her.

"Bloodwood royalty," Brix whispered in Grim's ears as they sat down to dine. He gave her a questioning look, but she just grinned at him and handed him a cup of wine.

"They say they will sing ballads about what happened here," Tanner said now, shaking his head. He was paler than usual, but had not lost his good cheer. Only, a shade of melancholy passed now over his features. That was something Grim had perceived in all of them. They had come a long way from their days on the Old Road. A distance that was not measured in miles.

"They call it the Siege of the Well," Kestrel said. "Where few fought many."

"And too many died," Doctor Emery said, raising his cup in a toast.

The others joined him.

"A ballad..." Grim murmured, taking a drink, and for the briefest moment of paralyzing fear felt as though soft fingers prodded at the edge of his mind. Had that been just that, he wondered, for the Fae out there? A ballad, an entertainment? A game played with pieces on a board, like Emery and Suhlwen did?

The gentle touch retreated, and Grim wished that, whoever they were, they had been entertained. He was grateful the nightmares had gone, and that was enough.

When he came back to the present moment, the others were talking amongst themselves.

"The healers said at least two weeks," Tanner was saying. He touched delicately the bandages at the end of his shortened leg. "And then the artificer will fit me with his contraption, and I'll have to learn to walk again."

"You can help me put my notes in order in the meantime," Doctor Emery said. "We can stay in the Well, I am sure, there is plenty of room–"

"A bit draughty, but dry," Brix said with a chuckle. Emery hid his thoughts behind a sip of wine.

"I do not know what your plans are," Kestrel said casually, with a sly glance, "but I have it on good authority that all of you would be welcome to stay in the Bloodwood as long as you wish."

Grim gave a look at Brix, a grin splitting his face. "What did I tell you? Honorary elves."

ACKNOWLEDGMENTS

I have a long list of people I need to say thanks to.

My brother Alessandro for keeping the fort while I was writing this book.

My friends Lucia, Marina, Paola, Emanuele, Roberto, Marco.

The boys and girls keeping the Lifeboat afloat.

Dave, Eckhard and Mark for motivating me to write in English.

Aconyte Books for giving me a voice and Charlotte for bringing life to it.

And a huge thank you to all the readers and the *Descent* players out there. Cheers!

ABOUT THE AUTHOR

DAVIDE MANA was born and raised in Turin, Italy, with brief stints in London, Bonn and Urbino, where he studied paleontology (with a specialization in marine plankton) and geology. He currently lives in the wine hills of southern Piedmont, where he is a writer, translator and game designer. In his spare time, he cooks and listens to music, photographs the local feral cats, and collects old books. He co-hosts a podcast about horror movies, called Paura & Delirio.

karavansara.live
twitter.com/davide_mana

Epic fantasy of heroes and monsters in the perilous realms of Terrinoth.

Legends unite to uncover treachery and dark sorcery, defeat the darkness, and save the realm, yet adventure comes at a high price in this astonishing world.

WRATH OF N'KAI
JOSH REYNOLDS
THE LAST RITUAL
S.A. SIDOR
LITANY OF DREAMS
ARI MARMELL
MASK OF SILVER
ROSEMARY JONES
THE DEVOURER BELOW
CULT OF THE SPIDER QUEEN
S.A. SIDOR
THE DEADLY GRIMOIRE
ROSEMARY JONES
IN THE COILS OF THE LABYRINTH
DAVID ANNANDALE
DARK ORIGINS
GRIM INVESTIGATIONS
LAST RESORT
WELCOME TO THE ZOMBIE APOCALYPSE. TRY NOT TO DIE.
JOSH REYNOLDS
PLANET HAVOC
IN SPACE EVERYONE SCREAMS
TIM WAGGONER
AGE OF THE UNDEAD
MAYHEM. MAGIC... ZOMBIES!
C.L. WERNER
TERRAFORMING MARS
IN THE SHADOW OF DEIMOS
JANE KILLICK
TERRAFORMING MARS
EDGE OF CATASTROPHE
JANE KILLICK
THE FRACTURED VOID
TIM PRATT
THE NECROPOLIS EMPIRE
TIM PRATT
THE VEILED MASTERS
TIM PRATT
EXPLORE AMAZING NEW WORLDS
ACONYTE
ACONYTEBOOKS.COM
PATIENT ZERO
AMANDA BRIDGEMAN

WORLD EXPANDING FICTION

Do you have them all?

ARKHAM HORROR

- ☐ *Wrath of N'kai* by Josh Reynolds
- ☐ *The Last Ritual* by SA Sidor
- ☐ *Mask of Silver* by Rosemary Jones
- ☐ *Litany of Dreams* by Ari Marmell
- ☐ *The Devourer Below* ed Charlotte Llewelyn-Wells
- ☐ *Dark Origins, The Collected Novellas Vol 1*
- ☐ *Cult of the Spider Queen* by SA Sidor
- ☐ *The Deadly Grimoire* by Rosemary Jones
- ☐ *Grim Investigations, The Collected Novellas Vol 2*
- ☐ *In the Coils of the Labyrinth* by David Annandale *(coming soon)*

DESCENT

- ☐ *The Doom of Fallowhearth* by Robbie MacNiven
- ☐ *The Shield of Daqan* by David Guymer
- ☐ *The Gates of Thelgrim* by Robbie MacNiven
- ☐ *Zachareth* by Robbie MacNiven
- ☑ *The Raiders of Bloodwood* by Davide Mana

KEYFORGE

- ☐ *Tales from the Crucible* ed Charlotte Llewelyn-Wells
- ☐ *The Qubit Zirconium* by M Darusha Wehm

LEGEND OF THE FIVE RINGS

- ☐ *Curse of Honor* by David Annandale
- ☐ *Poison River* by Josh Reynolds
- ☐ *The Night Parade of 100 Demons* by Marie Brennan
- ☐ *Death's Kiss* by Josh Reynolds
- ☐ *The Great Clans of Rokugan, The Collected Novellas Vol 1*
- ☐ *To Chart the Clouds* by Evan Dicken
- ☐ *The Great Clans of Rokugan, The Collected Novellas Vol 2*
- ☐ *The Flower Path* by Josh Reynolds

PANDEMIC

- ☐ *Patient Zero* by Amanda Bridgeman

TERRAFORMING MARS

- ☐ *In the Shadow of Deimos* by Jane Killick
- ☐ *Edge of Catastrophe* by Jane Killick *(coming soon)*

TWILIGHT IMPERIUM

- ☐ *The Fractured Void* by Tim Pratt
- ☐ *The Necropolis Empire* by Tim Pratt
- ☐ *The Veiled Masters* by Tim Pratt

ZOMBICIDE

- ☐ *Last Resort* by Josh Reynolds
- ☐ *Planet Havoc* by Tim Waggoner
- ☐ *Age of the Undead* by C L Werner